Praise for *USA Today* bestselling author
KINLEY MacGREGOR

"The talented Kinley MacGregor [is at]
the top of my 'must read' list."
Teresa Medeiros

"Her admirable flair for the comic
is sure to entertain."
Publishers Weekly

"Humor and passion are the trademarks
of any Kinley MacGregor book."
Christina Dodd

"[MacGregor] packs hours of entertainment
between the pages."
Oakland Press

"Warm, witty, and wonderful."
Stephanie Laurens

"A spirited new voice in adventure romance . . .
[She] will bring a smile to your lips. . . .
Keep your eye on Ms. MacGregor."
Romantic Times

By Kinley MacGregor

RETURN OF THE WARRIOR
A DARK CHAMPION
TAMING THE SCOTSMAN
BORN IN SIN
CLAIMING THE HIGHLANDER
MASTER OF DESIRE
MASTER OF SEDUCTION
A PIRATE OF HER OWN

Kinley MacGregor

Master Of Seduction

AVON BOOKS
An Imprint of HarperCollinsPublishers

AVON BOOKS
An Imprint of HarperCollins*Publishers*
10 East 53rd Street
New York, New York 10022-5299

Copyright © 2000 by Kinley MacGregor
ISBN: 0-06-108712-2
www.avonromance.com

First Avon Books paperback printing: July 2005
First HarperTorch paperback printing: January 2000

Avon Trademark Reg. U.S. Pat. Off. and in Other Countries, Marca Registrada, Hecho en U.S.A.
HarperCollins® is a registered trademark of HarperCollins Publishers Inc.

Printed in the U.S.A.

10 9

MASTER
OF SEDUCTION

For Ken, the precious wind beneath my wings.

Je t'aime toujours.

1

The diary of Lady Ashton, 1775

*B*lack Jack Rhys is the fiercest pirate to ever roam
the raging seas. Every sailor alive fears to mention his
name aloud lest it summon him up from the very bowels
of hell.

'Tis said to see his ship is to see your death, for he
gives no quarter, shows no mercy. Once his prey is spotted, he is relentless in his pursuit and will not cease until
he claims his prize.

Jack Rhys is a man possessed of a mysterious legend.
A man possessed of numerous talents.

Tonight, I have met said man and discovered for
myself just how hypnotic a creature he is. Aye, he is
fierce and wild and untamed, but more than that, he is a
spectacular specimen of manliness. And though I ache to
have him for my own, I know only too well that no
woman shall ever claim him.

With a sigh in my heart, I have resigned myself to the fact that I spent but one glorious night with the Master of Seduction. For one moment in time I held the unattainable, and tasted the full delights of my gender. There is no other man who can come close to matching Jack Rhys and so I end this small entry with the same sad note that I ended last night.

Farewell, Jack Rhys. May you always avoid the gallows.

Charleston, South Carolina, 1780

This was her night of supreme triumph.

Lorelei Dupree smiled in satisfaction as Justin Wallingford whirled her about the crowded dance floor. After all these years of waiting, of knowing deep inside her heart that he was the only man for her, she had finally heard his proposal.

And what a proposal it had been. Wearing his immaculate British uniform, Justin had tapped on his wine glass with his monocle until he'd held everyone's undivided attention. Then the haughty, much sought after lieutenant had begged for her hand in the presence of Charleston's social elite.

Oh, but it was a glorious evening. She would treasure the memory for the rest of her life.

As the music finished and she left the dance floor on Justin's arm, Lorelei caught the pleasure in her father's smile. In his mid-sixties, Sir Charles Dupree, the most renowned Tory in Charleston, still held the striking handsomeness that had marked his youth. With his powdered wig rolled in the latest fashion, and wearing his dark blue jacket with the heavy gold embroidery, he looked quite dashing.

"I shall fetch us a cup of punch," Justin offered before leaving her side. As he made his way through the crowd, several men clapped him on the back and nodded in her direction.

Lorelei paused before her father. "You're looking smug this evening," she teased.

His smile widened. "And you, little Lori-Angel," he said, taking her extended hand and bestowing a fatherly kiss on the backs of her knuckles, "are as breathtaking as your mother."

She blushed at his compliment.

He kept her hand in his and held it tightly. He'd done that much tonight, as if fearing her coming marriage would somehow separate them. But Lorelei knew better. Nothing could ever come between her and her beloved father. He was her Saint George who had slain every evil dragon that had haunted her childhood.

"How is it Justin has left you free for this dance? I thought you had promised it to him alone?" he asked.

She raised her white lace fan to her face and whispered behind it, "I'm afraid I'm the one to blame, Father. My toes needed time to recuperate."

He laughed. It was common knowledge that Justin, a man of numerous talents, had never mastered the art of dancing.

"If you'll please excuse me," she said, reluctantly withdrawing her hand, "I see Amanda and Annabeth heading out to the balcony. I must speak with them."

"Ever as you wish, sweetest." That had always been his answer to any request, large or small.

3

Lorelei gave him a quick peck on the cheek before she skirted through the groups on the edge of the ballroom floor to seek out her friends.

The cool breeze outside was fragrant with magnolias as it whispered through the sculpted shrubs that surrounded the balcony. Crickets and frogs sang to the night while Amanda, Annabeth, and Martha fanned their flushed cheeks in the privacy of the ivy-covered balcony.

Annabeth was the daughter of the local magistrate. Fair of face, she was pleasingly plump and had a cheerful disposition. Tall and thin with brown eyes, Martha had been Lorelei's very first friend. And the ever beautiful, perfectly coifed Amanda was either Lorelei's closest friend, or her worst enemy, depending on the mood they were in.

"Oh, Lorelei," Annabeth breathed as she joined them. "You're so lucky to have Justin dote on you so."

"Aye," Martha agreed. "I think he's the most handsome man at the party."

Lorelei looked to where her fiancé stood inside with a group of other British Regulars. His father had commissioned Justin's lieutenant's rank just last year.

He *was* a handsome man. Tall of frame and slight of build, he had laughing blue eyes and was probably second only to her father when it came to indulging Lorelei's whims. The two of them had known each other all their lives and she looked forward to spending the rest of her life with him.

Amanda poked her arm with her closed pink fan. "Be warned, Lori," she said, her tone dire. "My mother told me a woman only has a month after the wedding before her husband tires of her and seeks another conquest. What will you do when Justin no longer responds to your charms?"

Lorelei laughed and brushed Amanda's words aside with a cheerful reprisal. "Not respond to my charms? Surely you jest. There's not a man born I can't wrap around my little finger." She lifted up her hand and quirked her pinkie finger to illustrate her point.

Amanda rolled her eyes. "You have a high opinion of yourself, *Miss* Dupree."

Lorelei recognized the swipe Amanda was taking by reminding her of her less than noble heritage compared to Justin's impeccable lineage. The fact that Lorelei's mother had been born of a notorious, illicit affair was more than well known.

Not one to be insulted, even subtly, Lorelei arched a brow at the fragile blonde. "It may be arrogant to you, *Lady* Amanda, but I know the secret of how to handle a man."

"Oh?" Amanda asked, her face a mockery of a surprised expression. "Then, please," she said, extending her arms as if to receive a great gift of enlightenment. "Do tell us this incredible secret."

Annabeth and Martha stopped fanning themselves and leaned closer in their eagerness to hear Lorelei's every word.

Lorelei smiled mischievously, then let fall her greatest weapon. "The secret is you must treat a man like a dog."

Annabeth gaped. "A man is like a dog, you say?"

Lorelei brought her hand up to her lips to remind Annabeth to keep her voice down. Though Lorelei and her friends were alone in the shadowy alcove of the balcony, anyone could walk within hearing range. Most especially one of their nosy chaperones.

"You're telling us that we are to treat a man like a lapdog?" Annabeth repeated, careful this time to keep her tone low enough for only their group.

"Exactly," Lorelei repeated. "In order to keep a man loyal, you have to treat and train him very much like you would a pampered pet."

"Who told you this?" Martha demanded.

Lorelei knew her eyes must be twinkling with her mirth. "My mother told me the secret when I was but twelve. 'Twas the same secret her mother had given her. And it works. I tell you, I've had nothing but success with the method."

"My mother says petulance and pouting work best for bending a man to your whims," Amanda contradicted.

Lorelei bit back the reminder that Amanda's father was a known lecher who kept two mistresses in town. Unlike Amanda, she would never be so cruel as to embarrass her friend with such a statement. "Fine then, you use your method and I'll continue mine."

Martha glanced inside the open doors to where Justin stood in a regal pose as he lectured the soldiers in his group. "I'd like to hear more of this theory," she said to Lorelei. "After all, you're the only one to ever attract the notice of Justin Wallingford."

"Aye," Annabeth agreed.

Lorelei cast a quick glance inside to make sure no one could hear, then drew her friends closer. "Very well, remember what we were told as children about dogs. Never show them any fear. They can smell it and it makes them mean. Men are the same. They

6

know when a woman is afraid and they use it to control you."

"Yes, but some of them are vicious by nature," Martha said.

"As are some dogs!" Annabeth added, pleased with herself that she had caught the metaphor.

Lorelei nodded. "And as with a pet, you must make sure you establish from the beginning exactly who is in control."

Amanda smirked. "Everyone knows the man is in charge. Why bother?"

"The man doesn't have to be."

Annabeth's blue eyes widened. Martha's mouth fell open and Amanda fluttered her fan in annoyance.

"What are you saying, Lori?" Annabeth whispered. "That *we* are in charge?"

"That's scandalous!" Martha gasped. "Whoever heard of such?"

"Who runs the household?" Lorelei asked, ignoring Martha's question.

"We do, of course," Martha and Annabeth answered in unison.

"And who makes sure the man is kept comfortable, served his favorite foods, and such?"

They exchanged puzzled looks.

"The wife, correct?" Lorelei prompted. "She makes sure her husband is treated with the proper regard and she is the one who sees after his care, just like you would do a treasured pup."

Annabeth frowned. "I suppose that's true."

"Thank you," Lorelei said. "Now, if you wish to train a man to listen to you, you never shout, you whisper. They take extra special care to listen to a quiet tone, while they automatically shut out loud ones. And just like you would a dog, when he comes at your bidding, you reward him. That way, he'll always come instead of ignoring you or putting you off."

"This is ridiculous," Amanda spoke again. "Justin would die if he heard any of this from you, and I shan't listen to anymore of this nonsense." Snapping her lace fan closed, she lifted her head haughtily and returned to the party.

Lorelei shrugged away her rancor. "No matter what she thinks, I tell you there's never been a man born I can't handle. You've seen it yourselves. When it comes to men, I could write a book of lessons."

Annabeth sighed forlornly, her large bosom heaving with the weight of it. "I wish I knew how to handle a man."

"As do I," Martha chimed in. "I always get flustered whenever one comes near me."

Martha looked past Lorelei's shoulder and her pale face flooded with color.

Lorelei turned her head to see Justin standing in the open doorway with two cups of punch in his hands. The light from inside shadowed most of his face, but even so there was no mistaking the half-peeved, half-shocked look on his face.

"Excuse me," Martha and Annabeth said as they gathered their skirts and rushed back to the party.

Justin arched a brow at Lorelei as he sauntered onto the balcony and placed their cups on the narrow ledge.

"A dog, am I?" he asked, humor dancing in the blue depths of his eyes.

Instead of being mortified, Lorelei laughed. "Here, Fido, come, sit."

He dutifully sat on the marbled railing where she'd patted her hand, then gave a soft canine whine.

Her smile widening, she gave him a quick pat on his powdered wig. "Good boy."

He reached out and pulled her into his arms. "Give me a kiss, wench."

Shaking her head, Lorelei placed her hands on his biceps and removed his arms from her. "Absolutely not."

He sighed and became instantly peevish. He reluctantly released her. "Why not?"

"There's a party inside, you cad. Someone might see."

He scoffed, then scooted off the railing. Reaching out, he took one of her curls between his fingers and rubbed it with his thumb. "You've caused quite the scandal by not wearing a wig tonight."

She pulled back from his grasp so that her hair was removed from his hand. "'Tis the latest fashion," she said defensively. "I read that no one will be wearing a wig by this time next year."

"Don't be so testy. I think your hair is quite pleasing."

"Thank you." She took her citrus punch from the railing and sipped it.

Justin grew quiet for a moment while the music and voices swirled around them. When he spoke, she had to strain to hear him. "Do you have an answer for me yet? Will you help me catch a pirate?"

She cradled the porcelain cup in her hand. So, that was what had been on his mind this night. His stupid wager against Roger Tilden about which of them could capture the nefarious Black Jack Rhys. It was a foolish wager in her opinion, not that Justin ever asked her opinion, mind you.

But far be it from her not to participate in such an adventure. "Do you have to ask? You know how much I love intrigue."

His face relaxed. "Then tomorrow night. I've already arranged everything with the tavern's owner. We'll tell your father I'm taking you to the play."

She tried to look stern with him, but she had a terrible feeling she failed miserably to hide the gleam in her eyes. "How did you know I would go along with your mad plan?"

"As you said, I know how much you love intrigue and I knew you were only making me wait for your answer to torment me with your usual grace."

"Lori? Justin?" her father's deep authoritative voice broke them apart. "Don't you think it's time to return inside?"

Lorelei snapped open her fan with a flick of her wrist as Justin offered her his arm. Side by side, they stepped into the ballroom.

To her immediate consternation, Justin led her to the dance floor, where he set about trampling her feet. It seemed an eternity had passed before the song ended and she could send him for more punch.

$\mathcal{M}$organ Drake paused in the doorway of the grand party with his notorious friend by his side. The people here tonight, most especially the British Royal Navy, which hunted Black Jack Rhys on a regular basis, would be stunned to learn he was in their midst. But then Jack thrived on danger. He defied death at every turn with a bitter, taunting laugh.

How many times had Morgan seen the man walk up and shake the hand of whatever official had just sworn to catch that black-hearted pirate, or die in that effort?

The one saving grace that kept Jack from the gallows was that he wasn't what he seemed. In this party of nobility, high officials, and spies, Jack Rhys wore the arrogant stoicism, powdered wig, and court dress as if he'd been born to it.

He'd come to this party with his only friend, Morgan Drake, devout Patriot and, in Jack's opinion, devout fool. But Morgan didn't mind his friend's epitaph. For he knew the truth of Black Jack Rhys.

Jack Rhys had a heart.

It was a heart Jack did his damnedest to deny, a heart he'd tell anyone he'd been born without. But Morgan had known the man too long and had seen him act contrary to his words too many times not to know the truth of it.

Morgan took a glass of sherry from a passing servant. He waited until they were alone before he turned to Jack. "What name will you be using tonight?" he asked.

"Count Arnaulf Hapsburg, I think."

Morgan's lips quirked up in humor at one of Jack's old favorites. "From Bulgaria?"

"Why yes, young pup," he said, cloaking his voice in an authentic accent. Bulgarian was one of about fifteen languages Jack spoke fluently. "Is there any other save *moi?*"

"Very well, *Count*, I shall leave you momentarily to find your bedmate."

Jack's gaze narrowed speculatively.

Morgan turned his head to see an attractive red-head quickly fanning herself next to a group of matrons. Her vivid hair color stood out among all the white and pastel colored wigs the rest of the crowd wore, and that marked her independence even more clearly than her choice of fanning. "I wouldn't have thought her your type."

Jack tipped his glass back and drained it. "Since when do you know my type?" His voice was scarce more than a growl meant to intimidate.

But Morgan knew. In spite of Jack's words and angry tone, Jack had never taken a virgin, nor would he do so tonight. He might dance with the girl, even pass a few words with her. But in the end, he would go off with a hungry widow.

Jack, for all his caution, was a devout creature of habit.

"Happy hunting," Morgan said to him as he spotted the Patriot spy he'd come to the party to meet. "I'll see you back at my ship in the morning."

Jack inclined his head in a subtle nod, his gaze still riveted by the woman before him as he placed his empty glass on the tray of a passing servant.

Her dress was a pale yellow silk, opened in front to show a quilted yellow panel. The low square neckline showed off the top of creamy breasts he could well imagine taking in his hand.

And her long, graceful neck. . . .

Jack had always been partial to a woman's throat, to the feel of her heartbeat teasing his lips as her heart raced in response to his expert touch. In his opinion, it was one of the most erotic places on a female body.

There was only one part he liked to taste more.

She darted rather quickly out of her current group and crossed the room to stand with two couples. Her harried movements reminded him of a dove being pursued by some beast as it tried to find a safe place to rest.

He smiled.

Morgan had been right, she wasn't his usual type. He liked his women tall, thin, and breathtaking.

Though attractive, she wasn't the classical beauty who normally turned men's heads, and if he didn't miss his guess, her pale skin was splashed with freckles her white powder couldn't hide.

But there was something striking about this woman. She had hair as dark and rich as mahogany with golden streaks laced through. She possessed an aura of warmth and happiness that seemed to glow from within her.

Watching her, he felt like a wilted flower that had just received a ray of sunshine after a long, cold winter. It was a strange feeling. One he'd never before known.

And he found himself wondering about the color of her eyes. . . .

Lorelei had spent the last twenty minutes avoiding her next promised dance with Justin. He would have the rest of their lives to stomp her toes. But if she were to carry out his ruse on the morrow, she would need both her feet intact.

Seeing him rise on the tips of his toes to scan the

crowd for her, she ducked and moved to stand with Amanda's mother, Lady Whitney, who was talking to the dowager Mrs. Darcy.

"My dear?" Lady Whitney asked Lorelei, her face pinched with worry as she gave her a regal perusal. "Are you all right?"

"I feel a little faint," Lorelei offered as an excuse for her odd behavior.

Mrs. Darcy touched her lightly on the arm. "I know exactly what you mean, Lori. I regret that I had my maid lace my stays so tightly tonight. Been near fainting myself."

With an imperial flick of her hand, Lady Whitney motioned for Amanda to join them.

Once Amanda was there, Lady Whitney turned to Lorelei. "Can you have your father arrange an introduction for Amanda to meet Count Hapsburg?"

"Count *who?*" Lorelei and Amanda asked simultaneously.

"Count Arnaulf Hapsburg," Mrs. Darcy said with a childish giggle. She put her gloved hand up to shield her mouth as she spoke in a loud whisper. "Why girls, don't tell me you haven't seen him?"

"I don't remember a Count Arnaulf Hapsburg being on the guest list," Lorelei said, wondering who the stranger was.

"Well, someone must have brought him," Mrs. Darcy said excitedly. "I heard he's descended from the royal family!"

Lady Whitney lifted her chin and looked down her hook nose to Mrs. Darcy. "I have no doubt. You can *see* his good breeding. 'Twould be obvious to anyone that he is royal."

Lorelei and Amanda exchanged frowns.

Then there was a flurry of feminine voices near them, some of them quite silly and high-pitched.

"Count Hapsburg is coming this way!" someone said. "Pass me my smelling salts."

"He's going to ask someone to dance," another woman said.

"Please, let it be me," the first woman begged.

Lorelei strained to see this mysterious count, but she was too short to see over the high wigs of the older women. In fact, she couldn't even tell from which direction he was supposed to be coming.

"He's after my Amanda," Lady Whitney said, her voice filled with glee. "Pinch your cheeks, dear, and for heaven's sake, straighten up."

As Lorelei searched the crowd for the newcomer, she caught Justin's eye. He raised his eyebrows in relief, smiled, and headed straight for her.

Oh, bother, he was after her now. Her toes twitched in memory of those polished black boots crushing them.

"Excuse me, please," she said to her group as she sought to find another safe corner of the room.

Lorelei was still looking back over her shoulder, to where Justin was making strides through the crowd, when she suddenly ran into a wall.

Only it wasn't a wall, she realized as she placed her hand upon it to steady herself.

It was a broad, rock-hard chest.

Her sight focused on the elegant, black silk, double-breasted cutaway beneath her hand. She slowly trailed her gaze up the embroidered cream waistcoat to his stand-fall collar, the stark white, lace-edged stock, and then to his . . .

Oh my.

Eyes of pewter stared down out of a face she'd never before seen in reality. It was the face of some perfect, ancient statue. His features sharp and angular, there was something predatorial in his gaze. Something that reminded her of a hawk watching a hare it wanted desperately to devour.

He gave her a smile that turned her legs to jelly.

"Forgive me, *mademoiselle*," he said in a deep, stunning timbre, his voice rich with a foreign accent.

Lorelei wanted to respond, but for the first time in her life, words failed her.

"I trust you're unharmed?" he asked.

She returned his beguiling smile, her throat finally loosening enough for her to speak. "I'm fine, thank you. I only hope I didn't offend you too much with my clumsiness."

He gave a low, rich laugh that made her insides flutter. "Please, feel free to run into my arms anytime you feel the urge."

"There you are, Lori," Justin said, coming up to stand beside her. His gaze raked the stranger with malice and it was only then she realized her hand hadn't left the man's chest.

Lorelei jerked her hand away with a very undignified gasp.

"I don't believe I know you, sir," Justin said with ice in his voice as he forced himself between her and the man.

"*Count*," the man corrected in a voice every bit as arctic. "Count Arnaulf Hapsburg."

Arnaulf turned his gaze to Lorelei and she grew warm inside at his heated perusal. "And you, *mademoiselle*?"

She sensed the anger and jealousy in Justin, but

too much a gentleman to show anything save proper manners, he answered for her. "Allow me to present my . . ."—he paused for emphasis—"*fiancée*, Miss Lorelei Dupree."

Nervously, Lorelei extended her hand to the count and gave a proper curtsy.

His warm hand covered hers. Long, tapered, and well-manicured, his fingers were obviously those of a gentleman, and yet she felt rough calluses on his palm that belied the noble title.

He bowed low before her upraised hand. His warm breath tickled her flesh, sending chills all the way up her arm. And when his lips touched the back of her hand, he gave an impudent nip with his teeth.

Startled, she felt her blood race through her veins and straight to a foreign part of her body that thrummed in sudden need.

"'Tis the greatest pleasure to meet you, *mademoiselle*," he said in that voice that wavered somewhere between thunder and warm honey.

When he neglected to release her hand immediately, Justin clicked his heels together and made a curt bow to draw the count's attention. "I am Lieutenant Justin Wallingford."

Immediately, the count dropped her hand. His features grew still and masked, and some heated emotion sparked within the count's eyes. It was raw and primeval, and if Lorelei didn't know better, she'd swear it was hatred.

"So, you're the youngest son of Gabriel Wallingford."

"You know my father?" Justin asked, stiffening his spine with pride.

The count's smile was cold, formal. "Why, yes, yes I do. He's an old family friend."

There was definitely something hidden in those words. Lorelei was certain of it.

The count continued to scan the crowd. "Is he by chance here this evening?"

Justin shook his head. "He's not due back into port for another week."

Disappointment flashed across the count's features an instant before he hid the emotion. "Pity."

The count turned to face Lorelei. "I see the dancers are getting ready for the next set. Might I have the pleasure of your company, Miss Dupree?"

"Lorelei doesn't like to dance," Justin inserted before she could even part her lips to respond.

The count ignored him and gave her a bold, assessing look. "*Mademoiselle?*"

"I would love to," Lorelei said before she thought better of it.

By the look on Justin's face, she could tell it was the wrong answer. So be it. She could handle him well enough. He would forgive her on the morrow. He always did.

She took the count's proffered arm and he led her to the floor. As soon as they took their places, the music started.

Surrounded by his strong arms, Lorelei felt jittery and nervous, like a young girl facing her first dance at her debutante ball. The count's appealing scent of sandalwood and ash filled her head.

With every precise, perfect step he took, she could feel the raw power of him. He was like a caged lion just waiting for the chance to pounce as he swept her around the floor.

Against the dandies and pale faces of the crowd, his tanned, handsome face stood out. But it was more than that. There was definitely something dangerous about this man, as if he were hiding something from her.

She could feel it deep within her soul.

Was he a Patriot spy, or perhaps a double agent working for England? He could even be one of the blockade runners that had been flooding into Charleston since the British had overtaken the port city and sealed it off.

"Have you been in the Colonies long?" she asked.

"I've never been anywhere long."

"Not even Bulgaria?"

"Lately," he added with a disarming smile. "I haven't been anywhere long lately."

Again, she sensed he was hiding something from her and she was determined to find out what. "Might I be so bold as to ask who invited you to the party?"

His eyes danced with humor. "I don't want to talk about me, *mademoiselle*. Tell me about you."

"Me?" she asked with a frown.

"Yes, tell me how an enchanting creature such as yourself became engaged to a pasty-faced English-man."

Anger flared and she sputtered for a moment. "Justin is not pasty-faced."

He looked to where Justin stood to the side of the floor, watching them like a cat protecting its kitten. "He is no match for you, *milovidnost*."

"I don't understand that last word."

"It's Bulgarian, and you are avoiding my point."

Regaining her lost composure, she looked up at

him from under her lashes. Lorelei was a master when it came to the art of flirtation and she knew the ploy he was using. It was one she'd confronted numerous times—disparage the competition. How many times had a man belittled the object of her affection while holding himself up as the very model of her perfect mate?

Taking the upper hand, she decided to spoil his advantage. "And just what sort of man would you suggest for me?" she asked coyly. "Yourself, perhaps?"

His arms tensed around her and his eyes turned dull. "Forgive me, *mademoiselle*. I have overstepped my bounds." He broke off their dance and left her standing in the middle of the ballroom looking after his departing form.

Lorelei frowned. He wasn't supposed to do *that*. She had assumed he would pass words with her, not leave her standing in the middle of her party like some discarded kerchief.

Of all the bizarre men. . . .

Justin approached her and led her from the floor. "Is anything amiss?"

Lorelei shook her head as she glanced back to where the count had vanished. How could she possibly explain to Justin this strange feeling inside her?

Dare she tell him that for one mere instant, she had actually been attracted to another man?

2

The following night, the noisy tavern was filled with smoke and more unwashed bodies than Lorelei had ever smelled in her entire life. For the last two hours, she'd been avoiding hairy hands and thwarting rude advances as she listened to the seamen's conversations for any tell-tale word of Jack Rhys.

It was sort of eerie, really, when she thought about it. One of these men could be the pirate who was rumored to have killed more men than the pox that had ravaged Charleston the year before.

Why, he could be that short man in his fifties at the bar who kept looking at her, or the young man sitting alone by the fire as he nestled up with a tankard of ale. Perhaps he was the solitary man in the corner who kept checking the door every time it opened. . . .

What *would* such a man look like? Would he be tall or short? Dark-haired or fair?

Surely such brutality would show on his face. Wouldn't it?

Lorelei approached the table where her latest four customers sat. She set their tankards down before them. "Will that be all for you?" she asked, affecting the gruff tone of a tavern maid. "Or can I bring you some food?"

One man narrowed his gaze on her rump. "I'll be having me some of this fine dish right here!"

With a newly practiced sidestep, Lorelei avoided the swipe the man directed at her backside.

"Come now, ducky," she said with a note of warning in her voice. "*This* dish'll be giving you a bad case of indigestion, not to mention the scalding burn I'll deliver your cheek if you handle me wrong."

Laughter broke out among the other three men at the table.

"Better watch out, Danny," one of his companions, an older man of about sixty, said. "She looks as though she could do it, too!"

Lorelei balanced her tray up on her shoulder. "And if not me, rest assured my lover behind the bar over there will have all your heads."

In unison, they turned to see Karl, the tavern's owner, as he hefted a huge barrel of rum over one shoulder and placed it up on the rack above his head. Though only half an inch taller than Lorelei, he was built as stout as an oak and everyone who frequented the Boar's Head was familiar with Karl Harringer's nasty temper.

"You and that ugly bugger?" the youngest man at the table sneered. "I don't believe you."

Lorelei tucked her tray beneath her arm. "Hey,

Karl," she shouted to where he could hear her over the din of noisy conversations. "Who's your love?"

Karl's bear-like face cracked into a semblance of a smile. "Only you, my sweet Lori, only you."

Smirking, she looked back at the four men whose faces were now pale. "You still be wanting to sample some of me fare?" she asked the seaman.

He hid his answer in his tankard.

Satisfied she had thwarted his advances, Lorelei made a round of her tables.

As she neared the back of the tavern, she caught Justin's furious glare. He had shed his British Regular's uniform in favor of a homespun jacket and plain buckskin breeches. Even so, he still held an imperious look to him that marked him as the youngest son of Lord Wallingford. Well, that and the way he sat ramrod stiff, as opposed to slumped over his mug like the rest of the tavern's occupants.

He'd also forgone shaving this morning. He'd told her it was to make him look rough so that he would fit in with the seamen who frequented the tavern. In her opinion, it made him look silly.

But then not half as silly as his posturing, which had him constantly propping his hand on his hip before he remembered his role and dropped his hand back to his side.

Justin narrowed his gaze as she approached him and she could sense he wanted to strangle her. She was an outrageous and outspoken flirt. He'd always known that, and it had aggravated him since the day he'd finally taken notice of her.

In truth, she took great pleasure in tormenting him. All her life, she'd pushed the boundaries of tolerance just to see what she could get away with.

Justin claimed it was her father's fault. Her father had always been far too indulgent of his only child, far too liberal with her education, and far too tolerant of her mischievousness.

"You're looking a little pale, ducky," she said saucily as she neared him. "Be needing another tankard of ale?"

His face dire, he declined. "Any word of Black Jack?" he asked.

She shook her head and dropped her accent as she pretended to wipe up a spill on his table. "There are a couple of pirates in here, but so far none are Jack Rhys."

He glanced to his men, who were sitting at the table with him. The two of them had strict orders to see Lorelei to safety the instant Black Jack Rhys showed up.

"You be careful," he warned.

"What?" she asked as she tucked her dishrag back into her sash. "With you, your men, and Karl? Who would dare harm me?"

He grabbed her arm as his gaze burned into hers. "Lorelei," he cautioned again, pulling her closer to him. "This isn't one of those stupid games we played as children. Black Jack Rhys would kill you in an instant."

She crinkled her nose as she tried to pull her arm from his grasp. "He'd have to catch me first, and I've yet to meet a man who could."

Justin sighed in aggravation and released her arm so that she could leave him.

As it had done almost continuously for the last two hours, the front door opened, ushering in a wonderful breath of fresh, clean air. Lorelei started to turn toward the door when all of a sudden, strong arms wrapped around her waist and hauled her back toward a darkened corner.

"Well, well, what have we here?"

The stench of ale and foul breath choked her. "Let me go," she demanded in the same imperious tone that had made numerous grown men flinch.

She couldn't see the man, but he raised one filthy hand up to grope at her breast.

"Ach, now, be nice. I'll pay you well, I will."

Terrified, Lorelei looked to Justin's table. He'd risen to his feet and she could see his desire to help her. Just as he took a step forward, one of his men grabbed his arm and shook his head no.

Justin sank slowly back down.

How dare he!

She seethed, infuriated by his submissiveness to a man who ranked below him. Oh, when she got out of this, he'd be more than sorry. And get out of this she most definitely would. She wasn't some meek little maid to be raped in the back room of a tavern.

Her desperation overriding her fear, she stomped the man's instep.

He cursed sharply and released her.

Lorelei rushed out from the corner toward the door, which had just swung open again. Before she could reach it, the man seized her once more and slung her around to face him. For the first time, she saw his black beady eyes and greasy dark blond hair. His ugly face contorted by rage and lust, he shoved her back against the wall and started pawing her body with his huge hands.

"I said let me go!" she insisted, struggling hard

against his grip. She tried to use her tray as a shield to force him back, but he wrenched it from her hands and tossed it to the ground.

"The woman made a request. You *should* obey her."

Though low of tone, the deep-timbered voice seemed to roll across the room like thunder. Heavy, thick, and powerful. There was something very familiar about that voice.

She looked up and . . .

Her heart stopped.

The first thing she saw were eyes of deep, dark gray. Pewter eyes that held a smoldering fury inside their cold, deadly gaze. Pewter eyes that belonged to Count Arnaulf Hapsburg.

Instead of his impeccable court attire, he now wore a white linen shirt open at the neck, and his sleeveless, dark green embroidered waistcoat was unbuttoned and hanging open. Long blond hair fell midway to his back while the candlelight flashed against the long, wicked saber at his side.

He reached out and placed a hand on her accoster's shoulder. "Did you not hear me?"

"This is between me and the girl."

"The girl wants no part of you and you should honor her good taste." One corner of his mouth turned up into a mockery of a smile. "Now unless you release her, it's going to be between you and *me.*"

There was no compassion in his eyes while he waited impatiently for her attacker to decide.

The brute swallowed as sweat beaded on his forehead. He removed his hands from her and straightened his jacket with one hard tug at the lapels. "I beg pardon, miss," he said at last. "I meant no harm." And with those words spoken, he quickly rushed out the door.

Relieved, Lorelei stared up at the same handsome face she'd admired the night before. A face that, like Justin's, was covered with a full day's growth of beard. Instead of looking silly, his added a rugged quality to his chiseled features.

"What happened to your accent?" she asked.

The count faced her with a wry half-smile, then used the line men had been using with women since Adam and Eve. "I beg your pardon, what are you talking about?"

"You, why are you here, dressed like that? Speaking like that?"

He frowned at her as if she'd lost her wits. "I'm sorry. You must have me confused with someone else."

Lorelei knew the game. It was the same one Justin had used when she'd caught him in an intimate embrace with Sophie Polke. The cad had actually tried to tell her she was seeing things.

She'd seen things all right—seen her fiancé's hand groping Sophie's backside!

The whole thing was the old *Let's make the woman feel stupid so that she'll leave it alone* ruse. A man only used it when he was hiding something.

In that instant she knew what it was.

Dear Lord, he's Black Jack Rhys.

She knew it. Deep in her bones and with every ounce of instinct she'd ever possessed, she knew this clever man was the only one who could thwart so many attempts to capture him.

And you danced with him!

Taking a deep breath for courage, she realized the only way to get out of this would be to play along with his lie. Let him think that he'd convinced her she was wrong.

"Oh," she said, trying to look contrite. "You're right. I . . . I must be mistaken. Thank you for helping me."

Jack stood aside as she rushed away from him like Satan himself was in pursuit. He'd seen the recognition in her eyes just moments before she'd vacillated to his logic.

Damn the intelligent wench.

Watching her cross the room, he saw her head straight to her pasty-faced Englishman.

Jack growled low in his throat. He'd come here tonight to meet Morgan and the Patriot spy who wanted them to run supplies through a British blockade. Only the three of them knew Black Jack would be here tonight.

So then, who, of the three of them, was the traitor?

Well, he could easily account for himself. He hadn't told a soul he planned to come here. And though he'd had plenty of people betray him over the years, Jack knew Morgan would never act dishonorably.

But the spy would.

Which meant Morgan was sitting in a trap and didn't know it. Jack sighed. Once again, he was going to have to pull Morgan out of the fire. Damn that boy's Patriot heart. Causes were for fools.

Heading for Morgan, he went to tell him the *wonderful* news.

Morgan was sitting at a table to the right of the bar. He looked up and nodded at Jack's approach. "There you are."

Jack ignored his greeting and slammed his fist straight into the jaw of the spy.

Morgan arched a curious brow as the man slid slowly to the floor. "What did he do? Wear the wrong color coat? Or is it his stock you find offensive this time?"

Jack leaned over the table. Resting his fists on the rough top, he narrowed his gaze on Morgan. "I'm assuming he's the one who told the Regulars we'd be here tonight. Did I hit the wrong man?"

Morgan's eyes widened. "What?"

Satisfied the shock on his friend's face was sincere, Jack smiled grimly. "We walked into a trap."

Lorelei looked triumphantly at Justin. "See. He's Black Jack. He just struck a man for no apparent reason."

"For all you know, Lori, the man seduced his wife."

Lorelei straightened and eyed Justin with malice. "I'm telling you it's *him*. Don't you recognize him from last night? He was playing Count Hapsburg no doubt to gather information about—"

"Lori, please," Justin said, his voice laden with stressed patience. "That man doesn't look anything like the count. He's obviously just some poor sailor come in to get a drink. The count was a good head taller and fair dripped with princely bearing. That man there is obviously a bluestocking. Besides, use your head, why would Black Jack Rhys come to the aid of a tavern whore?"

"I beg your pardon," she ground out. "I'm not a whore."

"You know what I mean."

She threw her hands up. How could he be so dense?

Infuriated, Lorelei turned on her heel. "You want proof. I'll give you proof." She took three steps toward Jack and shouted. "Hey, Jack Rhys."

The man she watched didn't move.

"See," Justin snapped. "He didn't even flinch. I told you it wasn't him."

Lorelei bit her lip. He hadn't moved, but everyone else in the tavern had looked. She had her proof.

She returned to Justin's side. "Just go arrest him. If I'm wrong you can let him go."

"If you're wrong, I'm a laughingstock."

Uhat are we going to do?" Morgan asked Jack, trying to look nonchalant and failing miserably.

Unfortunately, Jack was all too used to dealing with these situations to be rattled by this latest bout of treachery. "I want you to walk out of here like nothing's wrong. No one, other than our unconscious lump on the floor, knows who you are, so you're safe." He glanced to the spy on the floor. "At least until *he* wakes."

"What about you?"

"Don't worry about me."

"Jack . . ."

"I may have been spawned in the gutter, Morgan,

but I'm not going to die in it. Now go on, get yourself to safety."

Reluctantly, Morgan rose from his chair and did as Jack wanted.

It was only after Morgan had closed the door behind him that Jack dared a look to where Lorelei stood arguing with Justin.

Now *this* was amusing.

The moron had brought her here, no doubt, to listen for word of Jack Rhys, and as soon as she found him, the moron refused to believe it.

What did she see in that man anyway?

Women. He'd never understand them.

Jack knew he should leave before Justin realized who he was. But in truth, he was enjoying this little drama too much to leave. Besides, there was no trap from which he couldn't escape. No man or woman who could hold him.

Well, a naked woman in bed could hold him for a little while if she appealed to him.

And Lorelei Dupree appealed to him greatly.

He slid his gaze appreciatively over Lorelei's back. The short skirt fell several inches from the floor, giving him a nice view of her trim ankles. They were shapely and petite, and he wondered if they were covered with freckles like the bridge of her nose.

She gestured furiously toward him, then fell silent when their gazes met and locked.

Jack felt as if he'd been struck by lightning. Time seemed suspended as they stared at each other. The droning conversations faded until all he could hear was the thrumming of his own heart.

Jesus, but there was magic in that woman's gaze.

Some unknown alien power he'd never before encountered.

All he wanted to do was cross the room, pick her up in his arms, and carry her off to a bed somewhere and make love to her for the rest of the night.

And it was then he made a decision.

He'd intended to leave Lorelei out of this. But if Wallingford wanted her involved, so be it. He wasn't the kind of man to look a gift horse in the mouth. Fate had thrown her into his path twice and far be it from him to question what fate had in store for him.

Justin came to his feet. His face flushed with rage, he walked stiffly to where Jack stood.

It took all the control Jack possessed to break eye contact with Lorelei so that he could meet Justin's peeved expression.

"Forgive me, sir," Justin said before casting a quick, superior glance toward Lorelei. "I'm sorry to disturb you, but could you please tell me, are you Jack Rhys?"

"Aye, lieutenant," he said with a wicked grin. "You have your man. The question is, can you keep him?"

Justin's eyes widened and he fumbled for his sword. "It's him, men!" he shouted. "Seize him!"

Laughing at Justin's ineptitude, Jack reacted in an instant. He shoved Justin out of his way. The two men who had been sitting with Justin led Lorelei toward the door.

Jack unsheathed his sword and raced after them with only one thing in mind.

Lorelei Dupree.

Two plain-clothed Regulars emerged out of the

crowd and blocked his path to the door. He laughed at them. Did they really think they could stop him? He'd thwarted entire fleets sent out to destroy him.

Black Jack Rhys was not so easily taken.

With only a handful of moves, he disarmed them and was back on the trail of his target.

Jack rushed through the door to see Lorelei being helped into a cart. One of the soldiers with her turned to face him and unsheathed his sword.

This was rich, Jack thought with a smirk. Did the man honestly think he could protect her? That anyone could keep Jack Rhys from taking what he wanted? No one stood in his way.

Ever.

Just as they crossed swords, a shot rang out. Jack felt a sharp pain across his right shoulder blade. Glancing behind him, he saw Justin holding a smoking flintlock.

His jaw locked in anger, Jack sidestepped his foes and leapt to the back of the cart to survey the damage. Blood seeped from the wound, but the bullet appeared to have been deflected by a bone. Though painful, it wasn't enough to kill him.

It was just enough to make him mad.

No one drew blood from Black Jack Rhys! Tasting vengeance on his tongue, he took three steps toward the front of the cart, tossed the soldier next to Lorelei to the ground, then took his seat. Before she could move, Jack grabbed the reins and slapped them across the horses' backs.

The cart lurched sharply, then sped forward.

Lorelei turned in the seat to stare back at Justin as they sped away, her face frozen in a state of shock.

"Lorelei!" he heard Justin scream as they left him behind.

Her cheeks paling, Lorelei faced Jack. "What are you doing?"

"'Twould seem, fair lady, that Black Jack Rhys is abducting you."

3

Lorelei's heart hammered in fear and yet as she stared at Jack, there was an air of playful good humor about him. His eyes were alight. He didn't seem to be the cold-blooded killer of legend. He seemed more like a mischievous child completing a prank.

"What are you going to do to me?" she asked.

He looked at her, his face boyish and charming. "Believe it or not, and I'm sure you won't, I mean you no harm."

She scoffed. "Am I supposed to believe that the most wanted pirate on earth has abducted me and means me no harm? Surely, sir, you take me for a fool." And Lorelei was anything but a fool. It was time she parted company with Black Jack Rhys.

As she attempted to jump from the cart, the pirate grabbed her arm and pulled her back toward him. "I told you you wouldn't believe it."

Struggling against his hold, Lorelei drew back to slap him.

His face turned dark, foreboding. "Don't." That one word carried more power in it than a raging hurricane.

Not willing to test his brutality, she settled down and eyed him warily. "You don't really expect me to just sit here quietly while you abduct me?"

"That's exactly what I expect you to do."

"You haven't been around many women, have you?"

When he spoke, his voice was empty and strange to her ears. "I've been around enough."

"Well," she said, "they certainly didn't teach you any manners."

"I'm a pirate," he scoffed. "What, would you have me spout poetry?"

She stiffened her spine at his reprimand. "You didn't appear the pirate last night at the party. You were a gentleman then."

"Yes, well, you didn't appear to be a tavern whore last night, but—"

"Don't you say it," she snapped, her vision dulling at the second time someone had insulted her so.

He laughed again. "I apologize, Miss Dupree. I have no doubt of your innocence."

Her fear multiplied. "Is that why you intend to rape me?"

He pinned her with a furious glare. "I have no intention of raping you."

"Then why this elaborate abduction?"

"Why not?" he asked flippantly. "I was there, you were there, Lord Pasty Face was there. It seemed like a perfect opportunity."

The knot in her stomach drew tighter. She tightened her grip on the back of the seat as the cart rattled along the dirt road. "An opportunity for what?"

He didn't answer as he veered the horses to the left fork in the road that headed toward the docks. He glanced back over his shoulder, then he looked at her. "Let's pretend it's a game, shall we?"

Was he serious? Or just insane?

"A game?" she gasped in indignation. "A game of what?"

"Of chance and chase."

Could the man never answer a straight question? At any other time, she might have respected his quick thinking; however, it was her future they were talking about and she wanted to know what this man had planned. "Meaning what?"

"Meaning you, my little guppy, are the bait I intend to use to lure a shark out of his nest."

"I don't understand."

"I know you don't," he said, his gaze veiled. "I don't want you to. Suffice to say, you're going to be my guest for awhile."

Lorelei could see the docks up ahead. She had no intention of allowing him to take her on board his ship. She'd heard too many tales of what men like Black Jack Rhys did to the unfortunate females they captured. "Thank you for the invitation, but I really must decline."

This time his laughter was evil. "I'm afraid I *really* must insist."

As soon as Jack slowed the cart to a pace that wouldn't injure her, Lorelei leapt from her seat. A loud rending of fabric sounded as the hem of her dress caught in the cart and tore a gaping hole in her skirt. Ignoring it, she hit the ground on her side with a fierce thud that knocked the breath from her. Even so, she refused to succumb to the pain. She pushed herself up from the ground and ran. Her legs trembling, she prayed she could make it to the alleys of the warehouses before he caught her.

She didn't.

Jack's arms wrapped around her and the two of them tumbled to the ground. As they fell, Jack rolled so that his body absorbed the impact and they came to land a few feet from the cart with Jack on the bottom.

Lorelei dug her elbows into his chest in an effort to loosen his hold so that she could rise to her feet. He groaned and tightened his arms around her until she could no longer move.

Lying atop him, she stopped struggling and stared down into those cold gray eyes. She licked her suddenly dry lips, afraid of what he might do to her now that he had her firmly within his grasp.

To her relief, he released her and stood. Before she could run again, he pulled her up from the ground and locked his hand tightly around her upper arm. "As I said," he ground out, "I really must insist."

When she tried dragging her feet and twisting out of his grip, he growled low in his throat, then picked her up and tossed her over his shoulder.

"Let me go!" she shrieked.

"I have no intention of renewing our chase." He locked his arm around her legs to keep her from kicking him.

As Lorelei drew back to pummel his back, she caught sight of the dark stain spreading on his shirt. Frowning, she touched it, then drew her hand back to see it covered in red.

It was blood.

"If you so much as pat that wound," Jack warned, "I'll see your back lashed with a whip."

Tempted to disregard his words and pound anyway, she decided the saner course of action would be restraint. This was a man whose very name symbolized murder, mayhem, and cruelty.

Besides, as large as he was, it would probably only make him angry. And she'd already had a good indication that Black Jack Rhys was a fearsome ogre when angered.

He carried her up a gangway.

"Jack!" She heard a man's excited shout. "Thank God, I was just . . ." The man's voice trailed off as Jack stepped aboard the ship.

"What the devil have you done now?" the man demanded.

Jack ignored him as he carried her across the deck, past crew members who stared at them in a mixture of curiosity and disbelief, and descended a ladder to the decks below.

The man followed behind them, his mouth opening and closing like a fish gulping for air.

Lanterns were placed on the wall every few feet, giving her enough light to finally see the bloodstain seeping across Jack's shirt. It was an ugly wound and she recalled the sound of a gun firing not long before Jack had tossed her poor escort to the ground and taken his seat.

The man trailing them was extremely handsome and in his early twenties. With black hair and brown eyes, he stood almost as tall as Jack. She had seen him earlier that night at the tavern talking with another man she had suspected of being a spy by the way he would draw silent at her approach and scan the room nervously while she served them.

But the man behind her had not been so cautious.

"Is this the girl from the party last night?" the stranger asked.

"Aye," Jack answered. "I told you, pup, you don't know me as well as you think you do."

"What is it with you and this woman?" the man asked Black Jack, looking somewhat dumbstruck. "Jack, you can't go around abducting heiresses. Are you insane?"

Jack snorted. "So I've been told."

"Make him let me go," Lorelei begged the handsome stranger. "Please don't let him keep me."

The man opened his mouth to speak, then closed it.

Lorelei heard footsteps as someone approached from in front of them.

"Tarik," Jack said in greeting. "Get the men ready to sail. We leave immediately."

"Aye, Captain."

Jack paused and Lorelei tried to see the newcomer, but Jack held her so that all she could see was the shocked look on the dark-haired man's face. Raising up, she bumped her head against one of the lanterns.

"Hold still, woman," Jack snapped. "The last thing you need is a concussion."

Lorelei balled up her fists wishing she could strangle the beast.

"And Tarik," Jack said, his voice thick with warning. "We were being chased. If they show up on the docks, aim to maim. Do what you have to, but try not to kill anyone."

"Captain?" the man asked as if the order confused him.

"Just do it. Tell the men I'll have the head of anyone who kills a Brit tonight."

"Aye, Captain."

Jack turned her to the wall as the man walked past them.

"Let me go!" she insisted, knowing it would do no good, but still feeling the need to try.

The dark-haired man stepped forward and gestured toward her. "You've got to let her go, Jack. She's more trouble than even *you* want."

Jack's low laugh was his only response.

Now the man trailing them looked as if he wanted to throttle Jack as much as she did. "Please talk some sense into him," Lorelei begged, hoping this stranger held some sway over her captor. At least he appeared to be more reasonable than the pirate.

"Enough of this, Jack. Let her go."

Jack ignored him. "Lay on, Macduff; and damned be him that first cries, halt, enough."

Shakespeare? she thought with a frown. The king of pirates was quoting Shakespeare?

"Very amusing, Jack," the dark-haired man snarled. "Need I remind you, Macbeth lost his head."

Jack said nothing more as he opened a door, walked to the center of a large cabin, and finally released her. Immediately, she ran for the door.

"Stop!" Jack roared in a voice so powerful that her body involuntarily obeyed.

He crossed the room and stood before her. His eyes devoid of emotion, he stared sharply at her. "I weary of chasing you, my lady. If you so much as take one step from this room, then I shall be forced to kill you for it."

She swallowed convulsively as the rumors of his ferocity played through her mind. No one crossed Black Jack Rhys and lived.

"Better dead than raped," she said, her voice cracking with nervousness.

Jack rolled his eyes. He turned to the dark-haired man. "Would you please tell the wench that rape isn't included on my list of crimes against nations?"

"Neither was kidnapping until tonight."

Jack's look could have forged steel. "You're not helping. And I haven't any more time to deal with either one of you." Jack directed his gaze back to Lorelei. "You'll be locked in here until we get safely past the Brits. Try to relax and stay low to the floor."

"Low to the floor?" she asked in confusion.

"Aye, you're less likely to lose your head should a cannonball come crashing through the wall."

"Is that a jest?" she gasped.

When he didn't answer, she turned to the dark-haired man. "Is he joking?"

"Nay."

Jack pulled a set of keys from his pocket. "Don't worry," he said with a taunting smile. "If the ship starts sinking, I promise I'll come back and unlock the door."

Her stomach sank faster than a capsized boat.

Lorelei was too stunned to move until after the two men had left the room and closed the door behind them.

Rushing to the door, she rattled the knob as Jack

locked it. "Nay!" Lorelei shrieked. "You have to let me go."

But it was no use. Jack locked the door and she listened as he and his companion walked away from her room.

Lorelei closed her eyes in defeat. Her fate was sealed and she was doomed.

Jack, I know you've—"

"Listen," Jack said, cutting Morgan off as they headed back topside. "I need you to deliver a message for me to Lieutenant Justin Wallingford."

"I don't care if it's to . . ." He watched as the name dawned on Morgan. "Wallingford?"

Jack nodded. "She's engaged to Lord Wallingford's son."

The color faded from Morgan's face. "You can't be thinking what you're thinking."

Jack rubbed his aching, wounded shoulder. He needed to get Morgan off his ship and tend his wound. The last thing he wanted was to bleed to death before he had a chance to even his score.

"Morgan, I don't have time to write the letter myself. I need you to do it after I'm gone. Tell Wallingford I'll be waiting for him at *Isla de Los Almas Perdidos*."

"This is suicide, Jack."

"No," he said, narrowing his gaze on the docks. "This is revenge."

Morgan glared at him for several seconds before he spoke again. "You know Thadeus wouldn't approve of this."

Jack felt a tick begin in his jaw as he thought

about old Thadeus. He'd been a kind, gentle man. A physician by trade and a sailor by choice, Thadeus had befriended Jack after he'd escaped and signed on to sail with Robert Dreck's pirate crew. When Robert had retired from piracy, the old man had chosen to sail with a merchant ship. A merchant ship that had turned Patriot at the outbreak of this bloody damn war. A ship Wallingford had captured eight months ago.

He'd been looking for the bastard ever since.

His eyes hard, he snarled at Morgan. "I'm sure Thadeus didn't approve of being tied to the main mast of the *White Dove* while Wallingford set fire to it, either."

Jack tried to step past Morgan, but Morgan grabbed his good arm and turned him back to face him. "I know you loved the old man, Jack. But let it go before you get killed."

Grimacing, Jack wrenched his arm free. "Let it go? This from a man out to destroy Isaiah Winston? How long have you been after that bastard?"

"That's different. He murdered my father."

"What the hell do you think Thadeus was to me?" How he hated hearing the pain in his voice. Jack prided himself on the fact that nothing ever touched him. But Thadeus had. In a life filled with pain, Thadeus had been the only salve he'd ever known. The old man's wisdom and kindness had been the only thing that kept Jack whole and sane.

There were times he hated the old man for not joining his crew. If he had, he'd be safe now. Instead, Thadeus had joined those damned Patriots and gotten himself taken.

There had been no survivors. Wallingford had

ordered his crew to shoot any man who escaped the flames.

Morgan and Jack stood there glaring at each other until Morgan finally sighed. "I'm sorry, Jack. I truly am. But this won't give you peace any more than getting yourself killed will bring Thadeus back."

Those words reminded him of the last thing Thadeus had said to him. *Just don't let yourself get killed before you make your peace, boy. Many's the soul who consigned themselves to hell without the devil having to lift a finger.*

Jack hadn't consigned himself to hell. The world had done that to him long ago. Now it was time for him to fulfill the doomed prophecy his mother had whispered in his ear since his early childhood.

"Are you going to write the note, Morgan?"

Morgan sighed. "I owe you too much to say no." His eyes turned to stone. "Damn you, Jack. I'll never forgive you if you end up like Thadeus."

Jack wanted something to say to comfort Morgan. But he couldn't give him any solace. Fate was fickle. They both knew that. One day fate, like everyone else in his life, would betray him.

It was expected.

"Go on, Morgan. I've got a lot to do."

Morgan gave a bitter laugh. "Have him meet you at the Island of the Lost Souls. You're a sick man, Jack Rhys. May God have mercy on your soul."

Jack watched him walk away. Morgan was the only person alive who understood the significance of that island. The only person who knew that part of Jack's past.

That part of his future.

Lorelei leaned over the wooden table in the center of her room with her chin resting on her folded arms. The cabin was larger than she would have thought, with a washstand and basin in one corner and a small bed to her left. Large windows were in front of her that allowed her to see the lighthouse light dappling against the midnight waves as she watched the coast of Charleston grow smaller and smaller.

It had been almost an hour since Jack had locked her in and left her here to contemplate her future.

And what a grisly future she imagined it to be.

She trembled in uncertainty. Poor Justin. He would blame himself for this. He wouldn't rest until he found her in whatever condition Jack left her in.

Deep inside, she wished she could blame Justin for this. But she'd been the one who agreed to this horrible night. She was the one who had identified Jack Rhys.

"You should have listened to Justin!" she hissed to herself. He'd warned her of the danger, but fortified by her own arrogance, she hadn't listened.

When was she going to learn to obey her fiancé and her father? How many more fiascos would she have to face before she learned her place?

The door to her room flew open.

Lorelei shot to her feet to meet the newcomer.

Black Jack entered. Though his face still bore a day's growth of beard, he'd changed clothes and washed himself. Even across the room, she could smell the clean scent of man, soap, and sandalwood.

His black trousers were snug against his lean muscular hips and thighs, and tucked into a pair of finely polished boots tipped with sliver inlays. The black cotton shirt was full and open at the throat, displaying a good hand's length of smooth, tanned chest that fair glowed in the low candlelight. He wore his long honey-colored hair pulled back into a queue that contrasted sharply with his dark-colored clothing.

The look on his face was both stern and sharp, intense and predatorial.

If not for who and what he was, he would have been an incredibly handsome man.

"What do you want?" she snapped, putting her chair between them.

A bitter smile curved his lips. "Still don't trust me."

"Should I?"

His face turned serious. "No, you shouldn't." He moved toward her.

Instinctively, she backed across the room until the wall stopped her retreat.

To her surprise, he paused at the table where she'd been sitting and placed a small brass key on the tabletop. When he looked up at her, he pinned her with his cold, serious stare. "This is the only key to this room."

Lorelei looked at the key that glinted like gold in the candlelight.

"You may keep the door locked for the entire trip if you wish."

She lifted her gaze from the key to his face. "You're really not going to rape me?"

Closing his eyes, Jack clenched his teeth, and bore the look of a man who was struggling for patience and losing the battle quickly. "No, Lorelei. I'm not going to rape you."

Could she really believe him?

He'd said himself he wasn't trustworthy. "Is this all just some elaborate game? Are you trying to make me trust you so that you can torture me with betrayal?"

"Been listening to stories about me, have you?"

"They're true, aren't they?"

He shrugged. "I guess it depends on whom you ask. What I've learned over the years is that truth is never so easy. And every person sees a different reality."

She thought about him at the party last night. The way he'd easily convinced people he was an aristocrat. He'd been a part of her world then, with the same stoic arrogance he bore here on board the ship where he was the absolute voice of authority. It had taken untold confidence and daring for him to walk into her father's party uninvited and not be caught. But then, he must have known that he wouldn't be challenged, had probably gone to numerous such affairs without ever being found out.

It was her first insight into this man. "You like to play with people's perceptions, don't you?"

He didn't answer her question. Instead, he moved to stand before her.

Lorelei glanced to the door, wondering if she could run through it before he caught her. Before she could try, he reached out and touched her cheek.

Though light, his touch and his heated gaze held her prisoner. His fingers were warm against her flesh.

"Little Lorelei," he breathed. "Named for a goddess and possessed with the inner strength of a warrior. I don't want you to be afraid of me," he whispered and in some way, those words soothed her. Against all sanity and reason, she believed him when he spoke.

"What do you want from me?" she asked.

His gaze dipped to her lips and when he spoke his voice was warm and welcome. "I want you to know that no one on board my ship will harm you. Most especially not me."

She swallowed at his words and at the spell they were weaving around her. What was it about this man that she found herself wanting to trust him? His scent clung to her, as well as the heat from his body. The tenderness of his flesh against her own sparked a flame deep inside that terrified her more than his ruthless reputation.

He lowered his hand to where he could feel the strong beating of her heart against his fingertips. "There," he said quietly. "No fear?"

"A little fear."

He laughed at her honesty.

A knock sounded on the door, intruding on the strange feelings that swept through her at his intimate touch.

Jack took a step back. "Enter," he called.

A tall, distinguished-looking black woman walked in, carrying an armload of clothes. She was dressed in a loosefitting skirt and sleeveless shirt of vibrant gold. Surely no more than a year or two older than Lorelei, she had a beautiful face and her hair had grown out naturally, forming an attractive frame for her medium brown skin.

"So," the woman said, her voice thick with a Carribean accent. "This be the poor child ya done gone and stolen from her family. Ya ought to be ashamed of yourself for such, Captain Jack. Ya've probably frightened the poor child out of her old age."

To her astonishment, Jack looked sheepish.

"Now ya best be going," she said to Jack. "Tarik say those British are closing in and he be needing ya topside for the fight."

"Fight?" Lorelei asked, her heart hammering once more.

Black Jack shrugged nonchalantly. "What can I say? It's a war. We're a ship leaving an occupied city in the dead of night. . . ."

"How can you find this funny?" she asked, agape at the humor in his eyes.

"Don't be so afraid, Lorelei. There's nothing to worry about."

"Death!" she snapped. "Death is most definitely something to worry over."

He placed his hand over his heart. "Then fear not, fair maiden. For your safety, I shall cast off those demon ships." He gestured toward the windows. "I shall smite them to the very depths of the ocean where they can never again pose a threat to your most cherished personage."

He took her right hand in his and bent low over it before kissing the back of her knuckles. His breath tickled her skin and she bit her lip to stifle the strange titillation that such a small gesture gave her. "I bid thee adieu, fair maiden."

Straightening, he gave her a heated look. "But before I leave and face my most dreaded foe, wilt thou not send me off with a kiss?"

Before she could protest, he stepped into her

arms and lowered his lips over hers. Too shocked to protest, she felt his arms tighten about her waist as his lips opened hers.

Her head swam as he explored her mouth with the gift of a master. Surrounded by the scent of man and ocean, and the feel of hard muscles flexing beneath her hands, she was entranced. Never had Justin kissed her like this! Never had he *felt* like this.

That one kiss went deeper than just her lips, her mouth. The heat of it spread through her body, setting fire to her blood and making her ache in tender places.

Just when she feared she could no longer support her own weight, he pulled back and stared down into her eyes. "Now, if death awaits, I can go happily to my grave."

"You are insane," she breathed.

"Nay, my dearest Lorelei, I am merely a man who has sampled the fruit of heaven. And, fate willing, on the morrow I shall sample the peaks," his gaze lowered to her breasts, which tightened in response.

Then his gaze moved lower. "And valley."

Heat stung her cheeks as she stepped away from him. "Never!" She gasped.

His smile grew wider. "Never, never, never, never, never." His hand moved to the top of her bodice, where a row of buttons secured the thin linen over her corset. "Pray you undo this button."

Her face hot with fury and embarrassment, Lorelei narrowed her eyes at the quote from King Lear. For the first time in her life, she was grateful for her father's passion that had forced her to learn Shakespeare's works. "Eyes look your last," she taunted. "Away you moldy rogue, away."

He laughed, deep and rich; it filled her ears with music. "You're mixing your plays."

She opened her mouth to retort.

A cannon blast sounded outside.

Jack ran for the door, then paused, turning back to face her. "Fair thoughts and happy hours attend on you."

And then he was gone.

Stunned, Lorelei stood frozen in the center of the cabin. She had no idea what to make of this man. On the one hand, he possessed the refinement of a gentleman capable of quoting the great bard and on the other, he was a known killer. His name was synonymous with death.

"Don't frown so, it's not so bad here," the woman spoke as she placed her armload of clothes and such on the table. She approached Lorelei with an air of open friendship. "They call me Kesi."

"Are you a prisoner here, too?" she asked, wondering why Kesi traveled with a shipload of pirates.

Kesi shook her head. "There aren't any prisoners on Captain Jack's ship. I'm the wife of his quartermaster, Tarik."

Lorelei frowned. "Black Jack Rhys allows you to travel with Tarik?"

"Of course. I am one of several wives on board. You'll meet the others tomorrow."

"I don't understand," Lorelei said, confused by Kesi's declaration. "I thought pirates only kept slaves or used women on their ships."

Kesi laughed. "Don't ya go listening to those tales, child. Some pirates are like that, but not Captain Jack." Kesi moved forward and took her by the arm.

"Come," Kesi said, pulling her gently. "We best be moving away from the windows and turn out the lamps. The British will shoot at anyone they see."

She led Lorelei to sit on the bed, then quickly extinguished the light. The room was bathed by moonlight as more cannons exploded.

"Don't worry, child. Kesi will stay with ya." Kesi sat down beside her.

Lorelei cleared her throat in an effort to dislodge the knot of fear that was almost choking her. "Does this happen much?"

"Not too often." Kesi took her hand. "Don't be afraid. No one here will harm ya."

"That's what Black Jack said."

"But still you don't believe him?"

"Can I?"

"Listen with your soul, child. What does it say?"

"It says I should have stayed home tonight and never, ever left my room."

The night sky flickered with light as two British frigates gave chase. Jack had ordered the black sails raised, which made it all the harder for the English to see them.

A few minutes more and they would be through it. As he stood near the anti-boarding netting, his thoughts turned to the woman who waited one deck below.

He'd never before met a woman who could quote Shakespeare back to him. But then, Lorelei had probably never before met a pirate, let alone one who could read.

He had Thadeus to thank for that. And he wondered who had taught Lorelei.

Had she been as opposed to learning as he'd been? Or had she embraced it?

Something told him that her tutor had probably had his work cut out for him every bit as much as Thadeus had. He couldn't see someone as vivacious as Lorelei sitting still long enough to read. Nay, she was the type who would prefer making mischief.

"Incoming!"

He jerked around at the shout.

His eyes used to the darkness, he could see the cannonball silhouetted by the moonlight as it arced for his ship. It seemed as if it moved in slow motion and he watched in shocked horror as it flew straight into the windows of the second deck.

Straight into the windows of the room he'd left Lorelei in.

4

Without thought of the British or the fight, Jack ran for the ladder to the lower decks with Tarik hot on his heels. He skidded down the ladder without touching a rung, then dashed down the narrow corridor at top speed. Their panic seemed to feed off each other as they raced toward the cabin where the two women were.

His heart pounding in terror, Jack pushed open the door, expecting the very worst.

A voice that wavered between ire and incredulity drew his gaze to the sight he longed most to see— Lorelei standing intact in front of Kesi.

"I can't believe it was a cannonball," Lorelei said once more.

Relieved more than he cared to admit, Jack paused in the doorway as Tarik entered and swooped Kesi up into his arms to hold her close against his chest.

"Ah, woman," Tarik scolded. "Ya scared me to death."

"What ya worrying for," Kesi said in his ear as she hugged him back. "It didn't even come close to us."

Lorelei approached Jack, her eyes large with a glaze of terror. She held her arms out in measurement. "It was this big."

"I think the poor child has lost her mind," Kesi said quietly as she stepped back from Tarik. "She started babbling the minute the ball landed."

"The ball didn't land," Lorelei corrected. "It tore down that wall." She pointed to the wall opposite the aft where the cannonball had splintered a good portion of the sturdy oak boards. It, along with the broken windows, was an ugly scar on his ship, but fully reparable.

"Nay," Lorelei spoke again. "I take that back. It *shredded* the wall."

To his surprise, Lorelei reached up and grabbed his shirtfront. Her soft fingers sliding against the flesh of his neck caused a chill as she clutched the material in her fist. Pulling him down until his nose almost touched hers, she whispered, "Have you ever had a cannonball come so close to you that you could see the maker's symbol?"

"Actually, I have," he admitted.

Her eyes widened, then grew dark with anger. "Fine then, you stay here, I'm going home now."

Releasing him, she started out the door.

"There's one problem, Lorelei."

She paused and turned her head to look up at him. "What?"

"The only way home is back through the British."

Her eyes lost their glaze and focused on him with malice. "I hate you, Black Jack Rhys. I really, really hate you."

Jack just smiled, too amused and too relieved to take her words to heart. "As long as I provoke some strong emotion from you, I can't complain. 'Tis apathy I fear, not hatred."

She balled her fists up at her sides, delighting him all the more.

"Are we through it?" Kesi asked.

It was only then Jack noticed how far back the cannon fire had drifted while they'd been occupied with the women. He looked at Kesi. "It sounds like it."

"I'll go make sure," Tarik said to Jack while he touched Kesi lightly on her arm. "Please, go to our room where 'tis safe."

"I'm going." Kesi stopped beside Jack as Tarik left the cabin to return to his post. "Where ya going to put the child now that her room is destroyed?"

Jack considered the possibilities.

He certainly knew where he wanted to put Lorelei. His own bed with him in it. Now, that would be a truly pleasurable voyage. His entire body burned at just the thought.

Her seduction would be easy enough if he could just get her to stay in his room. But *that* wouldn't be easy. . . .

Then, an evil thought struck him.

There was one place he could put her that would guarantee she would go running to his room for protection. One place that would be even more horrendous to a woman of such delicate breeding and sensibilities than staying in a pirate's private cabin.

"The room across the hall."

Kesi looked stunned. "Ya can't be thinking of doing that. How's the child to sleep in that room with all those . . . those things in there? Ya'll be giving her nightmares forever. She'll take one look and run for the door."

That was the idea.

But he didn't dare tell Kesi that. Instead, he used logic to sway Kesi to his side. "There's no place else to put her. . . ." He feigned deep thought for several seconds. "Unless she's willing to share *my* cabin."

He slanted a hopeful glance toward Lorelei and noted her stiffened posture.

He gave a forlorn sigh. "I somehow doubt she'd agree to that."

"The room across the hall will be quite fine," Lorelei said, confirming his prediction.

Kesi folded her arms across her chest. "She only says that because she has yet to see what's waiting for her in that room. You're being cruel, Jack Rhys. Remember such dreadful things come back to ya tenfold."

"I hear your warning, Kesi. Now you better take yourself off to your room before Tarik loses any more years off his life."

"I'm going. But ya better do right by that child, or ya'll be having a heap of problems to be sure."

Kesi quit the cabin.

Jack watched the fury in Lorelei's eyes change to concern as she realized they were once again alone. How he hated seeing that fear there. It was the fire of her gaze that warmed him. The fire inside her that he responded to.

"You had to put me in a room with a big window," she said, her voice still shaky.

Her ability to see humor in the most dire of situations intrigued him. Most women would be screaming and trembling. But she bolstered herself well.

"Frightened you, did it?" he asked.

Her look would have melted ice.

Jack couldn't resist taunting her more. "Ah, now, Lady Lorelei, go ahead and admit it. Your blood is racing through your veins and for the first time in your life, you're drunk with the sense of adventure."

"I'm quite certain I have no idea what you mean," she said, lifting her chin haughtily.

He moved to stand before her, then reached out with his hand and gently tilted her chin until she met his gaze. "Aye, you do. Our escape was exhilarating and I've seen enough of your spirit to know you appreciate it."

"Bah," she responded.

He traced the line of her soft, delicate jaw and he couldn't help wondering how much softer and more tender the flesh of her bare stomach would be. "Tell me, has your pasty-faced Englishman ever made you feel this alive?"

"Alive? You almost got me killed."

"Almost never counts. You almost got away from me on the docks, but you didn't."

She took a step back from him and crossed her arms over her chest as if to protect herself from him. "You're an evil man."

Well, Jack certainly couldn't argue that point. He was an evil man with a wicked intent where this particular woman was concerned.

He slowly walked around behind her and resisted the urge to draw her close. He leaned down to whisper in her ear. "Aye, an evil man who has just given you one of the most memorable experiences of your life. One I know you'll recount dozens of times to your children and grandchildren."

He brushed a silken strand of hair off her shoulder and noted the chills that sprang up on her arms, the tightening of her breasts beneath the thin cotton of her blouse. Closing his eyes, he imagined how sweet it would be to taste those taut peaks, to run his tongue over them. . . .

"I bet Jason never made your heart pound," he said to distract himself before he gave way to the raging fire of his groin.

Now that got her dander up again. She shook his touch away and took two steps forward. "*Justin* protects me!"

He duplicated her pose of crossing his arms over his chest. "I didn't see *Jason* protecting you tonight at the tavern. Where was he while you were being pawed by a boorish bear?"

"He was waiting for you," she said in triumph.

"Well then, I'm certainly flattered to know my capture is worth more than your virtue to him."

She put her hands up to her ears. "Stop it this instant. I'll hear no more of this from you. Justin loves me more than his life and you're just trying to confuse me."

He took her hands in his and brought first the right then the left up to his lips so that he could place a kiss on her knuckles. "Truth is often confusing."

She stiffened and removed her hands from his grasp. "Nay, the truth is never confusing."

"Then tell me, what is the truth?"

"The truth is that you are a black-hearted scoundrel who must be brought to justice. You attack defenseless crews and leave them to die."

His bitter laughter rang out. He cupped her cheek in his hand and turned her so she was forced to look at him again. "Since when is a shipload of men armed to their teeth considered defenseless? And what of the English navy? Do you consider them defenseless?"

She frowned. "But you—"

"I seem to be the one who has a wounded *back*, Lorelei, while Justin and his men sprung a trap." He cocked his head. "Tell me, please, how can a man ambush a ship on the open seas? Do you think me some magician who has a flying ship that can just fall out of the sky?"

"Stop this. I will not listen to any more. I know the truth. You're just trying to make me doubt Jason."

"Justin."

"Jas . . ." Her voice trailed off as she caught on to what he'd made her say. Her face flamed bright red. "I want you to take me home, right now."

"Take you home. Back to your safe little world where you may pass judgment on people without knowing the facts. Really, Lorelei, you do disappoint me."

"Do you think I care whether or not I disappoint you, Jack Rhys?"

"I know you don't. I'm simply a dastardly pirate unworthy of anything more than your contempt."

"Exactly."

"Exactly," he said with an exaggerated sigh. "Then come, Lady Lorelei, and I shall take you off to your own little room where you may hide from the harsh realities of life. It must truly be nice to grow up so comforted. I personally wouldn't know."

And with that, he ignored the angry indignation on her face, turned on his heel, and led her from the room.

Jack didn't know why it bothered him so that she was so quick to judge him. Before he'd left his cradle, he'd learned to ignore the biting epitaphs people gave him, and as years passed to even enjoy them.

It was just that she wasn't applying the correct epitaph, he decided. Aye, that was it. She saw him as a pirate when he wanted her to see him as a lover.

Women adored him. They had always done so, and he'd learned to expect women to pander to his whims and moods. But not Lorelei. Her resistence to him was more than just token. More than just annoying.

It was challenging.

And Jack Rhys loved a good challenge.

So long as it didn't go on too long.

And much longer from her was far longer than he wanted. 'Twas time to breech her prickly defenses and claim the wench.

They crossed the small corridor and he knocked thrice upon a door.

Drawing her brows together, Lorelei took a step back in trepidation. "Who's in there?"

Jack decided to play up the moment. "No one."

"Then why did you knock?"

He bent down until his face was level with hers and whispered in a dire tone. "I'm scaring off the spirits so they won't bother you while you sleep."

He savored the confusion on her face, then pulled a lantern from its holder in the hallway. He pressed his back against the door, then opened it and walked backward into the room so that he could watch her face.

With every step backward that illuminated the room, her face turned a shade paler.

Victory. Sweet, pleasurable victory was almost his. He could taste it. Or more to the point, he could almost taste her.

Her gaze darted around the room from one grisly totem to the next. "What are those?" She gasped.

"Heads," he said simply, as he glanced around the walls which were covered with approximately thirty dark brown heads in various states of contortions. "Shrunken heads to be precise. We picked them up some time ago from an island of headhunters."

He hadn't thought it possible, but she actually turned a shade paler. "An island of what?"

"Headhunters. They kill enemies and foreigners and shrink their heads."

Her face incredulous, she narrowed her gaze on him. "They didn't shrink yours."

Jack acquiesced. "True, but it's only because I was more ruthless than the chief and his men."

Her look turned dubious. "Why do you have all these heads?"

Jack set the lantern down on the dust-covered trunk beside the bed before he looked up and again locked gazes with her. "We were burying a load of treasure on a remote, uncharted island when we suddenly found ourselves surrounded by island natives."

It was a complete lie. First, Jack had never in his life buried treasure. He preferred to make investments with his ill-gotten gains. And secondly, the heads had been taken from a Spanish merchant ship. Jack's crew had decided to hang them in here to scare prisoners into divulging secrets. Jack had never allowed his men to use this room for such, though; he'd always thought the very notion was ludicrous.

On the morrow, he'd have to up their wages.

He stood beside Lorelei and cloaked his voice in a fearsome whisper. "Naked savages they were, screaming and trying to kill us with long, fearsome spears. But it didn't take much to turn the tables on them. A few slashes of me sword and gunpowder-packed grenades and we whipped them but good."

Suspicion clouded her eyes and he realized he was heaping it on a bit too thick. Retreating before he undid himself, he finished the story. "After we had routed them, the chief offered the heads to me, provided I spare his life and leave his island. He swore that if I decorated my ship with them I would never know defeat."

She caught her lower lip between her teeth as she again dragged her gaze around the room. No doubt the idea of sleeping in his cabin was starting to appeal to Miss Dupree.

Feeling impish, Jack grabbed one of the dark, grisly totems from the wall. "Would you like a closer look?" he asked, moving it toward her.

With a squeak, Lorelei jumped back into the hallway.

Jack smiled at her reaction. "It won't hurt you, really. They are quite dead, after all."

She curled her lip. "You're disgusting."

"Perhaps. But not nearly as disgusting as this room . . . hmmm?"

Bravely, she stood ramrod stiff, like a queen about to address her court. She raked him with a sneer before she spoke. "I would rather spend eternity in this room than five more minutes in your company."

Jack cocked an eyebrow. What ho? Had she really said that?

To *him*. To bonny Jack Rhys, the greatest lover on the high seas?

No woman had *ever* said such to him before!

His male pride offended, he stared at her in disbelief. "You would truly rather spend the night in here than in the comfort of *my* cabin?"

She answered without hesitation. "Your cabin will be quite acceptable provided you're not in it."

"And if I were?"

"Then I say make room amongst the missing heads. There shall be a new member of their group tonight."

Now this was wholly unexpected. He had mistakenly assumed that one look in this room would send her fleeing to his arms for safety.

No woman had ever, ever been *this* reluctant toward him before. He was, after all, a man of renowned looks. Not that he was vain about his appearance—well, not overly so.

Of course, there was the matter of his reputation, which at times was more than well deserved, but women in the past had found even that appealing. Aye, the allure of having a dangerous man in their bed had thawed many a woman's frigidity.

Lorelei was bluffing, he decided. She must be.

After returning the head in his hand to the wall, he approached Lorelei, who stood warily in the doorway.

"So then, you'd rather lie down with all these men here, than with me?"

Unflinchingly, she met his gaze. "As you said earlier, they are quite dead while you—"

"Are quite alive."

"Aye."

"Then I suppose the question is, whom do you fear more? Them or me?"

" 'Tis not a question of fear, sir. 'Tis simply a question of preference. I prefer their loathsome company to yours."

Impulsively, he reached out and stroked the soft underside of her chin with his knuckle. She veiled her gaze, but even so he knew his touch affected her. How could it not? "And do you truly find my company loathsome?"

"Aye, and despicable."

"Despicable am I?" he said, greatly amused. " 'Tis a pity then. I find you captivating."

She stepped away from him. "And I find myself captive, which I believe is the very core of our differences. Now, if you'll excuse me, I feel the need for solitude."

"Solitude? Why, my dearest Lorelei, I believe you'll have an army of guests to keep you company tonight while you sleep," he said, gesturing to the heads.

She shuddered.

"It's not too late to change your mind."

"About you? I'll never change my mind about you, *Black* Jack Rhys."

He tilted his head. "A fickle and changeful thing is woman ever."

"A faithless and *dreadful* thing is man ever."

"Does that include Justin?"

"Not hardly."

"Ah, just as I thought. He's not a man after all."

Her cheeks darkened in anger. "Here is the door, and there is the way through it. Now use it."

"Ever as you wish."

Her face lost all color and she looked momentarily bewildered.

Jack paused at her pallor.

"Never utter those words to me," she whispered.

Taken aback, Jack nodded. Whatever had caused her to react that way?

Regaining his composure, he cleared his throat. "Very well. I shall leave you to your new friends. But should you change your mind, you'll find my cabin at the end of the hallway," he said, pointing to the correct door. "You won't even have to knock."

"Don't wait up."

"Fine then, just make yourself at home."

"I shall," she said, then shut the door in his face.

Jack clenched his teeth as he swallowed the bitter taste of stalemate. She was a crafty one to be sure. High-spirited and delightful to a fault.

Her resistance merely added to the satisfaction he would gain from her surrender. It would be his greatest revenge and his greatest triumph.

And in spite of what she thought, he *would* have her. After all, he'd never in his life known defeat.

Lorelei breathed a short sigh of relief at being alone. Until she started to turn around and face the . . .

"Courage," she breathed to herself even as she cringed. "The dead can't hurt you."

No, but they certainly terrified her.

There were probably no more than three dozen heads strung up along the wall. But to her, it seemed like three thousand. And each one of the dark, leathery things seemed to be staring straight at her with those dark empty sockets that she half expected to glow with some inner demonic light.

Forcing her temerity out of hiding, she decided that this was one battle she would win.

"You are Lorelei Dupree," she said to herself in an effort to rally her flagging courage. "You are the granddaughter of Anne Bonny and Anne Bonny would never, *ever* let these heads scare her."

Nay, Granny-Anne would take the devil by the horns and wrestle him to the ground. And as her father so often pointed out, she was her grandmother made over.

With that thought, she gingerly plucked one of the nasty things off the wall by the leather cord that hung it there. Her upper lip curled, she held it at arm's length as she moved slowly to place it on the small bed.

Just as she stooped, a loud knock sounded.

Shrieking in alarm, she dropped the head and spun to the door, which was then flung open.

Jack stood in the doorway, his features stern and concerned. "What is it?" he demanded.

"*What is it?*" she repeated, covering her thundering heart with a trembling hand. "You knave, you scared the life out of me!"

He laughed.

"It's not funny."

"It is from where I stand."

Fury sizzled deep inside her and she wished she were a man just long enough to give the pirate the sound thrashing he deserved. "Fine then, I suggest you stand outside and leave me be."

"Ever—" He paused, then said quickly, "Absolutely. I only returned so that I could give you these."

He held an armload of clothes out to her. It was the same bundle Kesi had delivered to her in the other room.

Stiffly, she took it from him. "Good night, Captain Rhys."

He brought two fingers up to his brow, then swept her with a mock salute before he pulled the door closed.

Lorelei took long deep breaths until her heart stopped pounding.

"Just pretend he's the ogre and you're the damsel," she whispered to herself, recalling one of the games she and Justin had played as children.

Justin always came to the rescue. Never once had he failed her and she was certain that this time would be no exception.

A night or two, and Justin was bound to catch them.

A night or two. . . .

Lorelei swallowed as she placed the clothes on the chest beside the bed, then returned to collecting the heads. A night or two of battling the devil himself while she wished herself safely home.

Jack Rhys. Devil, pirate, scoundrel and . . .

Handsome. It was a superficial thing, but it was also very true. He was also charming and intelligent. Nothing like she'd been told.

"Who are you, Captain Jack?" she asked the last head as she dropped it on the bed, then covered them all with a blanket.

She carefully brought all corners of the blanket up until she'd made a safe bag for the heads. Trying not to notice how they clanked together, she opened the door and dropped them in the hallway.

Sighing in relief, she shut the door and leaned against it.

Now that should put a crimp in the pirate's plan. And good riddance, too.

Without the heads, the room was tolerable enough, she supposed. The small cot was set against one wall next to a plain wooden chest, the top of which was covered in dust. Tomorrow she would remedy that.

For now, she needed to rest.

Crossing the room, she laid down and tried to ignore the musty odor of the sheets as she calculated her next course of action.

If only she knew what that action should be.

After waking from her sleep, Lorelei brushed and plaited her hair while she debated what to do about her predicament. Since her room didn't have a window, she wasn't sure what time of day it was, but she suspected from the amount of activity she could hear it must be late in the morning. Little wonder, that. She'd spent a dreadful night, tossing and turning, waking at every little sound. She was worried about her father and what he and Justin must be going through.

They would be beside themselves, not that she was any better off herself. Even though Kesi had tried to comfort her last night, she still had her doubts about Captain Jack. And most especially about Captain Jack's intentions toward her.

Well, the devil take his intentions, and the devil take the man.

She was through playing this game with him. She'd spent half the night wondering why he'd taken her. Was it to get back at Justin for trying to trap him, or was the pirate after Lord Wallingford? Though the latter seemed farfetched, she couldn't help remembering the look on Jack's face when Justin had mentioned his father's name.

Jack hated Lord Wallingford. She was certain of it, and he'd told her she was bait. The thought sent a shiver over her. She had no intention of letting anyone use her, most especially not a man who was after either her fiancé or her future father-in-law.

Tossing her completed braid over her shoulder, she headed for the door.

She cracked it open and paused. The first thing she noted was that someone had removed the heads she'd collected. From that, she trailed her gaze to the captain's room. It wasn't too far away, and yet she wasn't quite sure if she had the temerity to venture there.

What would the pirate do if they were alone in his cabin?

Did she really want to know?

Or worse, what would happen if one of the crewmen found her alone on her journey?

As if in answer to her thoughts, she heard footsteps approaching from the right. She tensed, ready to dodge back into her room and slam the door shut against the interloper.

"Awake, are you?"

In spite of herself, she found the rich baritone of Jack's voice welcome music to her ears.

He sauntered toward her with a masculine swagger that told the world who ruled this domain. His hair was windswept and the dull light of the corridor glinted against the gold of the earring in his left ear. He had a mischievous look about him.

"Aye, I'm awake and I wish a word with you."

His eyes fair glowed as a slow smile spread across his face. He stopped just before her and she had two urges at once. One to take a step toward him, where she could better inhale the sweet masculine scent of him, and another to retreat to the safety of her room.

As if sensing her conflicted thoughts, he braced his arm on the door frame above her head and leaned down. "Aching to be alone with me, are you?"

"Hardly."

His sweet breath tickled her skin as he spoke. "Admit it, love, you find me irresistible."

"I find you irritating," she said with a frown. "You know, that's certainly some ego you possess. You must have an incredibly large room to accommodate the two of you."

His laughter rang out. "My cabin's actually large enough to accommodate all three of us." He reached out and smoothed a piece of hair on her braid. "And when it comes to my bed—"

"I have no interest in your bed," she said, cutting him off as an image of what his bed might look like burned through her. "Nor in anything else so personal about you."

Instead of being offended, he just shrugged nonchalantly. "More's the pity then. I've been told my bed, among other personal things, is quite exquisite."

"Are you trying to shock me?"

"If I were?"

"You'll have to do better. Didn't your mother ever teach you that crudity is no way to entice a woman?"

The playfulness vanished from his face. She had gone too far, and now upon seeing the black, grim look on his face, she had no doubt that this man was capable of the horrors attributed to him.

"You don't ever want to know what lessons my mother taught me," he said, his low tone frightening in its frigidity. "Now, if you'll excuse me, I have duties to attend."

"Wait," Lorelei said, unwilling to let him go until he had addressed her concerns. "I still have a matter to discuss."

Slowly, stiffly, he turned around to face her.

He had shot from playful to angry so fast that her head fair reeled from it. Never had she seen anything like it.

And people called her hot-headed.

"Yes?" he asked coldly.

Bolstering her confidence, she looked him squarely in the eye. "What is Lord Wallingford to you and why do you hate him so? He is the one you're after, isn't he? You took me because you knew Justin would get his father to come for me."

No emotions showed at all. It was as if she were addressing a statue. "Before you ask me those questions, little Lorelei, I think you should ask yourself if you want the answers."

"Of course I want the answers. Why wouldn't I?"

"Why indeed," he asked in return. "Tell me why you think I hate him."

"Because he's sworn to hang any pirate he finds."

He mocked her with his eyes. "How very naive of you."

"Then for what reasons?" she demanded, agitated by his superior attitude.

"Go back to your room, Lorelei," he said with a sigh. "You're safe in there."

"Safe from what?"

"From me, from life, from everything."

Frustrated, she ground her teeth. "Would you stop playing this game with me and simply answer my questions?"

Silence hung between them until he finally answered. "Yes, I took you to get Gabriel Wallingford to come for you."

"Why do you hate him?"

"Because it suits me to."

"And why is that?"

"Because it does."

Deciding that was probably the best answer she was likely to get, Lorelei retreated slightly. "You realize, of course, there were other ways to get his attention."

"True, I could have killed one of his sons."

He said it so matter-of-factly that it stunned her. "Then why didn't you?"

"It didn't suit my purposes."

She rolled her eyes at his redundancy.

The pirate moved to stand before her. Even though there was still a coldness between them, she could sense his desire for her. It was a desire she had felt since the moment of their first meeting and suddenly she understood.

"Is seducing me part of your revenge? That is what this elaborate abduction is about, isn't it? You could have taken Justin as easily as you took me and Lord Wallingford would still have come after you. But you didn't take him."

He nodded. "You're very astute."

She didn't know why, but his answer disappointed her. And it made her angry. "You're wasting your time, you know."

"Am I?"

"Yes. I love Justin."

"Love," he sneered. "Love is nothing more than the lie men invented to woo women to their beds without guilt."

"Do you honestly believe that?"

"Believe it? I know it to be true."

"Then more's the pity for you. A life without love is an empty one."

"A life without love is a happy one."

Heaven above, but he was dense. Or was he merely doing it to perturb her?

"You've never once known the thrill of being in love?" Lorelei asked. "Never felt your heart quicken when someone special approached you? Longed to spend every moment of every day with one person?"

"That's called lust."

"It's called love."

"Then yes, I've been in love countless times. In fact, I'm in love right now. For all I can think of is holding your naked body against mine, of tasting—"

"That's not what I meant," she said between clenched teeth as heat stole across her face.

"It's what you said."

Flustered, she drew a deep breath to settle the vexing anger he provoked.

His look deepened as he cupped her cheek in the palm of his hand and stroked her chin with his thumb. His touch burned her, and it took all her strength not to turn her face in his hand and taste the flesh of that palm.

Oh, but his touch was warm and magical and . . .

Inviting.

And she wanted to accept that invitation, she realized with a start.

He pulled her against his hard chest and captured her with one arm about her waist. "I could show you delights you've never before conceived, my sweet. Not once in all the times you and your girlfriends giggled together did you ever imagine what I can give you."

Wicked desire swirled in her stomach and a part of her begged for him to educate her. What would it be like to hold a man so handsome? So dangerous?

One whose touch filled her with such white-hot desire.

This was madness, and well she knew it. She was spoken for and he was an outlaw. A wanted man whose life would be forfeit the moment she was rescued.

No matter what her body thought, she was a creature of logic and logic dictated that she keep a goodly distance between them.

"The world will surely come to an end before I allow that to happen. The only thing I crave from you is your absence."

He inclined his head in mock sadness. "And that is the one thing I refuse to give you."

"Then you are in for a great disappointment."

Humor danced in his eyes. "You think so?"

"I know so."

"Now who is the one so cocky?" he asked.

"It's still you. I merely know the facts."

He laughed. "As do I, and the facts clearly state that no woman can resist me. Not for long anyway."

What arrogance, she thought, seething at him. He had to be the most conceited man to ever draw breath. And if there was one thing she hated, it was that type of cocksure attitude.

Well, it was time someone taught Black Jack Rhys a lesson in manners. Time someone showed him he was not the end-all, be-all of masculinity.

And she was certainly up to that task.

"I assure you, Captain Rhys, that I can resist your most dubious charms. You'd drop to one knee and declare your undying love for me long before I ever give myself to you."

"Is that a challenge?"

Lorelei thought it over. Was it? She'd meant it as a comparison, but now that the words were out, she pondered it.

There's not a man born I can't wrap around my little finger.

That boast had seemed so simple the night of the party, and yet as she stared at Jack, she wondered if maybe she'd met the one man she couldn't control so easily.

Nay, she decided.

This time Jack Rhys had met his match.

"Aye, 'tis a challenge. I'll claim your heart before you claim my body."

5

Jack's laughter rippled in her ears. "Jack Rhys down on his knee before a woman, declaring his undying love. Now there's a thought borne of pure fantasy."

"On the contrary," Lorelei said haughtily, fortified by her experience with the opposite sex. She remembered a time when Justin had also laughed at the idea. But in the end, she had won him over, and she was certain she would win this time as well. "Men, for all their denials, are susceptible to the same emotions as women. More so, in fact."

"And how do you figure that?"

"You live your life for vengeance. I live mine for peaceful tranquility. Tell me, whose life is more emotional, more volatile?"

"I can certainly tell you whose life is more boring."

"Ah, there ya are, child."

Lorelei turned her head to see Kesi coming down

the ladder Jack had just used a few moments ago. Kesi held a small basket in her arms that was covered with a green gingham cloth. "I was just bringing ya some bread and cheese to break your fast."

Once again grateful for the woman's kindness, Lorelei walked the short distance that separated them and took the basket of food from her hands. "Thank you, I am a bit famished."

"I thought ya might be." Kesi greeted Jack. "How's your shoulder doing?"

"Throbbing actually."

Kesi's eyes glowed. "Ya always say that."

The pirate walked forward to address them. "If you ladies will excuse me, I have duties to attend." He paused beside Lorelei and spoke in a whisper only she could hear. "And a seduction to plan."

Flames of embarrassment burned her cheeks. "You're wasting your time."

A light of self-assurance sparked in his eyes. "Nay, Lorelei, 'tis you who are wasting your denials."

Kesi frowned at them while Jack took his leave. "What was that about?"

Lorelei pursed her lips, not willing to share such an indelicate matter with a stranger. "Nothing important."

"Come on then, let's go topside and get a bit of fresh air. 'Tis truly a lovely day."

Lorelei hesitated. "Is it safe up there?"

"Aye," Kesi said. "You're safer here than anywhere else on earth."

"But the pirates—"

"They won't touch ya, child. Captain Jack already told them that he'd have the life of any man who so much as frowns in your direction. And ya can trust in the fact that none of them are willing to face the captain's wrath."

A chill crept up her spine. Jack must be terrible to intimidate his crew so. When scary men became scared, it wasn't a good sign.

"Now don't be giving me none of that sour frown," Kesi chided. "It'll make ya look old before nature intends. Now, come. The other women are all wanting to meet ya."

Shifting the basket to the crook of her arm, Lorelei followed her up the ladder to the main deck.

She supposed it was a beautiful morning, provided she didn't think about the fact she was on board a ship full of pirates and headed for an unknown destination while the king of the pirate brood had sworn to seduce her.

But then, given the number of rude stares she collected from the ruffian bunch as she crossed the deck a step behind Kesi, how could she think of anything else?

All around her, young men were stripped to the waist as they went about hoisting sails, cleaning the deck, polishing capstans, and doing a thousand other tasks. The high wind blew through her hair and carried aloft the bawdy songs and curses of the crew as they worked.

The dress Kesi had brought her last night fit everywhere except the bust, which was just tight enough to be annoying. It was a dark green cambric with short sleeves, but if the truth were known, she wished herself wrapped up in a thick, oversized woolen sack. Anything to keep the men from looking at her.

As they walked on, she noted a group of three

women who were standing together at the prow of the ship. The eldest, a matronly, plump woman in her mid-forties with salt and pepper hair, held a large silver serving platter while the younger two women were tossing bread scraps up to a circling flock of seagulls.

"Watch your head now, Alice, that last one about took your cap off," the elder said as she pulled a young woman of about twenty-four back from the circling birds.

"Go on with you, Mavis. I know what I'm doing," the younger woman snapped as she tossed another handful of bread at the birds. "Besides, 'twas your idea."

The third woman, a petite brunette, jabbed Mavis in the side with her elbow and nodded toward Kesi and Lorelei.

Releasing Alice's arm, Mavis beamed a bright smile that lit up her entire face. "Well, well. So this be our guest."

Kesi stepped aside for them to get a good look at her and suddenly Lorelei felt completely self-conscious, as if these women were sizing her up like a possible opponent.

"This be Lorelei Dupree." Kesi touched Lorelei lightly on the arm. "Poor child. Captain Jack done gone and stole her in the middle of the night."

"It's a bad thing for a man to steal a woman away in the middle of the night, indeed," Alice said with more than a hint of sarcasm in her voice.

"It is when ya not be wanting to be took," Kesi said.

"Oh, pay them no mind," Mavis said as she crossed the short distance between them. She clucked her tongue at Alice. "Alice is just jealous the captain carried you on board so easily. Poor Billy broke his back as he carried her out her parents' window."

"I resent your implication, Mistress Mavis. 'Twas not my weight that broke him." Alice's cheeks turned bright red. She stood before Mavis with her fists clenched and gestured to show Mavis how Billy had fallen. "He slipped from ladder on the way down."

Mavis snorted. "Says you."

"Ladies, please." Kesi moved to stand between them. "What's Lorelei to think with the two of ya carrying on so?"

"She's to be thinking we're a rude lot to be sure," Mavis said good-naturedly as she turned back toward Lorelei. "You'll have to forgive us. It gets so boring here that me and Alice pick on each other just so's we'll have something to do."

The knot in Lorelei's stomach loosened and she sensed a ready friendship from the women, as if they'd already accepted her into their group.

Kesi pulled the third woman forward. The girl crossed her arms over her chest and shyly tilted her chin down.

"This is Sarah Little. She's married to the cook."

Sarah inclined her head to Lorelei and offered a generous smile.

"She can't talk," Alice explained.

"But she can whistle like a lark and make a sweet biscuit that'll bring tears to your eyes." Mavis tossed the last bit of bread to the birds, then wiped her hand on her white apron. "My name's Mavis Browne and I'm the wife of the ship's navigator."

Alice stepped forward. "And I'm Alice Young-blood. My husband's Billy." She paused, looked past Lorelei's shoulder, then raised her voice. "And if he doesn't stop gawking at you, I'll make sure he sleeps alone for the next month of Sundays."

Turning her head, Lorelei saw one of the youthful sailors as his cheeks darkened. "I was only looking at you, love."

"Phew," Alice scoffed. "I saw where your eyes were, Billy-boy. And if you be wanting to keep 'em in your head, you'd best be tending your duties."

Billy gave her a charming grin before hoisting himself up one of the masts.

Sarah made several quick gestures with her hands before she took the platter from Mavis.

"She says welcome aboard and that she hopes ya won't think her a dullard for not speaking," Kesi interpreted.

Confused, Lorelei looked back and forth between Kesi and Sarah. "How do you know . . ."

"Her husband used to be a priest under a vow of silence," Mavis explained. "He taught her to speak with her hands. We all learned it so that we could talk to her."

Lorelei was elated and intrigued by the idea. "I would love to learn, too."

"And so we'll show ya, child," Kesi said. "But for the time being we all got chores to do."

Alice sighed. "Why is it you always say that, Kesi? I declare, you are addicted to your chores."

Alice took the platter and cast a parting look at Lorelei. "We'll talk later, after chores." Alice led Sarah off toward a ladder.

"Are you handy with a needle?" Mavis asked Lorelei.

"Why, yes, yes I am." It probably should irk her that she would be abducted only to work for her captors, but it didn't. After all, most anything would be preferable to sitting around and doing nothing all day.

"Then you can help me mend the men's clothes."

Kesi grabbed an empty bucket off the deck of the ship. "Then I'll leave the two of ya to it and tend my own work." She headed off in the direction opposite the one Sarah and Alice had taken.

Mavis led Lorelei over to a shaded spot on the deck where a large pile of shirts, pants, and socks waited. From where she stood, it was a daunting task.

"How long have you been working on that?" Lorelei asked. "Just since the dawn of time, or eternally?"

Mavis laughed and took a seat on a small stool under the overhang of the poop deck. "It's not as bad as it seems." She indicated another stool across from her and Lorelei took a seat. "I actually like doing it, since I can sit up here in the fresh air."

Unwrapping her breakfast, Lorelei had to grant her that it was a pleasant morning.

Mavis took a needle and white thread from a small sewing kit that was set next to her stool. "You go ahead and eat while I get started. You need to put some weight on yourself or you'll get blown overboard."

Lorelei laughed. Her friend Amanda would argue that point, but it was nice to hear the contradiction from Mavis. She uncorked the bottle of milk and poured some into the mug Kesi had placed in the basket. She saw a small green bottle laying in the bottom. Pulling it out, she uncorked it and took a whiff. It had next to no scent whatsoever.

"That be Kesi's sleeping tonic," Mavis explained.

"Sleeping tonic?"

"Aye, we've all had it at some point. No doubt she was thinking you'd be having trouble sleeping at night."

The truth could not have been spoken more plainly. Recorking the bottle, she returned it to the basket unsure if she would ever bother to use it. Still, it was nice to have it just in case it came in handy one day.

"So, how long have you traveled with the . . ." Lorelei paused as she tried to think of a word that wouldn't offend her companion.

"Pirates?" Mavis asked. "You can say the word. All of us here know what it is we do for a living."

Heat stung her cheeks. "I didn't mean to offend—"

Mavis interrupted her with a snort. "The truth doesn't offend me. Only lies do that." Mavis picked up a small white shirt that looked like it belonged to a boy. She started mending a small tear in the left sleeve. "I know you probably think of us as monsters, but let a woman who's lived twice as long as you have tell you that monsters exist everywhere. You'll find no more meanness on board this ship than what you're used to."

Lorelei wanted to argue, but refrained lest she alienate the only allies she could hope to have until Justin rescued her. Yet, she didn't understand how Mavis could rationalize the pirates' behavior. They were killers and bullies who traveled the seas just looking for hapless victims.

Of course, Mavis probably had to rationalize the violence in order to live with the pirates. Otherwise the guilt would no doubt drive her mad.

Mavis looked past her shoulder and her gaze narrowed speculatively. "Well now, Mr. Kit, did you finally decide to grace us with your presence?"

Lorelei looked up to see a boy of about eleven standing behind her. He was a handsome lad with brown hair and bright green eyes. He stared at her intently as if trying to size her up. She couldn't tell how he felt; he seemed to have Jack's ability to camouflage his emotions.

"What's your favorite color?" he asked Lorelei.

She frowned at such an odd question. "Yellow."

"Yellow," he sneered. "That's a girl's color."

"Now, Kit, watch your manners. You've not yet introduced yourself to her and already you're insulting her. At least let her think you a good lad until she gets to know you."

Shrugging aside Mavis's reproach, he took a step forward. "I'm Kristopher," he said, extending his hand to Lorelei. "Most folks call me Kit though."

Lorelei shook his proffered hand. "It's a pleasure to meet you, Kit."

He moved to stand beside her as he sized her up yet again. "So, you're the booty from last night. Kind of scrawny, ain't you?" He looked to Mavis. "We should probably throw her back. She's too little to keep. Barely enough flesh on her for a man to get a hold of."

Mavis's mouth dropped. "You little scamp!" she scolded, rising to her feet. "I'll tan your backside for that."

Before she could reach him, Kit took off in the opposite direction.

Stunned by his words, Lorelei watched him dart across the deck like a nimble cat before he dodged down a ladder.

"What an odd boy," she said as Mavis retook her seat. Maybe "crude boy" was more to the point. "Whose is he?"

"The devil's, if the truth were told," Mavis said under her breath. She sighed and picked up the shirt that Lorelei realized was Kit's and returned to mending the sleeve. "He's Captain Jack's son."

The unexpected news hit her like a blow. Lorelei looked once more in the direction Kit had flown. Jack Rhys had a child?

Where was the boy's mother?

"Who's his mother?" she asked.

"Don't know. I was told she died before I came here. Kesi said the captain took the boy in and has kept him ever since."

"That's rather unusual, isn't it?"

Mavis bit the thread in twain, then set the needle aside. "Most things about the captain are unusual."

Lorelei stood at the ship's railing, staring out at the ocean. Sunlight played on the white-capped waves as the ship skimmed over the water's surface.

For hours she had sat sewing with Mavis and now her entire body was cramped. Rubbing her neck, she tilted her head to stretch the taut muscles.

"Might I be of assistance?"

She looked over her shoulder to see the captain standing behind her.

"What do you want?" she asked.

He just smiled a smile that lifted her heart in spite of her. Without comment, he took a step forward and gently placed his hands on the tops of her shoulders. With a tenderness that astounded her, he massaged her cramped muscles.

Lorelei closed her eyes against the pleasure of his touch. His hands worked like magic, unlocking the tension and relaxing her.

"Better?" he asked.

"Hmm," she breathed, enjoying his expert touch too much to say anything more.

Jack delighted in the softness of Lorelei's skin as he rubbed the stiffness from her neck. The wind blew stray tendrils of her hair around them and the setting sun shone in her eyes.

But all he could really focus on was the small white buttons down the back of her dress. Buttons he could imagine opening with his fingers as he bared more and more of her flesh to his touch.

How he ached to run his lips over every inch of her, savoring her scent, her skin.

"Tell me, Lorelei," he whispered in her ear. "What were you thinking about when I approached?"

"Justin."

Jack ground his teeth in frustration. If it was the last thing he did, he would drive that man's name from her vocabulary.

"And now?"

"I'm thinking how much Justin would want to kill you if he saw your hands upon my neck."

His first inclination was to remove his hands, but damned if he'd do that and let her think he feared Justin Wallingford. It would be a cold day on the equator before he feared a milksop pup like that.

"And would you weep if he killed me?" he couldn't resist asking.

"For you?" she asked with a short laugh. "Why

I'd . . ." Her voice trailed off and, to his surprise, her gaze changed to a soft welcoming look. "Why yes, Captain Rhys. I would weep for you."

It was a game she played. He knew it as well as he knew his ship.

Still, the words resonated inside him. But not as much as the truth that should Jack Rhys perish, no one would ever weep for him.

"What a gifted liar you are, my lady. I shall have to remember that."

She stiffened at his words and pulled away. "That makes two of us then, Count Arnaulf Hapsburg."

"Ah yes, the good count," he said with a laugh. Then he cloaked his voice in the count's aristocratic accent. "But tell me truly, *milovidnost*, had I asked you to elope with me that night, would you not have followed me to the ends of the earth?"

"I wouldn't have followed you to the end of the corridor."

She was so quick to retort. So challenging to try to thwart. He'd never known a woman so sharp of wit and he adored that part of her personality.

"Lorelei, Lorelei, Lorelei, when are you going to admit that you liked me as a count. If I were one of your pasty-faced nobles, you'd have tripped over your own feet to be near me, just like all the other little chits at your party."

She arched a brow at him. "Would I? I seem to recall you're the one who sought me out."

She probed him with her stare, as if trying to see deep into his soul. "And why was that?"

"You were adorable."

Surprise flickered across her face. "Adorable?"

"Aye. Vibrant and ethereal," he said, tucking a

stray piece of hair back into her braid. "Like some fey mist seeking refuge from the woodsy floor where it was trapped."

"I beg your pardon?"

Jack leaned against the railing and spoke the truth he'd noticed about her that night at the party. "You were running from Justin. I saw you."

"I was running from Justin's boots, if you must know. Not from him."

"His boots?"

She cleared her throat and dipped her head down so he could no longer see her eyes. "He was trampling my toes."

He arched a brow at her disclosure. "That's why he told me you don't like to dance. How very noble of you to save his feelings," he scoffed. "Do you, by the way?"

She looked up. "Do I what?"

"Do you like to dance?"

She didn't say anything, but the look in her eyes spoke loudly. She did.

"So, you would condemn yourself to a lifetime of crushed toes to possess the title of Mrs. Wallingford?"

Her face glowed with conviction. "I would condemn myself to a lifetime of crushed bones to possess Justin."

Now that stung. Much more than it should have. "And what did dear Justin do to provoke this unwavering loyalty?"

"He makes me laugh."

"Laugh?"

"Aye. Laugh. He is my friend and my confidant."

"You know," Jack said, leaning down toward her,

"confidants make poor lovers. They know all your secrets."

"I wouldn't know anything about that."

He traced the outline of her ear with the tip of his finger. "I could easily educate you."

"I'm sure you would like to try. But as you can see, I have no interest."

What he could plainly see was the small goose-bumps on her skin that his touch caused, and her rapid breathing. Whether she admitted it or not, his touch warmed her.

"Well then," he said to humor her as he pulled away and straightened up. "Since you're not interested in me, allow me to escort you back to your room so that you can prepare for dinner."

"I should like my dinner in my room."

"And I should like your dinner served at my table." Or rather, he would like her served up *on* his table, to be more precise. Aye, he could feast on the likes of her flesh for weeks.

"Then I should like to starve," she said as if she knew his thoughts.

"Don't be childish, Lorelei. There's no need to waste away. After all, I'm sure you wouldn't want dearest Justin to see you bony and frail. You do have to eat or else you'll lose all your strength and you'll have nothing left to fight me with."

"In that case . . ."

She dutifully took his elbow and allowed him to lead her below.

"How is it you know gentlemanly ways?" she asked as they made their way to her room.

"How do you know I'm not a gentleman?"

"You're a pirate," she said simply as if that gave

her all the clues to his personality and mettle.

"Not all pirates are base-born," he dutifully reminded her.

"Are you a gentleman, then?"

Jack wasted no time in setting her straight about his birth. "I am the lowest of the low, Lady Lorelei," he said, pausing to bow before her as if they were being introduced for the first time. "You see before you the bastard son of a perpetually inebriated prostitute."

As intended, his words shocked her.

And before he could stop it, the rest of his story came out. "I grew up in the backroom of a sleazy Carribean bordello cleaning up after the whores and sailors."

Tears misted in her eyes. "I'm sorry. I had no idea."

Now it was his turn to be shocked as he returned to leading her down the corridor. It was an oversimplification of his past, but it was one he'd never tried to deny. He didn't hide from what his mother had been. Only from what he, himself, was.

And who his father was.

But her reaction confused him. Never had anyone reacted so . . . emotionally about his past. Not even him.

"Don't be. It made me the pirate you see before you today."

"Then I am doubly sorry," she whispered. "Given your intellect and talents, I'm sure with a better set of circumstances you could have gone far in life."

He stopped dead in his tracks, her words biting him deep and raising his anger. "I have gone from one end of this earth to the other. There are few things I haven't seen and fewer still I haven't done."

"But you've never loved."

Jack stifled the urge to roll his eyes. "Back to that, are we?"

"I think whether you want to admit it or not, everything comes back to that."

"You are a doe-eyed romantic." He opened the door to her room and stood back to let her enter. "We eat in one hour. I'll send Tarik for you."

Lorelei watched as the pirate headed off to his room. The man was infuriating.

And puzzling.

She didn't know what to make of him. Or even what to believe. He was a study of contradictions.

And deep inside she had to admit that she liked the challenge of the man. Liked the challenge of trying to unravel him.

She stepped into her room, then froze. Someone had been busy this afternoon.

Gone was her small cot and in its place was a well-made, intricately carved full bed. Her chest had been exchanged for a matching wardrobe, and a washstand and dresser had been brought in and placed to the right of the door.

Everything glowed from fresh polishing and the scent of lemon oil stung her nose. Indeed, someone had even put a vase of dried flowers on her dresser.

Closing the door, Lorelei was amazed.

Then she realized the color of the bed and the lace doilies—yellow. The entire room had been done up in her favorite color.

"What are you up to?" she whispered, knowing he

was the only one on board who wielded the authority to have her room rearranged.

At least it finally explained Kit's strange question.

But it didn't even come close to explaining the pirate's motivation. First he placed her in here with the shrunken heads to frighten her and now he made it a cozy haven.

Was he playing up to her?

Or was it simply an apology?

She almost laughed at the last thought. Jack Rhys apologizing to her. That was even less likely than him declaring his undying love for her over dinner.

"He's a crafty one," she said to herself. Then she spoke louder, as if addressing him through the walls. "But I'm not one of your lovers, Captain Rhys, nor will I ever be."

Nay, she was the one who would bring him under heel—not the other way around.

Well, she would bring him under heel if she could keep her wits about her. But every time they were together, her will seemed to melt. Her best intentions scattered.

Her gaze shifted back to the flowers and this time she saw the small note snuggled in amongst the yellow roses. Walking over, she pulled it out and read the crisp, flowing script.

Wear the green velvet gown. —Jack

"Not on your life!" she snapped. How dare he tell her what to wear. She wasn't some pup to fetch at his command.

She was . . .

Lorelei paused as she swung open the door of the wardrobe, which was crammed full of expensive gowns, bonnets, and petticoats. Even so, the green dress he referred to stood out plainly.

It was beautiful. Heavily embroidered with gold and lined with luminescent seed pearls, it was a gown fitted for royalty. In spite of herself, she trailed her hand over it, awed by the rich, deep softness of the material.

Maybe wearing it wouldn't be so bad. After all, she was supposed to bend him to her will.

Aye. Humor him for the night.

As with a pet, you must make sure you establish from the beginning exactly who is in control.

And tonight, it was she who would wield the power.

6

Jack studied himself in his dressing mirror as he tied his crisp linen stock. He couldn't wait for dinner tonight. For another match of wits with his captured prize. Imagine a woman like her bound in eternal wedlock hell to a man like Justin Wallingford.

The more time Jack spent with Lorelei, the more intrigued he was by her. He was determined not to see her suffer in bondage to a man who stomped her toes.

What other favored pastimes had she forsaken for the fop? The very thought of it made him seethe.

And for what?

For love. That idea made him nauseous. Why did women delude themselves with such foolish thoughts?

"Oh, but he *loves* me," Jack mocked to his visage. It was an effort not to puke.

Well, he had no one to blame but his own gender. They were the ones who played into women's fantasies, and all for a night's worth of pleasure.

A twinge of guilt pricked his conscience, but he quickly stomped it out. He wasn't his father. He hadn't lied to Lorelei, nor had he played into her concept of love. She knew he was out to seduce her—he had stated it clearly enough—and so she was fair game.

"Just don't let her fall in love with me," he whispered, his stomach churning.

If she so much as dared breathe those words, he would toss her overboard and let the sharks have her.

He'd never been foolish enough to stay with a woman long enough for her to have that delusion, and he lived in terror of some poor soul thinking she loved him.

"How positively revolting."

And it was.

A knock on his door distracted him.

"Enter," he called.

Tarik stuck his head in. "Dinner be ready, Captain. Ya want me to fetch her now?"

"Yes, thank you."

Jack smoothed the ruffled edges of his stock. Tonight was perfect. He was perfect, and in just a few minutes, he fully intended to charm the very drawers off Lorelei Dupree.

As she followed Tarik the short distance to the captain's dining room, Lorelei couldn't help but wonder if the Christians of the fourth century felt the same way as they were led to the Colosseum, for surely she was going into the lion's den.

He was such a clever lion, too. Golden and handsome, mesmerizing and deadly.

And determined to devour her one way or another.

Yet it wasn't in her to hide from him. Nay, her father had always stressed confronting fears and challenges. The pirate wouldn't force her, he'd made that clear enough. So long as he abided by that, she was in control.

Now. To make him fall in love with her. No simple feat, to be sure, but if she could get the ever-wandering Justin to propose, then she could certainly have one Jack Rhys down on his knees.

Tarik opened the door for her.

Lorelei stepped into the room and paused. Soft candlelight sparkled against the high polish of the mahogany dining table, which was set with fine porcelain dishes decorated with pale yellow flowers. Romantic dinner music filtered in from the open windows and she wondered at its source. The aroma of roasted duck and squash made her stomach rumble in anticipation.

It was a room perfect for seduction; at least she was certain that's what the pirate thought.

Well, he would learn.

"So," Jack said, stepping out of the shadows on her left. It took her a moment to recognize him as he was once again dressed in his elegant black suit, starched white shirt, and cream waistcoat. She'd forgotten just how stunning the elegant count was compared to the earthy and raw Black Jack Rhys.

"You wore the gown after all. I wasn't sure if you would."

Reminding herself of the game she played, she smiled coyly and smoothed the gold-laced stomacher with her hand. "It was such a small request, why wouldn't I honor it?"

He quirked a brow as he approached her with one arm held behind his back, looking very much the noble gentleman. "Well, if you don't mind honoring small requests, then might I have your hand?"

Suspicious, she hesitated. "For what purpose?"

He paused before her and she caught the crisp scent of sandalwood from him. It was a heady mixture when combined with the sea air and succulent food. "I made a small request. Surely you don't intend to deny me now?"

She bit her lip to keep from questioning him further. "Very well." Lorelei lifted her gloved hand.

Even through the soft kidskin, she could feel the heat of his hand as he lifted her knuckles to his lips and placed a chaste kiss on them.

He closed his eyes as if savoring something delectable. "You chose the rose perfume."

"Does it please you?"

"Very much."

He brushed her fingers with his thumb and an electric charge rushed through her body straight to the center of her being. She licked her suddenly dry lips and fought herself for control of the swirling emotions he provoked so easily.

She must do something to staunch her attraction for him before it was too late, or more to the point, to staunch his desire for her. As every moment passed she began to wonder if perhaps 'twas she who'd met her match this night.

The captain placed her hand in the crook of his elbow and led her toward the table. "No doubt you're thinking of wearing the lavender perfume next time to spite me."

She cocked a brow at his ability to read her so easily. "Perhaps I was thinking of asking for more rose to continue to entice you."

He held the chair out for her and she dutifully sat down. Once she was situated, he leaned down, and when he spoke, his breath fell softly against the flesh of her neck, adding flames to the already swirling fire inside her. "You've already enticed me, sweet. We both know what you really want to do is *repel* me."

She turned her face slightly to see the devilish look on his face. "Nay, not at all. I said I would make you fall in love with me and so I shall."

"And I said I would seduce you and—"

Impulsively, she placed her fingertip to his lips to silence him before he made his boast once more. "Shall we make this more interesting?" she asked, thinking that an added incentive might be just what she needed to keep both of them at bay. "How about a wager?"

He took her hand in his and lightly stroked the small buttons at her wrist. "A wager? I thought women profaned wagers."

Lorelei resisted the urge to close her eyes and savor the gentleness of his touch, which was sending out waves and waves of pleasure to her. "And men adore them."

"Well then, let's hear this wager of yours."

She dropped her gaze to his well-manicured thumb, which was now tracing small circles in her palm. His dark tan stood out sharply from the white kidskin and she noted a pale scar that ran along the top of his knuckles. "Should I win and you fall in love with me, you will cease being a pirate."

He dropped her hand with a short laugh. "That's hardly fair."

Looking up, she locked gazes. "Wagers seldom are."

"Very well, I agree." He thoughtfully stroked his chin as if considering something of great import. When he finally looked back at her, she had an eerie chill of premonition. "Now for your consequences. If I win, you will refuse to marry Justin."

She frowned at his request and at the underlying tone she caught in his voice. "Why does my engagement to Justin bother you so?"

His face stoic, he answered rather snidely. "It doesn't bother me at all."

"Doesn't it?"

He veiled his gaze. "It's simply a wager, Lorelei. You asked for something preposterous and I asked for something preposterous in return."

"If you say so," she said, but still she had a sense that there was more to it than he let on.

"I do." And with that he took himself off to his end of the table.

Once he was seated and had his linen napkin folded properly in his lap, he rang a small brass bell and two of his crewmen appeared to serve them. The pirates had attempted to dress themselves up in navy jackets and breeches, but one of them still wore a red bandana about his head and large gold hoops in his ears. The other was a bald man of about twenty with a rugged look to his face and two missing front teeth.

"Would ya be liking some rum sauce for the

chicken, Captain?" the bald man asked in a thick Cockney accent.

"It's duck, Kirk. And yes, thank you, I would like some sauce for it."

Kirk scraped the ladle across the bottom of the dish, raising the hair on the back of Lorelei's neck. He dumped the sauce over the captain's food, then smacked it twice with the ladle for good measure. "Duck, chicken, don't see much difference meself. It's all for the gullet in the end. Why, when I was a lad, we was lucky to have cabbage soup, much less anything as fancy as all this here."

"The captain don't care to hear your woes," the other sailor inserted. "Blimey, Kirk, can't you see the man is trying to impress the lady, and here you go off about cabbage soup and gullets. Where's your mind, man? Use it for something other than—"

"Tommy," the captain interrupted. "Kirk, we thank you for your service, but I believe silence might be in your best interest."

"Ach, now ya done gone and done it," Kirk muttered as he dumped more sauce over Lorelei's duck. "We'll be swabbing the decks tomorrow for sure."

"Me?" Tommy asked in a huff as he poured the wine in Lorelei's cup. "I wasn't the one—"

"That will be enough, men."

The two sailors glared at each other while they finished their various duties.

Lorelei waited patiently while they were served. The captain appeared as grand and noble as the highest, most well-born dignitary she'd ever seen, and she began to wonder if he'd been honest with her about his background. Surely the types of people one typically found in a bordello hadn't possessed the refinement of breeding the pirate showed so naturally. Nay, someone had trained him as effectively as she herself had been groomed.

But who?

And why?

With a regal wave of his hand, he dismissed his men.

Knowing the captain wasn't about to trust her with the knowledge, she cut a small piece of the duck and took a bite. She delighted at the delicate flavor.

Their conversation lagged until Lorelei finally found enough courage to mention to him the matter foremost on her mind. "I met your son today," she said after taking a sip of wine. "But then you know that, don't you? You sent him to find out my favorite color."

He wiped his mouth with his napkin before he answered. "Yes. I wasn't sure if you'd tell me."

"Why did you want to know?"

He leaned forward slightly, as if about to impart some great secret to her. "I find you fascinating and I want to know all about you."

"Ah," she said in full understanding. "Knowledge is power. The more you know about me, the easier I'll be to seduce." Like him, she leaned forward and met his gaze evenly. "And will you allow *me* such arsenal?"

He sat back slightly. "Perhaps."

A glimmer of hope appeared. It was certainly a kinder answer than the rude "no" she'd expected. Fortified, she asked the question that had intrigued her most of the day. "Then tell me, who is Kit's mother?"

"I don't know."

"You don't know?" she repeated in disbelief. "Sir,

'tis the father who can be in doubt. The mother is surely known, unless you . . ." Her eyes widened. "You kidnapped the boy?"

"Hardly," he said, his voice laced with aristocratic disdain. "Kit is my son. That is all anyone ever needs to know about the matter."

Lorelei watched him in silence. If he hadn't kidnapped Kit, and Jack was truly his father, then he must have known the boy's mother . . . intimately, at some point.

"Was she some passing wench you fancied? Or a lady of short acquaintance, perhaps?"

"She is none of your business and she has nothing to do with me."

By his tone, she knew the matter was ended. Any further inquiries would only alienate him from her. But oh, how she longed to know the truth. Why was he so secretive about the matter? Had he loved Kit's mother greatly?

She almost laughed at the thought. Nay, the captain disdained love too much to ever have felt it. Which made the question of Kit's mother all the more tantalizing.

Changing the direction of her thoughts, she asked him about the next item that intrigued her. "Then tell me why you became a pirate."

He swirled the wine around in his glass and sighed. "These are all boring questions. I became a pirate to make money."

"Why not be a privateer, or join the navy?"

"Because I refuse to answer to any man or government. On this ship, my will is supreme."

And it was. She knew that, had seen it firsthand on deck.

"Now my turn," he said, returning his glass to the table. "Tell me, other than thinking of Justin, what do you like to do?"

She puzzled over the strangeness of his question. "What do I like to do?"

"Yes. When you're all alone in your father's house and there's no one to disturb you. What gives you pleasure?"

That was harmless enough to answer. He certainly couldn't use that against her in any way. "Reading."

His look became one of intrigue. "And what do you like to read?"

"Poetry, mostly. I particularly like Anne Bradstreet."

He inclined his head to her, then recited one of her most favored poems.

"For riches doth thou long full sore? Behold enough of precious store. Earth hath more silver, pearls, and gold, than eyes can see or hands can hold. Affect's thou pleasure? Take thy fill, Then let not go, what thou may'st find For things unknown, only in mind."

Lorelei smiled at the quote, impressed that he knew it. She continued,

"Spirit: Be still thou unregenerate part, Disturb no more my settled heart, For I have vowed (and so will do) Thee as a foe still to pursue. And combat with thee will and must, until I see thee laid in th' dust."

Then together, "'Sisters we are, yea, twins we be, Yet deadly feud, 'twixt thee and me.'"

"You're very well learned," she said before taking another bite of her food.

"For a pirate?"

"Hmmm."

"I, too, like to read."

"And to quote."

"Exactly."

Fascinated by his ability to recall quotes so accurately and his great passion for literary classics, she couldn't understand his view on love. "How is it a man who reads so can also denounce love so vehemently? Most of the greatest works produced are based on love."

He lightly cleared his throat. "There is an old French proverb that sums my view up nicely. Love makes time pass; time makes love pass."

She took a deep breath and shook her head at him. "You are a true cynic."

"And you are a romantic dreamer," he countered. "Tell me, Lorelei. Tell me of your deepest, darkest secret. What passion burns inside such a romantic soul? What is the one wish you hold above all others?"

The answer was a simple one, but not one she was sure she should share with him. It was a dream that had brought her enough grief from her father and Justin, who thought it a great waste of time. Only her grandmother had ever encouraged her, and even she only grudgingly.

Still, it might give her a bit of temperance to add his sneering comments to the others she'd endured. After all, did she truly care what the pirate thought of her? So what if he mocked her as they did? She would be away from *him* soon enough.

"If I answer, will you do the same?"

He nodded.

Reconciling herself to his inevitable response, she spoke, "My one secret is that I should like to be a great artist."

"Really?" he asked. "I can just imagine you covered with paint as you get that little look on your face while you try to capture a scene."

"What look?"

"That little scrunchy thing you do with your face."

"Scrunchy thing?"

He nodded. "You're doing it now, in fact. Your brows are slightly creased and your eyes slightly narrowed as you try to delve into something's source."

She blinked several times to dispel whatever look he referred to. "I have no idea what you mean."

" 'Tis a pity then, it's a wonderful look for you."

In spite of herself, his compliment warmed her.

"And what does Justin think about your desire to be an artist?"

She looked down at her plate, too embarrassed and hurt to answer.

"Come now, Lorelei. Be honest with me."

Refusing to look up, she pushed the sweetened broccoli around on her plate. "Why should I answer when I know you'll just mock me?"

"So, he thinks it a foolish endeavor."

She swallowed the lump of sadness in her throat and rose to Justin's defense. "He's actually quite right. Once we marry, I shan't have time for such trivialities."

"And why is that?"

"I'll have to supervise the household and tend our children."

"While Justin pursues his military career."

"Yes."

" 'Tis a bit unfair, don't you think?"

"It's the way of the world," she said, even though deep inside she'd always resented that fact. 'Twas the very thing that had driven her grandmother to take to the sea as a young woman. But Lorelei had promised her grandmother years ago that she wouldn't try and fight the way things were. She would merely accept the world and abide by all its unfair dictates.

Reconciled to it, she looked up at Jack. "Now for you. What is your greatest passion?"

"Killing people."

Her heart stopped. Was that the truth? She wasn't sure, and his face and body gave nothing away. "I don't believe you," she said in an effort to test her theory.

"Don't you? I am a pirate, after all."

"Yes, you are. But you're not like other pirates."

"How are you so sure?"

"You travel with your son and you allow your crew to keep their wives with them. Why is that?"

"Because life is too short and we could die at any minute. The last thing I want is for my men to die alone."

"And what about you?"

"I am alone."

"Wouldn't you like to change that?"

"Hardly. I'm quite content with my life."

"Are you?" she asked quietly.

"Truly ecstatic."

Sensing his closure, she finished the meal in silence.

Once they had both finished, he stood and pulled her to her feet. Jack led her to the windows that looked out on a quiet, tranquil sea. The music from the deck continued to fill the air with its sultry tone as a gentle breeze rippled around her. "Where does the music come from?" she asked.

"My crew," he said. "They play every night around sunset."

Jack leaned back against the support beam next to the window so that he could watch her. Trying to ignore how nice he looked there, Lorelei forced her gaze to remain on the ocean.

"It's very beautiful, isn't it?" she asked.

"Very."

She was aware of every aspect of him. His long legs were stretched out before him, and she admired the way his breeches hugged his lean, muscular thighs and the fact that his coat only emphasized the breadth of his shoulders.

His gaze on her face felt like a tangible touch. Her heart raced. There were so many things about him she liked. And so many more she wished she knew.

The longer the silence stretched, the more nervous she became. She glanced at him and heat stole across her cheeks. She tried to focus her attention on the dark sea, but a few seconds later, she looked back at him to find his gaze had not wavered from her.

"What?" she asked in an effort to dispel her discomfort. "Have I grown a new head?"

He pushed himself away from the window and moved to stand behind her. Still, he said nothing.

Lorelei bit her lip in uncertainty as she felt the heat of his body reach out to her. Something sizzled between them, catching her off guard with its warmth.

"Tell me, Lorelei," he said at last. "Have you ever had a man kiss you here?" He touched the tender part of her neck just below her ears where she'd pulled her hair up into a cascade of curls.

"That is very forward of you," she said primly.

His fingers stroked her skin, sending a slow burn through her body. "Yes, it is. Have you?"

From the inside out, she ached for his touch, and yet she knew she should rebuff him. "No."

"Pity. It's terribly pleasurable. May I?"

"Never."

Move away! And yet she couldn't get her body to obey. All she could do was stand there, feeling his flesh against hers. Feeling the gentle caress of his breath against her neck and wishing for things she knew she had no right to want.

He took a step closer. Even though he touched her with nothing more than one hand, she felt surrounded by him. Consumed by him. "One day you'll beg me to kiss you there."

Gathering the tangled, fleeing shreds of her sense, she said, "One day the world shall end and I dare say that day will come long before I ever allow you to kiss me there."

"And what about your lips?" he asked, touching her there. Her legs turned to jelly as her mind begged for him to kiss her. "Could I kiss those?"

"You already have."

"And you liked it."

"I deplored it," she said, her voice breathless.

"Should we have another go at it to make sure?"

Before she could step back, he kissed her. Her head swam at the contact as her body sang in response to the fulfillment of her longing. She tasted the sweet wine on his lips as he invaded her senses and sent her reeling with desire.

Oh, it would be so easy to give into this man. To let him have his way with her. And yet it would be wrong. Not just because she was promised to Justin, but because she meant nothing to the pirate captain.

To him she was an object of vengeance. A pawn for his own satisfaction, and no matter how good he felt in her arms, or how treacherous her body, she refused to allow him to use her as if she were nothing more than a simple tool to help him complete a task.

She was a human being with feelings and emotions, not a lapdog to fetch at his command. Regaining herself, she pushed him back.

He looked down at her, and she saw the triumph shimmering in the steely depths of his eyes.

"You're not going to seduce me, Captain Rhys."

He smiled. "Methinks the lady doth protest too much."

"And methinks the pirate doth insist too much." She forced him to release her. Lorelei straightened her dress and patted the loose tendrils of her hair back into place. "Have you never failed?"

"Never," he said, as he brushed the sleeve of his jacket.

She ran her fingers through her hair, trying to straighten out her coiffure. Tilting her head, she brushed the curls away from her neck. "You really are incorrigible."

When she looked back at him, the captain's eyes held her prisoner. Unbridled lust glowed deep and he stared at her like a starving man before a banquet table.

"You had best leave."

She frowned.

"Leave, Lorelei, now while I can let you go. If you stay, I won't be held accountable for what happens."

Deciding it would be best to heed his warning, Lorelei quickly left the room and dashed back to her cabin.

She locked the door behind her and drew deep breaths to calm her racing heart. What had happened?

He'd been fine while he brushed at his sleeve and then he'd . . .

Men, they were indeed a strange, unfathomable lot.

But worse than his actions and words was the undeniable fact that she was terribly attracted to him.

There was something about the pirate that called out to her. It lured a primitive part of her body that she couldn't control, and that frightened her.

How long could she keep him at bay when he assailed her defenses at every turn?

And in truth, she liked battling with him. She found his views intriguing.

And his touch, delightful.

"Think of Justin," she whispered to herself as she summoned a mental picture of him in his uniform.

He was handsome and strong.

Just not quite as handsome as the pirate.

"Justin is safe."

But he wasn't exciting. He had never made her pulse beat like this, nor did he stir her body into flames by merely walking into a room.

"Stop it," she demanded, covering her eyes to banish the image of the pirate in his dashing black cutaway.

Beware the man who beguiles you, Lori-Angel, she heard her grandmother's voice in her head. *Those are the ones who won't commit to you. Oh, they'll show you wonders, to be sure, and they'll spin your head with their pleasurable ways. But in the end, they always leave you and your broken heart far behind. Believe me, 'tis better to have the simple hound than to follow the fox. Though the fox is fairer to behold, the hound knows where his home is and dutifully he stays, while the handsome fox is ever off to find new game.*

The pirate was definitely a fox. One that had told her exactly how happy he was with his life.

She would just avoid him. That was all there was to it. Forget her boasts and wager. She didn't want to even try to win. She just wanted Justin to come and free her from this confusion.

Admit it, old girl, what you really want is another moment of your pirate's kisses.

Lorelei closed her eyes in an effort to banish the truth. Well, she was certainly old enough for her wants not to hurt her. And Jack Rhys could find himself another pawn. This one was quitting the game.

7

Lorelei woke early to the sound of someone knocking rather forcefully upon her door. Rubbing the sleep from her eyes, she picked up the warm pink velvet wrap from the foot of her bed. Shrugging it on and then belting it, she crossed the room to crack open the door ever so slightly so that she could see who was disturbing her.

"Sorry to bother you, miss," an older sailor said. He had balding red hair and a leathery face that bore the marks of years of squinting against an unforgiving sun. "We was ordered to bring these things to you first thing like."

She frowned at the wooden crate in his hands and then her gaze drifted to the other five sailors standing behind him who held various items as well. The boxes appeared to contain art supplies, but how could that be?

"We won't be bothering you none. We'll just put them down and be on our way."

Embarrassed that her suspicion over their motives was so plain on her face, Lorelei stepped back and allowed them to bring in their wares. As the fifth man walked past, she noted the easel under his arm.

"Where did all this come from?" she asked, amazed at the variety and multitude of supplies as the first man placed his crate on the floor beside her bed.

Why, she didn't have this much in art supplies at her father's house!

"Henri paints," the older sailor said, indicating the younger pirate behind him who was busy setting up the easel.

The man he referred to looked up and smiled. He was a handsome man around her own age with laughing blue eyes which twinkled from beneath the overhang of jet-black bangs. His long black hair fell to mid-shoulder and he wore a thick, well-kept beard. "*Oui, mademoiselle*, the captain, he asked me if I had any canvas or paints to spare, and I told him that there is always plenty to share with a fellow *artiste*. 'Tis simply my greatest joy that you have all that you need."

"*Merci beaucoup*, Henri," she said, even though the words were quite inadequate for the gratitude she truly felt. "It was so kind of you to bring all of your supplies to me."

"Ah, *non, non, mademoiselle*," he said as three of the sailors left the room. "I assure you this is not all that I have. This is but a bit I had laying around on the third deck."

"And thank God he found some place to finally put it," the fourth sailor said irritably on his way out the door. He was around Henri's age, but with thick brown hair and a permanent frown. "I'm sick of tripping over the blamed stuff. Thought I was going to have to kill him to have any peace."

Henri snorted and waved his hand at the pirate who continued on his way. "Pay him no heed. Bart is a . . . a surly fellow who is never happy unless he has something about which to complain. Me, I like everything." He tapped the center of his chest. "I am a true *artiste*, not just a boat-rat."

Bart stuck his head back in the door. "I heard that, you frog."

Henri stiffened and eyed Bart like he was some disgusting blemish marring his boots. "Smile when you say that or I shall be forced to show you some manners."

Bart scoffed. "I don't need you to show me your girlie ways, Hank. And you'd best be getting out of here before the captain catches you eyeing his woman. Remember what he did to that fellow in Greece? I bet they still haven't found all that man's parts."

Henri paled.

"What did he do?" Lorelei asked, wanting desperately to know.

Henri licked his lips, his brows drawn into a stern vee. "It is not the type of thing one discusses with ladies. The captain, he is not always understanding and Bart is quite right. I should be going."

He moved to the door where Bart waited. "*Bonjour, mademoiselle*, should you need any more supplies, please do not hesitate to let me know." Henri turned on his heel and led Bart away from her room.

"*Please*," Bart mocked in a horrible rendition of Henri's French accent as they headed for the ladder, "*do not hesitate to let me know.* Lord, Hank, but you're ridiculous with that stuff. 'Tis a wonder you didn't drown her with your drool."

"As if you know any better. Tossing a woman over your shoulder and carrying her to an inn is not the way you treat a woman of breeding."

"Well, I don't know no women of breeding."

"And I am sure ladies the world over are now breathing a collective sigh of relief."

Laughing at their banter, Lorelei closed her door, then moved to examine the contents of the crates. There were brushes and paints, jars and charcoal, sketch pads, conti, turpentine—everything she could possibly need.

Without a doubt, it was the greatest gift she'd ever received. She knew the pirate king had done it simply to endear himself to her, but even so, it touched her.

You really should thank him.

It would be the polite thing to do, she assured herself. Even a scoundrel deserved thanks for a good deed.

Hurriedly, she shed her wrap and nightgown and chose a light yellow day gown. Once dressed, she pulled her hair back into a tight braid and tied it off with a yellow ribbon, then headed out of her room to the captain's cabin.

She knocked once on the door. At his answer, she opened the door and stepped into his room.

Lorelei hesitated at the mouth of the lion's den. She hadn't given much thought as to what his room would look like, but never in her wildest dreams would she have imagined this.

All four walls were lined top to bottom with bookshelves, which were brimming with books. Numerous leather-bound tomes were also spread haphazardly about the room. Three stacks of books were on his desk. Four opened books lay on a chest by his bed, and several crates that held even more books were littered about.

Sunlight poured into the room from open windows that allowed a pleasant breeze to circulate. The wood of his cabin was stained much darker than the light oak of her own room.

She could only see Jack's long legs, as he was lying in the center of a large four-poster bed which was covered with a rich red velvet spread embroidered with gold leaves and acorns. Thick matching drapes hung from the canopy, obscuring the upper half of his body from her.

There was also a large cherry table to her left and a plush stuffed chair set before it. The room looked more like someone's library than a captain's quarters.

Lorelei took a step further into the room so she could see the pirate's face. He was lying on his side, reading a book. His white, loose-fitting shirt was unlaced and hanging open to show a bounty of tanned, well-muscled chest. It was the most casual, natural pose she'd ever seen him assume.

But what held her attention most was the small pair of reading glasses he wore.

The incongruity of it stunned her.

He looked up at her. A warm, welcoming smile curved his lips. "To what do I owe the pleasure of this visit?" he asked, removing the glasses. His hands looked so large compared to the dainty glasses as he carefully folded them up and placed them on the chest beside his bed.

His gaze swept the mattress in front of him. "You haven't decided to yield victory so soon, have you?"

Resisting the sudden urge to flee, she said simply, "I merely came to thank you."

"Ah," he said, leaning his head slightly back. "Henri must have delivered his treasure." He picked up a small fob watch which was lying beside his book and checked the time. He set it aside and quirked his lips. "I'm surprised he waited so long. I don't think I've ever seen him happier than when I told him we had someone on board who shared his love of painting."

"It is surprising."

"What? That a pirate can appreciate art?"

"Yes."

"Well," he said cooly. "I'll certainly credit you with honesty on the matter. You didn't even blush."

His statement confused her. "I don't understand."

"You shouldn't judge people, Lorelei," he said in the same deliberate voice her father used to censure her behavior.

How she hated that patronizing tone, especially coming from a man like him. "But you *are* pirates. All of you."

"We are people first. Pirate is merely one small facet of who and what we are." He closed his book and eyed her for a minute. "Let me ask you a question, Lorelei. Who do you think farmers fear most? A pirate or a banker?"

What a ridiculous question. "A pirate, of course."

"Nay," he said solemnly. "A pirate never fore-closed a farm, nor has one ever repossessed someone's belongings simply because their crops failed. If you were to ask a farmer who makes his blood run cold, he would tell you 'tis the banker he fears."

The insult he gave stung her deeply. "Do not liken my father to a pirate or a bandit. He is a good man."

"You say that only because you know your father as a man and not as a banker. I assure you, he has plenty of clients who would say otherwise. Indeed, the night of your party I heard a group of men describing him as a heartless beast who never had an ounce of compassion for anyone."

Narrowing her eyes, she saw red. How dare anyone say such about the man who'd loved her all her life? Her father was a wonderful man. Kind, gentle, and generous to a fault. "Anyone who would say such a thing knows nothing of my father."

"True. They only know of a banker named Sir Charles Dupree."

She opened her mouth to retort, but could think of nothing to say.

Glancing to the floor, she considered his words. He was right. She'd heard those rumors of her father all her life, and she'd always discounted them. Through the eyes of a loving daughter, she saw her father as a shrewd businessman, but perhaps those who dealt with him on a daily basis saw him as something else.

Yet why did it bother the pirate so much that she judged people? "What makes you care so?"

"I have seen the consequences of judging people based on a handful of facts and a moment's worth of observations. It strips them of their dignity."

She found him perplexing. "You've used such

judgmental terms yourself. You called your own mother a prostitute."

"Aye," he said. "As I said, I've seen the consequences."

His double standard still baffled her. "Why do you care whether or not I judge people?"

"Because you're special, Lorelei Dupree." His answer stunned her. "You're not like other people and it pains me to see you do something so common when I know there's much more to you than that."

"How do you know?"

"I see it every time I look at you. You have a passion for life that burns so bright it almost singes me to be near it. Every time I see you suppress that fire it pains me." His gaze captivated hers. "I don't want anything to extinguish that fire."

"Is that why you sent the paints?" she asked quietly.

"Aye, I want to see you capture that passion on canvas."

"What if I can't?"

"You can. I've no doubt about it."

No one had ever said such to her before, nor had they ever encouraged her to do something she wanted to do. Her father and Justin had often indulged her, but never had they offered such support.

To think, when it finally came, it came from Black Jack Rhys. Pirate, rake, and . . .

She didn't want to finish that thought. The direction of her thoughts, along with the strange tenderness in her heart for him, was not something she wished to examine.

"All right, then," she said, deciding not to waste

this opportunity. If he wanted her to paint, then she would definitely oblige him. "I'll just need some fruit and an ornate vase or some sort of container, then—"

"Fruit?" he asked with a sneer. "You want to paint fruit?"

Why did he look so disgusted by her subject matter? Was there something about fruit he found distasteful? "It's what I always paint."

He hung his head. "Why does that surprise me?" he muttered under his breath as if exasperated with her. He looked back at her. Louder, he asked, "Did Michelangelo paint fruit?"

Warning bells sounded inside her. Jack was about to propose something to her. Something she would probably object to.

She knew it deep inside.

"He might have," she hedged.

A wicked, mischievous light shone in his eyes and she knew enough about the pirate to take a step back.

"Come now," he beckoned in a seductive half-whisper. "Don't tell me you've never wanted to paint *forbidden* fruit."

She swallowed in trepidation. Surely he wasn't proposing what she assumed he was proposing.

In spite of herself, her gaze dipped to the exposed flesh of his chest as an image of the statue David flashed before her eyes.

Heat stung her cheeks. Surely not even *he* would suggest she sketch him . . . sketch him . . . like that!

"Forbidden fruit?" she asked with a squeak.

By the light in his eyes she could see he was leaving her dangling intentionally. Oh, how the man loved to toy with her, and how she hated that she rose so often to his bait.

Just when she was sure her face could get no redder, he spoke, "Haven't you ever wanted to paint . . . people?"

Just as she suspected. Oh, he was clever. But if he thought for one instant that she was going to paint him in the altogether, then he was altogether wrong.

"I like fruit," she said crisply.

"Yes, but fruit is so very boring."

"Not really. It's actually rather fascinating."

He looked at her in disbelief. "What about fruit could honestly be fascinating?"

Well, he had her there. In truth, there was very little about fruit that she found interesting. But there was one thing about it—fruit was *never* dangerous. Nor threatening.

Come on, Lorelei, think of something or else he'll know you lie.

"The way light plays on it," she said at last, pleased with herself for finding an excuse.

Doubt was etched into his face. "And to think I actually assumed you were made of *braver* stuff."

Never let a man see your fear. They can sense it and they use it to control you. The words rang in her head. She had to do something to show him he didn't scare her.

"What do you mean by that?" she hedged again.

"I mean, here you are a grown woman with a man who is more than happy to volunteer himself to be your model and all you can do is request fruit. Really, Lorelei, what would Michelangelo say about it?"

Show them no fear.

"Meet me in my room in half an hour." Lorelei savored the confused look on his face. A slight frown drew his brows together while he looked askance as if trying to determine whether or not he'd heard her correctly.

"You won't be late, will you?" she asked, masking her face in pure innocence.

His frown deepened. "Nay. I'll be on time."

He thought she was up to something, she could see it plainly.

Let him wonder what.

"Then I shall await your pleasure," she purred, taking pure, evil delight in the new, stunned look on his face. She left him in his bed and returned to her room.

If the truth were told, she'd always wanted to paint a person, but no one at home would ever hold still long enough to allow her that. This was a once-in-a-lifetime opportunity to see if she really could paint a person and she wasn't about to let it go.

Of course, she would have to make sure he stayed across the room from her.

Yes, over by the wardrobe, perhaps.

She studied the area. She could pull her chair over there and . . .

No. It would never work. The captain wouldn't look right sitting in the yellow upholstered Chippendale. Besides, now that she looked at it, she wasn't sure if he'd fit in it, as large as he was. The straight back and carved daffodils just wouldn't compliment his true essence.

The bed, of course, was *completely* out of the question. She could never spend another restful night in it after seeing him on it. 'Twould be disturbing to say the least, not to mention completely scandalous.

Then where?

She turned around slowly, examining every corner of her room and every possibility of where she might put him. But to her dismay, she couldn't see him anywhere in her cabin.

Nay, when she closed her eyes there was only one place she could imagine him—in his own room. The rich textures and colors were decidedly masculine and decidedly dangerous.

If she truly wanted to capture a pirate's essence, that was the only room that would do.

"'Tis no doubt just what he wants," she whispered in warning to herself.

Be that as it may, she couldn't argue with truth. It was undeniable. Jack Rhys didn't fit in with yellow daffodils and white lace.

"Just pretend he's a piece of fruit."

That *might* work. Divorce herself from the man and don the true cap of an artist. Surely she could do that. She was, as he so bluntly reminded her, a woman full grown.

She could do that. Really.

Gathering her courage, Lorelei walked the short distance back to his room and knocked timidly.

At his answer, she pushed the door open.

He looked up from where he stood over his table. "Surely it's not been half an hour."

She shook her head. "I can't paint you in my room," she said simply.

He arched a puzzled brow.

"I was wondering if I might paint you in here."

His other brow shot up as he stared at her in astonishment. If she weren't so embarrassed, his look would have amused her. "Learned to trust me already?" he teased.

"Hardly. It's just this room is more fitting for you than my yellow cabin. I just can't imagine you surrounded by lace and . . ."

"Frou-frou?" he supplied.

"That word will suffice. May I?"

He gave her a courtly bow. "I am ever your servant, my lady. You may have me any place you choose."

There was innuendo in his tone and for once Lorelei decided to ignore it.

"Would you care for my help moving your supplies into my cabin?" he asked.

"If you don't mind."

"Not at all."

In no time, they had her paints, canvas, and easel set up in his room. Lorelei covered her awkward feeling by carefully laying out her palette and paints while the pirate finished his entry into the ship's log. She did her best to ignore how handsome he looked leaning over the book while he sat at his desk. If she didn't know better, he looked like any other businessman carrying out his daily task.

It was only as she was pinning on her crisp white apron that the irony of his task struck her.

"Why do you keep a log?" she asked as she finished rolling back the sleeves of her gown. "I wouldn't think you'd want evidence of what you've done to be found. Especially evidence written in your own hand."

He shrugged. "I've never denied who or what I

am. If my enemies take me, so be it. I'm a pirate and if death by a hangman be my fate, then I'll abide by my sentence."

There was no fear or cowardice in his stance or face as he spoke. It was as if he were merely commenting on the weather. She'd never before met a man who was so willing to accept the punishment for his crimes.

"Do you want to die?" she asked.

"No more so than any other, I suppose. But sooner or later we all meet that end."

Suddenly, a loud bell started clamoring. The captain froze an instant before he ran to a chest beside his bed and pulled out a flintlock and sword.

"A ship's approaching," he explained.

"Justin!" she breathed, thrilled at the thought that he'd found her so quickly.

The look on the pirate's face could have chilled the sun. "Stay here." Then he was out the door.

Relief washed through Lorelei at the thought she might be headed home. Closing her eyes, she savored the image of Lord Wallingford's ship and Justin's face as she stepped on board the crisply polished galleon that would take her back to the safety of home.

She couldn't wait.

Moving to the windows of the cabin, she looked out at the swirling waves. She strained all she could, but there was no sight of a ship, nor any other sign that someone approached, let alone a clue as to who it might be.

Too excited to care how foolish her actions were, she left Jack's cabin and went up to the deck to see her fiancé for herself.

A mad shuffle was taking place on board as cannons were prepared and pirates scurried to take their places.

"It's a ship all right, Captain," the sailor from the crow's nest called down to Jack. "But it ain't *Winsome Fate*. Looks to be a Spanish sloop."

Disappointment assailed her. It wasn't Justin come to save her after all.

"Is she navy or private?" Jack called up to his man.

"Too far to tell, Captain."

There was an eerie silence before another shout. "New ship to port aft!"

Two ships?

Lorelei's stomach fled south at the news. Dear Lord in heaven above, they were about to be caught in the middle of a serious battle.

It was then Jack caught sight of her. His eyes narrowed and he strode quickly toward her.

"This is no time for you to take a walk, Lorelei. Go below before you get seriously hurt."

Just then a small head bobbed up over a barrel to Lorelei's left. The pirate's curse brought heat to Lorelei's cheeks.

"Is there no one on board this ship who will listen to me," he said in a low tone that barely reached her ears. His face stern, he reached for Kit and pulled the boy by the scruff of the neck to stand before him.

His grip was so tight on Kit's shirt that his knuckles blanched, and she could feel his need to throttle his son. Instead of the stern reprimand she expected him to give the boy, the captain said in a calm voice, "Kit, I have a serious mission I need you to complete."

Kit's face wavered between the fear of punishment and hopeful enthusiasm. "Aye, Captain?"

"It's the most important one on this ship."

Hopeful enthusiasm won out. "Truly?"

"Truly. I need you to guard our hostage while I deal with these Spanish dogs."

Kit's gaze slid to Lorelei and she could tell guarding her rated right up there with swabbing the decks and cleaning chamber pots. "Guard her how?"

"I need you to take her to your room and make sure she doesn't leave it."

Kit's face fell and he pushed his lower lip out in a show of adolescent distemper. "But how can I help you win the fight if—"

"This is far more important," the pirate interrupted. "We must make sure no harm befalls her."

Kit sighed in resignation. "Very well, Captain. I'll keep her below."

Lorelei didn't like to be manipulated so, but she knew the pirate was right. The deck was no place for Kit, or for her. And unlike Kit, the last thing she wanted was to see battle firsthand.

"Come on," Kit snapped. "We'll be safest in my room." He led her in the opposite direction of her own cabin, toward the center of the ship.

When he finally opened the door to his room, Lorelei paused, staring at the interior.

From where she stood, it looked like Armageddon had struck and nothing had been left standing. Clothes and wooden pieces of all manner of toys and ship parts were strewn about. It was strange to see the room, for it showed quite vividly Kit's transition from boy to man. Wooden soldiers and ships were littered alongside a wench and ropes that bore various knots.

Two large medieval-style pennants hung along one wall with a dragon rampant on one and a gryphon reposed on the other. His unmade bed was designed much like Jack's and if she didn't miss her guess, there was a crocheted black sheep tangled in the bed covers.

"I apologize for the mess," Kit said as he darted to the bed to toss a shirt over the sheep. "The captain gets on me always for it, but I don't get many visitors. Just the captain when he eats dinner with me."

"He does that a lot?" she asked as she closed the door behind her.

"Almost always." Kit took a match from a silver box next to his bed and lit two more lanterns to help her see. "I keep telling him I'm too old for it, but he doesn't seem to listen."

Lorelei smiled at the image of the pirate king coddling his son. "He still sees you as a child?"

Kit rolled his eyes and blew out the match. "I'm sure I'll be a grown man one day and still he'll cut up my meat for me."

She smiled at the forlorn note in his voice. "My father treats me the same way."

"But you're a girl," he said, as if that were an excuse for her father's overprotectiveness.

He picked up the armload of clothes from his chair and tossed them to the center of the room so that she could sit.

Deciding she couldn't relax in this room while it was in this condition, she set about collecting the wooden toys. "You love your father?" she asked.

"More than my life," Kit said with conviction. "He's the best captain ever to sail."

Lorelei placed her gathered toys in a carved

wooden chest that was set next to his bed. The chest was a beautiful cedar piece with coiling dragons carved all over it. In the center of the lid, the boy's name was carefully inscribed into a small cloud, Kristopher Alec Rhys. But what stunned her more was when she looked to the inside of the lid and read the poem that had been carved there:

There once was a little boy named Kit,
who was loved much more than a bit.
With eyes of green and hair of brown,
he had a smiling face that seldom frowned.
And though his room was seldom neat,
perhaps this chest will help achieve that feat.

She traced the writer's initials with her fingertip—JR. Jack Rhys? Could the poem really be the work of Jack Rhys?

She closed the lid.

"Do you like it?" Kit asked as he started folding some of the clothes.

"It's very nice."

"The captain made it himself. It was a gift for my fifth birthday."

Lorelei moved to stand next to him, where she could help fold his clothes and place them on the bed. She bit her lip in indecision as a thought struck her.

Would Kit be as closed about his mother as the captain?

It really wasn't her place to pry, and yet she wanted desperately to know.

Deciding this would probably be the only person on the ship who would answer her questions, she took a deep breath and asked, "Kit, tell me about your mother. How long was she married to the captain?"

He paused while folding a shirt and cocked his head as if trying to remember. "I'm not sure. The captain never said. He just told me that he fell in love with her the first time he saw her. Said she was a beautiful woman with very gentle ways."

Her chest tightened at his words.

She felt as if someone had just struck a blow to her. For some reason she didn't want to think about, it hurt her that he had loved this other woman, that he had lied to her when she'd asked him about it. "So, he loved her much?"

"Aye. She loved the two of us with all her heart. He said her last thoughts were of me and that she told him she'd always watch out for me from heaven."

She cleared her throat of the sudden knot that choked her. "How old were you when she died?"

Kit took a stack of folded trousers and dumped them in a small wardrobe by his door. "Three, I think. I don't remember her at all. I just know what the captain tells me about her."

Cannon fire roared and the ship shook. Lorelei gasped at the nightmarish repeat.

"That'll be warning shots," Kit told her.

"Warning shots?"

"Aye, we fire them to warn the captains we're serious about battle."

She heard the response as cannons in a distance fired. "Sounds like they're pretty serious as well."

His eyes troubled, Kit nodded. "There's a lot of people who want to kill the captain."

For the first time, Lorelei saw the pirate as something more than a bounty. She saw him through Kit's eyes. He was the boy's father. The man Kit treasured as much as she treasured her own father. Not a pirate or a brigand to Kit, Jack Rhys was the one who chased away his dragons and fears.

Without him, Kit would be orphaned and completely alone.

The boy chewed his lip and stared at the door as if debating whether or not he should run for the deck.

Lorelei knew his thoughts. He no doubt wanted the comfort of his father's presence, wanted to hear his father tell him everything would be all right.

"Kit," she said, moving toward him. "Would you hold me? I'm scared and I know that would make me feel a lot better."

He ran into her arms and as Lorelei held onto him, she didn't know which of them was more terrified.

"We'll be okay," he said in a wavering voice. "No one can beat the captain. Really. He's the best at everything."

She smiled at the youthful belief and at Kit's attempt to reassure her. "I'm sure you're right."

For what seemed like hours on end, the cannons roared and the ship rocked. At times she was certain they'd taken a straight hit, but no water ever seeped into the room and time seemed to pass slower and slower.

Just when she was certain she could stand no more, a loud thunderous clamor of voices rang out, then the bell sounded.

Kit raised his head so quickly, he bumped her chin. "We won!" he shouted.

"Are you sure?"

"Aye. That's the victory bell." He scrambled from her arms and ran out of the room.

On trembling legs, Lorelei forced herself to follow after Kit.

When she climbed out to the deck, the pirate men were in high celebration.

"Lower the red flag," the captain called to Tarik as he caught Kit up in his arms.

"We won, we won!" Kit shrieked, hugging his father.

Jack just smiled. "Of course we did, boy. You didn't really think I'd let them Spaniards get a hold of us, did you?"

Kit pulled away from his father and walked around the standing members of the crew to congratulate them.

Then the captain turned and met her gaze. The smile faded and something hot flickered in his eyes. "I trust you fared better this time?"

Stepping closer, Lorelei looked out at the Spanish ship which was a few hundred feet to their right. The ship was sinking and the crew was in a mad scramble to launch their lifeboats. "What's to be their fate?" she asked.

"Whatever God intends," he said, then raised his voice to Tarik. "Raise sails and make haste."

"Aye, Captain."

"Are we running from the other ship?" Kit asked in horror.

Jack laughed. "Never. 'Tis your uncle Morgan's ship out there to port aft. We'll let the Spanish think he scared us off."

"Phew," Kit said, curling his lip. "Why does he get to play hero while they hunt us down?"

The captain ruffled his hair. "One day you'll understand. Now off with you. I heard Sarah made your favorite tea biscuits and was looking forward to giving you one."

Kit scampered across the deck.

Taking a step toward the pirate, Lorelei looked up at him. "Why *are* you allowing Morgan to play the hero?"

"Why not?"

"Why?"

He smirked. "If I didn't explain myself to my son, why do you think I'd explain myself to you?"

"Because I'm old enough to understand."

"And I'm old enough to know better than to explain myself to anyone."

Lorelei clenched her teeth in frustration. He was a strange man, to be sure. He wasn't just the pirate she'd called him. There was much more to this man than that.

"I'm surprised you're not plundering their cargo."

He snorted. " 'Tis a warship no doubt sent out to hunt me down. It would only be a waste of time to search her. Besides, I have more important matters at hand."

"Revenge?"

He feigned shock. "Hardly. I have an appointment for a portrait with one of the most attractive artists I've ever captured."

Her mouth opened in disbelief. "Do you take anything seriously?"

"Only battle. Which, as you can see, is now over. We're still weeks away from our destination and I intend to enjoy the trip."

"I'm glad one of us will."

"Ah, Lorelei," he said, stroking her cheek and

raising chills along her arms. "I can guarantee you that you'll look back quite fondly on this journey in your old age."

"I sincerely doubt it." And even as the words left her lips, there was some small part of her that wondered if he were right. This was probably the last great adventure of her life. Once she married Justin, she would be bound to the hearth tending his parties and children. Planning dinner menus and balls.

Her life would be . . .

Boring, she realized with a start. Her life had always been a bit boring. 'Twas what motivated her to ruffle her father and Justin so much.

Adventure isn't worth the price you pay for it, little Lori. Take it from someone who knows. Granny-Anne's words had always been with her.

Along with the stories of heartache her grandmother had suffered. Heartache that had tainted the joy of her grandmother's smile and dampened the sparkle of her eyes.

Long ago, Lorelei had promised her grandmother that she would never seek adventure, and never disobey her father. And though there were times when she stretched that promise to the limits of its elasticity, she had always tried to suppress the same wild spirit and need to exert her will that had led her grandmother to complete ruination.

Nay, she scolded herself. She didn't need to exert herself. Her father showed great latitude in accommodating her personality.

Still, she couldn't honestly deny the fact that this would more than likely be the only great adventure she would ever encounter in her life, and that made her all too aware of how accurate Jack's prediction was.

"Now, if you'll excuse me, Miss Dupree. I have men who need my help. Why don't you go back to my cabin and finish mixing your paints."

And with those words, she found herself dismissed.

Miffed, she straightened her spine and headed back to the pirate's cabin.

Jack watched as Lorelei left the deck. He hadn't meant to be so curt with her. He'd lived too many years of his life with people who took advantage any way they could, and he wasn't about to start opening up now.

The less people knew about him, the safer he was. In more ways than one.

Even Morgan, as well meaning as he was, would occasionally bring up a subject that was still too raw for Jack to face. And at those times, he regretted his drunken verbosities, which had given such details of his past to Morgan.

Lorelei was nothing more than a passing fancy. She would suit him well for the next few weeks, but after that she would return to her world and he . . .

Would probably be dead.

Sighing, he headed for Tarik and vowed to think no more of Lorelei and the strange feelings she evoked inside him.

8

For several hours, Lorelei had been sketching Jack's room in her pad while she waited for the pirate to join her. But after a time, she ran out of objects to draw and grew quickly bored. Without the pirate's presence, she couldn't even begin the painting, for she wasn't sure how she wanted him to pose.

She paced around his room for a short while, then sat at the polished table.

Just an hour ago, she'd made one more attempt to go above, but Kesi had stopped her, saying that there was nothing Lorelei could do to help the wounded who were being tended. She'd tried arguing at first, wanting to help the men who were suffering, but Kesi wasn't one to be denied.

Yielding to Kesi's plea, she had returned to the captain's cabin and paced until she'd grown too bored to do even that.

With a sigh, Lorelei lifted her head up from her

crossed arms and glanced over to the log the pirate had been writing in earlier. Reaching out, she pulled it to her and began to idly flip pages.

Numbers flashed on one page and she paused to look them over.

November 3, 1777
1000 pieces of eight paid to Simon Platt for loyalty, 800 pieces of eight paid to Robert Gehrig for same.

Lorelei frowned. Jack rewarded his men for loyalty? How strange. It didn't make sense to her until she flipped more pages.

April 14, 1778
Made port in Barbados. Overheard three men talking of Simon Platt, who had told them he lost his leg while escaping me. Told them I had nailed him to the mast and had lopped off his leg so that he would bleed to death on his burning ship. Platt also said that he escaped the flames when the wood snapped and that he was the sole survivor. Sent another 800 pieces of eight to Morgan for payment to Platt for a job well done. That should quell a few of the men chasing me and I need to make mention of the deed when next in port.

Lorelei's mouth dropped in disbelief. Truly interested now, she began reviewing the pages in earnest and as she read, she found out a lot of intriguing facts about Captain Jack Rhys. Including the reason why he allowed Morgan to pick up the survivors of the Spanish ship.

"Why, Jack Rhys," she breathed. "You have a bleeding heart."

He really did. According to his log, he allowed his men an equal share of all their ill-gotten gains, as well as the right to vote on how the ship was run and how long they sailed each year before making their way to a small island in the south Atlantic where many of his men had families that didn't wish to sail with them. And when he lost a member of his crew, the surviving family members were paid a hefty yearly stipend to live on.

There were also detailed accounts of not-so-friendly encounters with enemies, and entries where he'd been forced to punish certain members of his crew. However, none of them showed the pirate acting unjustly, or doing anything a military commander wouldn't do in a similar situation.

But what caught her attention most were the number of times he would entertain a crew's officers while their ship was being looted. Lorelei read that on one occasion the unloading of cargo on a British ship took a full week and the pirates provided music and meals to the officers the entire time.

Could it be true?

And yet why would he lie in his ship's log?

She heard someone approaching. Slamming the book closed, she returned it to its spot and quickly laid her head down upon the desk to pretend she napped.

The door opened and the captain stepped in. Lorelei looked up and noted the pallor on his face, as well as the blood stains that covered his shirt.

"Are you all right?" she asked, rising immediately to her feet.

He looked at her and she realized he had forgotten she would be here. "I'm fine," he said as he walked to a cabinet hanging next to his bed. He pulled out a bottle of rum and took a liberal swig.

He wasn't fine. Lorelei knew that. Whatever had happened had shaken him. It scared and confused her to see him like this. He'd always been so sure and calculating in the past.

This Jack Rhys was strangely vulnerable. Strangely human.

"What happened?" she asked.

He took another drink, then replaced the bottle. Ignoring her question, he moved to his trunk and retrieved a fresh shirt. As he pulled his shirt off, Lorelei caught sight of the numerous scars marring his chest and back. Her stomach lurched. Never in her life had she seen anything like it. One long scar down his back looked like a burn mark, while others were easily identified as sword wounds or bullets.

Not to mention the bandage he still wore from Justin's sneak attack.

Once he had replaced his shirt, he tossed the dirty one into a small canvas bag. The pirate took one deep breath and faced her. "Tommy lost his left arm," he said at last.

"Tommy?"

"Aye, the older man who brought the paints to your room this morning. A piece of shrapnel caught his arm in the fighting."

"Will he be all right?" she asked, moving to stand before him.

His jaw tensed. "Doubtful. Most men die a few days after such an injury."

Aching to reach out and soothe the pain on his

face, she refrained. He wasn't the type of man a woman coddled, and no doubt he would see her effort as patronizing. "I'm sorry."

"Are you?" he asked, his voice laced with venom. "You'd roast the lot of us if you could."

"That's not true."

"It's not?"

And for the first time she realized it really wasn't true. She didn't want the pirate's head for what he'd done to her. In fact, he hadn't done anything to her, beyond teasing, and perhaps a little tormenting. Certainly nothing that was worth his life, let alone the lives of his crew.

He's a pirate, she remind herself.

Perhaps, but he wasn't what she thought of when she envisioned a pirate. A hardened pirate would be the one to lop off a man's arm and laugh over the deed, not stand before her so upset over it.

"No," she said, "it's not true. I told you before that I don't like to hurt people."

"So you did." He walked over to where she'd placed her easel and palette. He picked up a brush and ran his thumb over the bristles. "I don't really feel like sitting for your portrait right now. Perhaps later."

For some reason she couldn't name, Lorelei didn't want to leave. She wanted to stay and make him feel better.

Smiling, she gave a half-hearted sigh. "Why is it every time I want to paint someone they use that as an excuse? Now you know why I paint fruit. It can't get up and move."

* * *

Jack watched her as she headed for the door. Part of him wanted nothing more than to be left alone, while another part didn't want her to leave.

It was the first time he sensed she wasn't fighting him, judging him.

What are you going to do once she leaves? Sit around and mope over the fact that you let a man get hurt? You couldn't have stopped it. You did your damnedest to keep him from being harmed. What happens during battle isn't your fault.

He knew that. Still, it pained him, but not half as much as letting Lorelei leave.

"Wait."

She turned around with an arched brow. "Hmm?"

"I'm not like the other people you've known."

"That is very true."

"Well then, far be it from me to put you off. Come, *madame artiste*. Let me see what you can do."

Her smile warmed him. "Very well," she said, crossing the room. Taking his arms, she led him over to the red stuffed chair near his windows. "Sit here."

Jack did as ordered.

Lorelei stared at him for a few minutes, then moved around the room looking at him from different angles. Her brows were furrowed in thought and she looked so scrumptiously adorable that Jack wondered how long he could contain himself before he yielded to his temptation to kiss her.

"This won't do." Arms akimbo, Lorelei sighed.

"What's wrong?"

"Everything. You just don't look . . ."

"Pirate enough?"

She crinkled her nose at him as if his answer

annoyed her, though why it should, he couldn't fathom. "No—natural enough. I want to capture you."

Jack rose and approached her. "And I want you to capture me."

"Jack," she said with a note of warning in her voice as she caught his arms and forced them back to his sides.

He smiled. 'Twas the first time she'd ever used his name and it sounded wonderful in that sweet contralto of hers. He traced the line of her jaw with his thumb.

"Close your eyes," he whispered.

"Are you going to kiss me?"

"Shh," he whispered again. "Trust me."

He saw the doubt in her eyes and then to his surprise, she complied. Jack traced the petal softness of her lips with the pad of his thumb. Her skin was as pale as the purest cream and the freckles slashing over the bridge of her nose reminded him of nutmeg. Aye, she was a rare beauty with fire and intelligence the likes of which he'd never before seen.

"Think of me," he said, leaning closer to speak in her ear. "Tell me what you see."

He expected her to say a pirate with a sword raised, but what came out momentarily stunned him.

"I see you as you were the night at the tavern. With your hair hanging loose about your shoulders." She opened her eyes and gave him a smile that sent heat straight to his groin.

"You did it!" she said with a laugh.

Then, to his utter amazement, she threw her arms around him and hugged him.

Startled, Jack couldn't move. It was an easy, friendly hug. The kind that denoted pure affection. The kind of hug Jack Rhys had never before had. In fact, it was the only hug Jack Rhys had ever had from anyone other than Kit.

Unaware of the peculiar feelings inside him, Lorelei ran about the room like a squirrel. "I know exactly what I need." She returned to his side and started pulling him toward the bed.

Jack quirked an eyebrow.

"I want you on the bed."

"Interesting. I could say the same about you."

She rolled her eyes. "Come now, this is serious art. I want you like I found you this morning. Lying on your side facing the door."

He'd rather have her on her side facing him. Naked.

And one day soon, he would. For now though, he would play along and build up her confidence in him. Let her think she had control of the situation and once she dropped her guard, he would pounce.

Obliging her wish, Jack lay on his side. Lorelei propped pillows up around him. The soft scent of rose assailed him as she adjusted his stance and he took a moment to savor the womanly warmth of her being so close to him.

Aye, her breasts were just an arm's length from him. So close, and yet he didn't dare reach out for one the way his body and soul begged him to.

Clenching his teeth, he fought against the inferno that threatened to set his very pants on fire.

"Perfect," she declared at last. "Except for one thing."

"Which is?"

She reached out and pulled his hair loose of the leather tie and began fanning it around his shoulders. Jack sucked his breath in sharply between his teeth. There was something about the feel of her hands in his hair that burned him through. Not to mention the fact that her breasts were eye-level with him now. So very close that he could reach just a little to cup one. Or lean his head ever so slightly forward to suckle her.

He ground his teeth together, the torture of it almost more than he could bear.

The urge to pull her to him was overwhelming, but to do that would cost him dearly, for no doubt she would run out the door, damning him with every step.

This was Lorelei, the artist, and she didn't see him as a man. Right now, he was about as human as the ridiculous fruit she'd painted in the past. And if he played along with her wants, perhaps she'd let him show her his . . . banana.

Lorelei paused. "What?" she asked.

"What?" Jack repeated, concerned for a moment that he might have spoken one of his thoughts aloud.

"You've got a strange look about your face, as if you know some private jest."

Jack forced the smile from his face. "I was but thinking of you, my sweet. That is why I smile."

She straightened and gave him a calculating stare. "You know what I think?"

He arched a brow.

"I think you're so used to charming women that you do it without thought."

"Is that a fact?"

She nodded. "I'm quite certain of it. I think

everything you do is a calculated effort to get you what you want."

"And what is it I want?"

She crossed her arms over her chest and presented him with the stance of a military commander ready to do battle. "I won't let you use me, Jack. I'm as much a person as you are, which means I'm not the pawn you captured. I won't let you hurt the admiral any more than I'll let you hurt Justin. He's a good man."

Jack felt his body grow rigid at her words. If only she knew the truth of the Wallingfords. Knew just what an evil, vile man she protected so passionately.

"I promise you, Lorelei, he's not the man you know. And he is wholly undeserving of your devotion."

"I say you're wrong."

It was on the tip of his tongue to tell her the truth about Wallingford. To let her know just what sort of monster he was. But Jack held his tongue. He wanted to win her honestly. He wouldn't stoop to such ignoble tactics. Those he left to people such as Wallingford.

"Then I'm wrong," he breathed. "I was wrong to take you from your family, and if I had a decent bone in my body, I would return you home this instant."

She froze at his words and looked at him expectantly.

"Unfortunately, I lack any decent bones."

Her eyes narrowed and before he could blink, she reached out, grabbed the pillow he was reclining on, jerked it from beneath him, then whacked him on the head. Jack roared with laughter as she continued to pummel him with the pillow.

Seizing a pillow of his own, he counter-attacked.

She paused for only an instant before she renewed her attack, her laughter filling his ears as she pushed her offensive.

Jack backed across the bed and watched in satisfaction as she climbed aboard, too intent on his defeat to mind where she was going. She pulled her weapon back from him and caught the pillow against the carving on his canopy. A loud rending of fabric was quickly followed by a shower of goose feathers.

Jack smiled in triumph. "I win."

And before she could realize his intent, he pulled her against his chest and gave her the kiss he'd been wanting to give her since she'd first started posing him.

Her arms closed around him as she opened her lips to allow him to explore the sweet honey of her breath.

"Spoils to the victor," he whispered as he deepened his kiss.

She laughed deep in her throat, exciting him even more.

"And vengeance to the victim," she whispered before she shoved him back and unsheathed the sword from his hip. She moved slowly from the bed, all the while holding his sword before her. "I want you to take me home."

Conflicted emotions tore through him. One was the lust that still pounded in his loins, another a cold splash of treachery. Had all of it been a ploy so that she could trick him?

He'd never been one to tolerate such, and yet he couldn't quite believe she'd orchestrated the entire match. Nay, no doubt she had merely seized upon the opportunity.

Either way, she wasn't about to get what she wanted. Jack answered to no one save himself and no one would ever dictate his life again. "I really can't."

"I know how to use this, Jack," she said in warning. "And I *will* use it unless you take me home."

Jack moved from the bed and crossed his arms over his chest. With studied nonchalance, he approached her. "Had you wished to see my sword, my lady, all you had to do was ask. In all honesty, 'tis what I've wanted to show you since the night I danced with you at your father's ball."

She arced the blade toward his throat. "I'm warning you."

He should probably be terrified, he thought, but then he'd had great swordsmen corner him in similar fashion numerous times in his life. They had never trapped him and it would take more than this slip of a woman to do so now.

Jack moved slowly to his walking cane, which was propped between his chest and the wall. She didn't flinch as he picked it up and rolled it between his hands. Still, he noted the suspicion on her face as she waited for him to try something to disarm her. "Aye, you do look as if you've held a man's sword in your hand before."

Anger flickered in her eyes, but she didn't yield to her temper.

"I take it your father gave you sword lessons along with your reading, writing, and arithmetic?"

He pulled the thin épée from its cane sheath. He'd teach her to pull a sword on him! Swinging it around to disarm her, he was momentarily baffled as she parried his thrust with an expert move.

Astounded, Jack advanced only to have her take the upper hand. He actually took a step back from her approach. "You really have been taught."

"I was taught *well*," she said smugly.

His sword flashed in the light as she brought it down against the épée in his hand. He had seen few men her equal. She thrust at him and he barely sidestepped the move. He twirled around as she passed behind his back. Jack grabbed her in his arms, trapping her in his embrace. Her mouth opened in surprise and he planted a fierce kiss on her lips.

Lorelei shrieked in indignation, then stomped his instep. Pain exploding up his leg, Jack pulled back with a hiss. He barely parried her next move as he hopped away from her.

"That was vicious," he said, forcing himself to focus on something other than the agony of his toes.

She didn't respond verbally, but the lunge she took at him spoke loudly enough.

Jack dipped his blade below hers and wrested the sword from her grasp. Releasing the hilt of his own so that both swords hit the wall to his right with a loud clatter, he took her extended right hand in his own and pressed her back against the wall.

Her breasts heaved against his chest as she struggled to calm her racing breath. In spite of the fact she had just tried to skewer him with his own sword, he smiled.

"I much prefer to fight with pillows," he said, then dipped his head to kiss her lips once more.

Lorelei's head swam as much as her emotions at his touch. He had defeated her. It had been years since anyone could claim that, and yet this pirate had swept her sword from her hand with ease.

And now his kiss was melting her control in the same effortless way.

What was it about this man that made her crave his touch so?

It was his charisma and charm, his masculine aura of authority. Like some wild, untamed beast, he fascinated her. Here was a man of raw, unmitigated power. A man who lived by his own terms, not those dictated by others.

He took what he wanted and made no apologies.

Right now he wanted her. And if the truth were known, she wanted him right back.

Terrified by that knowledge, Lorelei pulled away from him. "Please, let me go."

In his eyes she could see her tiny request gave him pause. He released her. "I can't take you home, Lorelei."

"It was worth a try," she whispered.

"And a noble try it was, too. I'll certainly grant you that." The humor faded from his face. "I'll let this episode be forgotten. But never, ever cross swords with me in front of my men."

"I understand." And she did. Her grandmother had told her numerous stories of how important it was for a captain to maintain the respect and control of his crew. That was one of the reasons she had waited until they were alone to attempt it.

Jack retrieved the swords, then locked them inside his trunk. "Who taught you to fight?"

Lorelei chewed her lip as she debated what she should tell him. Deciding the truth couldn't hurt her any, she sighed. "My grandmother."

His face was a mixture between disbelief and incredulity. "Your grandmother?"

Savoring his uncharacteristic look of surprise, she confessed the whole of it. "She was Anne Bonny. I'm sure you've heard of her."

He started to laugh, but then something made him change his mind. "You're serious?"

"Aye, very."

Respect shone in his eyes. "Did she teach you anything else?"

"Aye, to be wary of pirates, especially those named Jack."

This time he did laugh. "Well, that certainly explains your daring passion. I bet you're the perfect image of your grandmother."

"So I've been told."

"And yet you would marry a British lord. How do you think that would make your grandmother feel?"

"Proud, actually," she answered. "She regretted the actions of her youth until the day she died."

"Regretted her freedom at sea?" he asked as if the very thought was inconceivable.

" 'Tis what she always said. But in all honesty, I think she loved it more than she ever dared let on. I think what she truly regretted was losing Calico Jack."

"Your grandfather?"

"Aye. She loved him terribly." Lorelei sighed, her heart aching for her grandmother's loss and the suffering her grandmother had endured after she'd returned home to Charleston. "She said she never should have disobeyed her father, that she should have stayed at home dutifully rather than give her heart to a pirate. 'Twas the worst mistake of her life and she paid for it every day."

Jack's frown deepened. "I can't believe she would ever regret her days at sea."

"I can. I saw for myself the sadness in her eyes."

"Perhaps the sadness was from the fact she left the sea behind?"

Had she not felt so sorry for her grandmother, she could have almost laughed at Jack's male persistence. At his inability to believe not everyone loved the sea as much as he did. "Nay, I know better. Had she wanted to return to the sea, she could have. Her father even offered her the opportunity."

"She refused?"

She nodded.

He crossed the room to stand before her. "So, to atone for *her* mistakes, you're willing to make your own?"

"I don't understand."

"You can't marry Justin."

She looked up at him. "Why?"

"Because he's not right for you. He's selfish and cold, and in time that life will devour you."

"You don't know him," she insisted.

"I know him better than you think. I saw the way he treated you. Like a possession to be guarded. He even endangered your life to advance his own career."

"I was the one who agreed to go to the tavern."

"But he shouldn't have asked that of you." Jack touched her face, his fingers sliding along her cheek in a gentle caress that sent heat tearing through her. How she ached for him in the most improper way! "He should never have exposed you to that rough and dangerous crowd. I've seen those kinds of men do things to women that would give you nightmares for the rest of your life. Every time I think about how close you came to peril, I want to beat Justin to a bloody pulp."

"He wouldn't have let harm befall me. I know it."

"But he did," Jack said, his gaze probing hers. "You're here with me now. He couldn't stop me any more than he would have stopped that man who accosted you. Justin isn't the right man for you, Lorelei."

There was so much earnestness in his eyes, and something more. Something deeper that called out to her. "I asked you the night of the party what sort of man would you suggest for me, and you turned and walked out. Why?"

He froze his hand against her cheek. "Unlike Justin, I'm honest with women. I don't promise love everlasting. I promise only what I can deliver."

"Which is?"

Sighing, he dropped his hand from her face and moved away from her. He stopped in front of his armchair and looked out the windows of his cabin. When he spoke, she could barely hear him. "A wonderful time in my bed, and a note in the morning when I leave."

How typically male. Her grandmother was right. A woman could never count on one to abide by his word. They would say anything to get what they wanted, then leave the first chance they got. "That is so shallow, Jack."

"That is reality, I'm afraid."

"Reality?" she scoffed. "*Love* is real. Lust is—"

"Liberating."

"Fleeting!"

He looked back at her, his face and eyes empty. "And love isn't?"

"Nay," she breathed, trying to make him see the truth of her words. "Love is wonderful."

He snorted. "Love is a weapon used to destroy."

"That's not true."

" 'Tis more than true. The only one in life you can count on is yourself, and only a fool would allow another person to have the ability to destroy them."

How could he be so blind? So unwilling to see the truth of life. The truth of love.

"What about Kit?" she asked. "I know you love the child. Do you doubt it?"

She narrowed her gaze on him as she thought of another way to make him see her point. "And what of Kit's mother? He told me you loved her more than your life."

In that instant she had an epiphany. "That's it, isn't it? You mourn for her as my grandmother—"

"I told you I didn't know his mother," Jack inserted, cutting her off.

Confused, she tilted her head slightly as she thought over what Kit had told her.

Jack took three steps until he stood before her. The rage in him terrified her. He was angry and cold, and she had no idea why.

"Let me tell you of love, Lorelei. Kit's mother was a prostitute in some port I can't even recall. When I turned her offer away, she asked if I preferred little boys. Her own little boy to be precise."

She couldn't have felt any worse had he struck her. Was he serious?

"What?" she gasped.

"I was as appalled as you are," he said, his lips curled in disgust. "I, who have traveled the world and have seen every nightmare imaginable, was laid low by her offer. So I bought him from her for a silver guinea."

"But Kit said—"

"Kit doesn't know the truth," he said as the anger fled his face to be replaced by sadness. "I never told anyone the truth of his mother until now. And for an obvious reason, I would keep the truth from him. I may be a pirate who will sooner or later wind up at the wrong end of a noose, but I sure as hell am better than what his mother had planned for him."

He swallowed and stared straight at her. "Now I ask you, where was *her* love for her child?"

"She was obviously deranged," Lorelei said, unable to believe anyone could do such a thing to a small child, let alone her very own. "My father would die before he allowed anyone to harm me."

"I'm delighted for you," he said, his voice cold, empty. "In my world such loyalty doesn't exist."

She reached up and touched his face, wishing there was some way she could make him see the world through her eyes. "I'm sorry, Jack. I'm sorry that you believe that, because love does exist."

"Then believe it if you will. I can only hope Justin, unlike his father, is man enough to honor his obligation to you."

"Why do you hate the admiral so?"

"My reasons are infinite," he said with conviction. "And they are my own."

"And you're not one to share the intimacies of your mind, are you?"

"Nay."

Lorelei ground her teeth in frustration, wishing she knew some way to reach him. But he didn't want to be reached and until he did, there was nothing she could do except make peace with him.

"Then come, my doubting pirate," she said, dropping her hand from his face and taking his arm. "If I can't defeat you with my sword, then allow me to capture you with my brush."

Lorelei placed him back on the bed. He looked perfect in that spot. There was a casual, sensual quality to Jack; even while reclining he radiated power and authority. She didn't know if she could quite portray that on canvas, but she was eager to try.

Seizing up her palette and paint, she began mixing the colors to see if she had any talent for human form.

And so the afternoon went. Jack lay on the bed watching her intently while she attempted to portray his personality on canvas.

A soft breeze whispered through the cabin while the sounds of the sea and crew echoed through the room. It was strangely peaceful and soothing.

Jack didn't try to talk to her and he seemed content just to watch her.

She wondered if he'd ever been this compliant with anyone else before and deep inside she knew the answer was no. She'd learned so much about him today, seen things in him she'd never have guessed were there.

But it was his kindness that stayed with her. He had saved Kit when most men would have simply walked away.

He cared for his crew. And if she admitted the truth, she wished that he could come to care for her.

"You're smiling," Jack's voice broke the silence. "What are you thinking about?"

She felt heat rush to her cheeks. "Nothing in particular."

"You're lying."

Clearing her throat, she wiped her brush off on a cloth. "Very well, Jack. I'm thinking of you, if you must know."

"Me?"

"Aye, I was wondering if anyone could ever save you."

9

A stern frown creased Jack's brow as he took her words in. "Save me from what?"

Lorelei shrugged as she dipped her thin brush into the light gold color she'd just mixed, and tried to paint the highlights in his hair. "From yourself."

His response was a rude snort that reminded her of a wounded boar caught in a trap. "That is the one thing I don't need saving from."

"I think you do," she argued.

"And I think you may be deranged."

Lorelei inclined her head to him as she swept her brush around the outline of his hair on her canvas. "Perhaps. I've been accused of worse."

Jack shifted ever so slightly on the bed. He raised his head, flexed his wrist a bit, then went back to leaning his cheek against his fist.

His hair fell away from his shoulders and his shirt opened a little more, baring the flesh of his chest almost to his waist. Beneath the stark white linen, bronze muscles contracted and relaxed with each breath he took.

Heaven, but he was a handsome man.

'Twas a pity he was all too aware of that fact. And even more so that she wasn't immune to those looks.

"What makes you want to save me anyway?" he asked.

Her brush between her teeth, she smudged the paint a tad with her little finger. She wasn't really sure she ought to answer his question. If she let him know what she truly thought, he would just be after her again like some mad beast in heat.

She took the brush from her lips and looked back at him. He was leaning forward ever so slightly, his shirt accentuating every curve of his muscular chest. His eyes were bright and she saw the burning curiosity there that enchanted her.

Before she could remember her earlier protest, the words came tumbling out of her mouth. "Because I don't think you're as bad as they say."

"Oh?" Jack said as his face brightened into a beguiling smile that showed just how intrigued he was by her observation. "I can name you a thousand men who would say differently."

No doubt he could, too. She knew three off the top of her head who would call him a loathsome devil in need of a noose. But regardless of what Justin, her father, and Lord Wallingford thought, she could no longer see Jack that way.

Pausing, she sought a way to divert the conversation from this new thread and herself from a line of thoughts that would only serve to get her into trouble. "Now look, you've gone and moved."

Jack dropped his arm and turned to lie fully on his back. He stretched like a languid cat and she did her best not to notice the tight linen that outlined his chest to perfection—or the form-fitting buckskin pants that hid a part of him she found herself strangely curious about.

She'd actually seen a man naked once. Well, Justin when he was ten. Hardly a man, but still, she had seen *it*.

She'd been out riding with her governess, who had gotten lost in the woods. Lorelei had been trying to find her when she stumbled across Justin and his brother, who were in the process of taking a swim.

His brother had still been clothed, but Justin had already stripped himself and was heading for the water. It had been such a strange sight. That odd little piece of flesh below his waist flapping about like some stubby, overgrown worm. She'd stared at it for several minutes, dying to know what it was.

It was then she'd heard her governess approaching and had quickly taken herself away from the area. For weeks, the sight had haunted her and she'd wanted desperately to ask someone about it.

Too shamed and embarrassed, she'd kept her secret to herself always.

It had been several more years before she understood what that thing was and what it did. That day, Lorelei had decided she never wanted to see one again.

Until now. Now she found herself intrigued. What would Jack's look like?

An inferno burst across her face at the very thought. *Lorelei Dupree, what in goodness sakes has gotten into you! Well-bred young women never, ever, think of such things. Ever! Your father would take a strap to you.*

What *had* gotten into her to make her think such a thought?

Thank goodness Jack couldn't hear her shameful musings. Instead, he took a deep breath, sat up in bed, and laced his shirt closed.

"Sorry, my sweet," he said, and to her further dismay the compliment actually warmed her. "I had to move. I just couldn't stand it anymore. I fear all this inactivity has strained even my patience. Besides, 'tis time I made my rounds and checked the crew."

Lorelei didn't say anything. How could she? She couldn't even look him in the eye. Wasn't sure if she could *ever* look him in the eye again after thinking about *that*.

He approached her easel and paused to look at her work while he retied the leather cord in his hair. "Well, aren't you the talented one, Miss Dupree."

Lorelei beamed at the compliment. But still she kept her eyes on her palette lest he somehow intuitively perceive her previous thoughts.

His portrait was better than even she had hoped. Except for his eyes. She couldn't quite get the shade right. That light, steely blue was almost impossible to portray. Never mind the fire and raw intelligence that flickered deep within his gaze.

"You made a nice piece of fruit," she said to him.

"Any time you need a piece of fruit, my lady, you may call my name," he said, leaning forward to whisper against her neck.

His breath fell against her throat, tickling her. Her chest constricted and she feared she would no longer be able to breathe. She could feel him beside her as if he were touching her. She wanted to feel him touch her, if the truth were told.

"That you already are, Captain Rhys," she said in a breathless whisper of her own.

"Then may I ask that you take a bite of me?"

His shocking words hit her like an icy splash of water. "I beg your pardon?" Without thinking, she looked up to meet his tantalizing smile.

He lowered his gaze to her lips. "I most certainly want to take a *bite* out of you." He encircled her with his arms, preventing her from pulling back.

Lorelei trembled in his embrace, knowing that if he didn't let her go, she might, in fact, surrender to him and to the aching longing that beat inside her. "I thought you had to check your crew."

"They can wait. But you—"

"Need to clean your cabin," she said, interrupting him. "I have brushes to soak and canvas to . . . to . . . Well, I just have things that need to be done. Right away."

Ignoring her rambling comments, he brought one hand up to stroke the sensitive flesh of her neck just under her ear. Chills spread through her as her senses reeled from the heat of his touch. He brushed her braid aside, exposing the back of her neck to his gaze. Jack moved his hand to touch her hairline there, and asked for the second time since he'd taken her hostage, "Have you ever had a man kiss you here?"

"Certainly not," she gasped.

And then he did.

Lorelei moaned at the unexpected pleasure that assailed her as his lips grazed her neck. He drew his arm tight about her waist and a thousand ribbons of pleasure spiraled through her body.

Pull away! her mind shouted. But she didn't want to. She wasn't even sure if she could.

Jack surrounded her with warmth. It was the most incredible thing she'd ever before felt.

"I want you, Lorelei," Jack breathed in her ear. "I want to feel your entire body against me, to taste every inch of your bare flesh."

She didn't know what to say because right then, she wanted the same thing. He just felt too good. His touch too seductive, his body too wonderful.

Jack moved his lips to her mouth and plundered it like the pirate he was. She savored the taste of him, the smell of ocean and man.

She grabbed his shirt in both fists, clinging to him, needing to press herself closer to him.

Heaven help her, but she wanted this man for her own. And just as she was sure she was doomed beyond redemption, a knock sounded on his door.

"Captain? I be needing a word with you."

Jack pulled back with a fetid curse that made her blush. He took one look at her and snarled toward the door, "It can bloody well wait."

Then he was on her again. Lorelei surrendered herself to his touch. She couldn't fight him. 'Twas more than her mortal senses could do.

"Captain, it be urgent," the voice insisted.

This time, Jack tore himself away from her. He took two steps back, his breathing every bit as labored as her own.

"Go, Lorelei," he whispered to her. He doubled over and grimaced as if someone had struck him a fierce blow.

Never one to argue with logic, Lorelei did as he commanded her. She rushed from the room and almost ran over the poor pirate in the hallway.

Muttering a quick apology, she continued on her way without looking back.

Once she was safely in her room, she slammed the door. But as she did so, she made a terrible discovery. What she was really running from was herself.

Jack trembled from the weight of his need. From the pure agony of pent-up lust and desire. Even now he could smell her sweet perfume clinging to him, feel her body pressed against his, and imagine all too well how much better she would feel naked in his arms.

Gerald, one of the first men who had ever signed on board his ship, stuck his head in. "Blimey, Captain," he said in a fearful voice. "I had no idea I was intruding."

Jack clenched his teeth and glared at the man, wanting to tear Gerald's head off his shoulders and stick it on a pole. "What do you need?" he growled.

"There ain't nothing I need right now, Captain. Nothing at all. You just go right ahead and do whatever it was you was doing and I'll just make myself scarce."

His sight darkened even more. "Why the hell didn't you do that when I told you to?"

Gerald tore off like a frightened rabbit that had just stumbled upon a hungry wolf pack.

His body still throbbing, Jack crossed the room and slammed the door shut. How he wished to all that was holy a squall would overtake them. He needed a good dosing of ice-cold water to stamp out the painful flames stabbing his groin.

Much more of this and they'd start calling him Mad Jack the Pirate.

"Little vixen," he snarled, angry at himself for letting her get to him this way. He'd always been the one in control, and yet the scent of her drove him to near madness.

One moment more and he would have forced himself on her.

Why?

She certainly wasn't the most attractive woman he'd ever seen. She wasn't the most charming or beguiling, and yet there was something about her he found irresistible. Something that called out to him in the most alarming way.

What he felt for her went beyond plain lust. It was something almost tangible, something frightening and . . .

It was something he had no wish to confront.

"I'll just stay away from her," he said, pouring some water into his basin. He washed his face and splashed the cold water over his neck.

Aye, that was the answer. Avoid her. It would be better to cede defeat on the issue of her seduction than to have her possess any part of him.

How, you fool? his reason demanded. *The ship's not that big.*

And the temptation of her was just too great.

"I'll bed the wench and be done with it."

Aye, that would purge her from his system. A few quick tumbles in his bed and all would be right again.

Wouldn't it?

"It bloody well better!"

Lorelei ate dinner alone that night in her own cabin. Jack hadn't bothered to even send word to her. Not that she had wanted him to.

Still, it would have been common courtesy for him to take dinner with her, his captive.

A knock sounded.

Her heart pounded at the thought that he'd come to her room after all. "Enter."

The door opened to admit Alice. Concealing her disappointment, Lorelei greeted her with feigned enthusiasm.

"We thought you might want to join us topside for awhile," Alice said.

It would certainly be better than sitting in her room, bemoaning her situation and the fact that Jack had better things to do than waste time with her. If he wanted to do whatever it was he was doing, then fine with her. She would entertain herself.

"I would love to." Lorelei folded her napkin and placed it on the tray beside her plate. "Just show me where to take this," she said, indicating her tray.

"We'll get it later."

Lorelei followed her up to the main deck where men were lounging about, some of them still eating their meals.

A group of three sailors held instruments in their hands, a guitar, drum, and fife, and they were playing a beautiful ballad while another sailor sang in a deep tenor. Several other groups of pirates were off together playing cards or dice.

It was a rather congenial scene, one which might be found in any small town, she thought as she trailed along behind Alice across the deck. One of camaraderie and friendship. No doubt their shared time and experiences had forged strong friendships between the sailors.

On the poop deck, Mavis and Kesi sat with their husbands and Billy, who was smoking a pipe while he leaned back against a coiled rope.

"There she be," Billy said as they joined the group. "I told you Alice could get her out of hiding."

Lorelei blushed at his words. "I wasn't hiding."

"He's just funning with you," Alice said as she sat down beside him.

"Come, child," Kesi said, motioning for her to sit to her right. "We're just watching the sun go down."

Lorelei sank down beside Kesi and studied the men around her. A few of them appeared truly gruff, but most of the crew were young men no older than twenty-four or so.

"Rain's coming," Tarik said as he studied the ribbons of pink lacing the dark blue and orange horizon.

"How can you tell?" Lorelei asked as she looked out at the beautiful sunset.

"I can feel it in me bones."

They fell silent for a few minutes. Then Tarik and Billy began playing a game of dice while Alice opened a small hemp bag and produced yarn and a set of knitting needles.

Lorelei watched as Alice set about knitting with expert skill and if she didn't know better, she'd swear 'twas a baby blanket Alice was making.

"Do you do this every night?" Lorelei asked the small group.

"Aye," Kesi said.

A soft breeze blew in from the ocean and the sounds of the waves enveloped Lorelei with a sense of peace. Though it was too bizarre to comprehend, she actually felt safe on board this ship of miscreants.

Was this how her grandmother had felt when she'd sailed on board her grandfather's ship?

She'd often told Lorelei of card games and songs they'd sung all those years ago. But never had any of that seemed real to her. Her elderly grandmother hardly looked or acted the type of woman who would run off to sea with her lover. If not for Granny-Anne's infamy, and her ability to handle a sword, Lorelei would have completely discounted her stories.

But they were real, each and every one. She knew that now.

"Hey, young Kit," one of the sailors called from across the deck. Lorelei looked to see Kit and Jack climbing up to the main deck. "Isn't it time for you to be in bed?"

Kit stuck his tongue out.

"Kit," Jack said with a hint of laughter in his voice. "Don't be rude."

Unaware of her, Jack urged Kit toward a group of men playing cards while he talked with the man who had spoken. A few minutes later, Kit went rushing back to his father with a winning hand.

Looking at the cards, Jack smiled at the boy and congratulated him before he patted his back.

She smiled at the sight and warmth rushed through her. Whether he admitted it or not, Jack loved that boy. A boy who had no relationship to him whatsoever.

You know what I miss most, Lori, she heard her grandmother say. *I miss your grandfather's laughter. The way he could make me feel happy when I was doing nothing more than looking at him. One day, I hope you'll know exactly what I mean.*

Lorelei tensed at the thought. Wherever had that come from? She certainly didn't feel *that* for Jack. 'Twas Justin who made her happy.

Placing her knitting in her lap, Alice leaned over and said to her, "He's a handsome man, isn't he?"

"Who is?" Billy snapped, pulling his pipe out of his mouth. He scanned the crew as if looking for a man to pulverize.

"The captain, Mr. Bill," Alice snapped to her husband as she wound her hand in another length of yarn. "And I'm not talking to you."

Alice looked away from him and met Lorelei's gaze. "You know, he once took a bullet for my Billy."

"He took more than that to keep me safe," Tarik added as he tossed his dice against the edge of the ship. "There's not a man on this ship what doesn't owe his life to the captain for one reason or another."

"And I owe him for you," Kesi said as she snuggled up into Tarik's arms. "I'd have never known you if he hadn't shown up at my father's party uninvited."

Tarik smiled as he stroked her chin. Their love for one another was more than apparent.

"*Pardonnez-moi, Mademoiselle* Dupree."

Lorelei looked up at Henri, who was bestowing a handsome smile her way. He wore a pair of white breeches and shirt with a tan waistcoat embroidered in blue. His long hair was secured in a queue and he looked rather dashing and debonair.

"They are about to play a jig and I was wondering if you might care to join me for the dance?"

Lorelei wasn't sure what to answer. The last thing she wanted was to be the center of everyone's attention.

"Ah, go on," Alice said, setting her knitting aside. "Kesi, Tarik, Billy, and I will all join you."

Tarik looked up from his game like he wanted to argue, but one glance at Kesi's arched brow stifled whatever objection he'd been planning to make.

You shouldn't do this. And yet the fact that Henri had gone to such efforts on her behalf made her refusal impossible. "I would be honored."

He beamed, and held his arm out for her.

Lorelei took his arm, then warned him, "I'm afraid I don't know how to dance a jig, Henri. I hope you'll forgive me if I trample your toes."

" 'Twould be my pleasure to have you grind my toes to dust, *mademoiselle*. But then you are not so inept, I think. *Non*, you will be a most excellent dancer."

"How can you tell?"

"Your *joi de vive*. Surely such passion as yours is not merely limited to your ability to paint."

He took her hands in his and arched them up and away from their bodies.

"I certainly hope you're right," she said as the musicians began playing.

Lorelei did her best to keep up with the intricate steps, but still she trampled his toes about as much as Justin abused her own. Henri didn't seem to mind, though. In fact, he merely laughed about it and kept giving her hints on how to improve. Even though she was doing a terrible job of it, she enjoyed trying to match his steps.

By the time the music stopped, she was breathless and completely disheveled. Exhilarated, she patted the wayward strands of her hair back into place, then straightened her skirt, which had shifted slightly while Henri had twirled her about.

Henri turned to her and whispered, "I hope you're a better *artiste* than *danser, mademoiselle*."

She laughed, until she caught sight of Jack, who had come forward to watch them. The raw hunger tinged by fury in his eyes froze her where she stood.

However, since Henri had his back to Jack, he was completely unaware of his captain's displeasure. His face was alight while he gave her a stiff bow. "Thank you for humoring me, *Mademoiselle* Dupree. It's been a long while since I had a proper woman dance with me."

Deciding to ignore Jack, she purposefully directed her gaze to Henri. "It was truly my pleasure."

He held his arm out for her.

Casting a "So there!" look to Jack, she curled her arm into Henri's and allowed him to lead her back to where Tarik and the others were regrouping.

She forced herself not to look back to where Jack was no doubt scowling at her, and walked over to the railing. She leaned against it so that she could focus on the ocean. But in truth, she could still feel Jack's gaze on her like a physical touch. Henri moved to stand by her side and then duplicated her pose, leaning his arms against the railing.

Henri was about as handsome as Jack and he was definitely kinder. Why, then, didn't he make her heart beat faster, or her body ache the way Jack did?

Point of fact, why had Justin never made her feel that way?

Unwilling to examine that thought, she asked Henri, "How is it you learned to paint?"

"*Mon père*, uh, my father, he was a painter."

"Really?"

"*Oui*, he studied in Paris. But like so many others, he could never make a living doing what he loved to do."

"That's a pity," she said, feeling for the man. "I take it he taught you?"

Henri shrugged and looked a bit sheepish. "What can I say? He tried, but I . . . I was not an apt *étudiant*. I was determined not to make his same mistake. I listened to my mother when she said such things were a complete waste for a man, and so I ignored my *destiné*."

It was obvious that it bothered him that he had forsaken his father's work. Poor Henri. "Is that why you became a sailor? To make a better living?"

"*Non*," he said with a hint of bitterness in his voice. "I was working the docks in Paris unloading ship cargo to help feed *maman* when a press gang caught me and sold me to an English ship that was in the harbor."

"Oh, Henri," she said, reaching out to touch his hand and offer him comfort. "It must have been terrible for you."

"*Mais oui*." He gave her hand a gentle pat. "Worse so, for I spoke no English at the time. I had a hard time learning what it was they wanted from me."

"Did one of the sailors teach you?"

"*Non*, a few lashes of the whip along with a few kicks of the boot and I learned very fast what it was they wanted me to do." He shook his head and sighed. "At the time, I thought, Henri, you *stupide* fool, for this you gave up art."

Her heart went out to him and all he'd suffered. "How is it you became a pirate?"

The right side of his mouth quirked up and he laughed. "Captain Jaques took the English ship a few years back. He offered freedom to those of us in chains if we swore ourselves to his service."

"And for that you were willing to have yourself hanged by the authorities if you are ever taken?"

He tilted his head. "Better that than to serve the English crew who paid me nothing and treated me like a dog. After the horrors I witnessed, one day of freedom is worth the possibility of death. I would rather die a free man than die a slave."

She knew numerous men who felt the same way. Numerous men she'd grown up with who were fighting a war at home for just that ideal.

Henri turned slightly sideways so that he could look at her. Lorelei kept her gaze on the waves and the ever darkening sky. "I think, *mademoiselle*, that you understand that need?"

"I do," she whispered. "Much more than you would think."

Henri reached out and smoothed a strand of her hair which had come free of her braid. "You are a brave woman, Lorelei."

"Not half as brave as you, Henri," Billy said, drawing their attention back to where he sat on the deck with Alice.

Billy inclined his head in the other direction.

Lorelei turned to see Jack glaring at them with a fierce scowl.

Henri quickly removed his hand from her.

Billy clucked his tongue. "He hasn't looked that mad since we heard of what Wallingford did to the *Dove*."

That drew Lorelei's attention away from Jack and his temper.

"What did the admiral do?" she asked, hoping he would be more forthcoming with the information than Jack had been.

Billy exhaled a wreath of smoke, then tapped his pipe against the deck of the ship. "After he took the ship in battle, he ordered the crew tied up and the ship burned."

Her stomach lurched. Lord Wallingford? Surely not. "Nay," she argued. "He would never do such a thing."

"The one they call 'Butcher Gabe' has done much worse than that," Henri said, drawing her attention back to him. "I heard he captured a colonial merchant slave ship and when his men found guns he suspected were for the Patriots, he ordered it burned as well." Henri's eyes turned dark, angry. "There were over eight hundred men and women chained below the deck. It is said you could hear their screams for leagues."

Lorelei tried to reconcile their stories with the fatherly man she knew so well. It was true the admiral was quite stern, but could he truly be capable of such atrocities?

Before she could think better of it, Lorelei looked at Henri. "Haven't any of you ever done such?"

The entire group looked offended. "We don't kill defenseless men and we've certainly never butchered women," Tarik sneered. "You'll find no cowards on board this ship."

"I'm sorry," Lorelei quickly amended. "I didn't mean that, it's just I've heard similar stories of Captain Rhys and his crew, about how unmerciful all of you have been to captives."

"You can't believe all you hear," Billy said. "Most of us are here simply to make enough money so that we can leave piracy behind and be wealthy men who live to a nice old age. We do what we have to do to survive, but we do no more than that."

"Then how do you know the stories of the admiral are true?" she asked.

"I used to sail on Wallingford's ship," Billy confessed, his lip curled by repugnance. "And I can tell you firsthand that we've never done half an act as heinous as what the *good* admiral would order on a daily basis. Wallingford has it in his head that he is acting on God and king's orders so any crime he commits is divinely ordained."

Dumbfounded, Lorelei stared at him. She'd actually heard the admiral say something very similar to that on several occasions.

Still, it couldn't be true. Could it? *Could* the man who'd held her as a young girl, and often referred to her as his adopted daughter, really be capable of such atrocities?

The hatred blazing in Billy's eyes was too sincere to be anything other than truth.

An ache started in Lorelei's head.

What of Justin? Was he what she thought?

You know Justin as well as you know yourself.

Or did she?

"They're just servants and slaves, Lori. Here to serve us, not the other way around."

She remembered those words from the day her

governess, Gertie, had taken ill. Lorelei had been fetching extra blankets when Justin scolded her for it. At the time his attitude had irritated her, but she hadn't paid it much attention.

Until now. Was that the attitude he showed to people when he wasn't with her?

Justin is noble! He loves you.

"You know, Lori, if you ever want me to offer marriage to you, you'll have to change your ways. I can't have my wife seen toting blankets to a mere servant. Good Lord, woman, you've a house full of people to command. Call one of them and order the blanket be taken. Really, next you'll actually be cooking a meal."

Pressing her hand to her forehead, Lorelei squeezed her eyes shut. There was nothing wrong with Justin's words. Her own father had said as much to her.

Jack had tried to confuse her since the moment she first met him. Now his crew was taking up his cause. She shouldn't listen to them. Justin and his father were good men. They had to be, or else everything she'd ever believed in was wrong. And she didn't want to be wrong, especially not about something that was going to affect the rest of her life.

"If you'll excuse me," she said to the group. "I'm not feeling very well."

Henri frowned. "You do look a bit pale, *mademoiselle*. Allow me to escort you to your room, *s'il vous plaît*."

"Thank you," she said, taking his proffered arm. He led her across the deck and down to the deck below.

And it was only when she was halfway to her cabin that Lorelei realized what she'd done. She had trusted a pirate to take her safely back to where she *slept*.

A quiver of panic raced through her as they approached her door.

"If you would like, *mademoiselle*, I shall ask Sarah to bring you some tea. It might help you feel a bit better."

"That would be very nice," she whispered.

Henri bowed low before her and placed a chaste kiss on her hand. "I do hope you feel better, *ma petite*," he said, straightening up. "Perhaps one day in the near future you will permit me to view some of your work. Captain Jacques said you were most talented, and it has been quite some time since I have had the pleasure of viewing another's work."

Clicking his heels together, he inclined his head to her with a gracious smile, then turned around and left.

Lorelei entered her room, her head spinning with images and thoughts. "Pirates who behave as gentlemen and gentlemen who burn ships," she breathed.

You should not judge people so quickly, Lorelei.

Jack was right. She'd judged people all her life and now those hasty judgments were making a mockery of her perception of the world. And right then all she really wanted was to go home, back to the way things were supposed to be.

Only she could never do that. Jack had taught her to see things differently. To see *people* differently.

Her thoughts turned to Gertie, her governess. She'd known her most of her life, but she didn't really know much about the woman who had dedicated her life to taking care of Lorelei. Did she have siblings? Did *she* like to paint?

Where did she go on her days off?

In her own way, Lorelei had been as callous to the woman who took care of her as Justin had been.

And just then, she didn't know if she should thank Jack for opening her eyes, or curse him.

10

$\mathcal{T}$wo weeks went by as Lorelei grappled with her confusion. Jack's men continued to treat her with courteous respect, and Henri had taken her under his expert tutelage. The Frenchman was incredibly talented, especially when it came to blending colors and using charcoal to shade.

She'd become good friends with Sarah and Alice, who would meet her every morning for breakfast. They would spend a little time on deck, then go off to their chores while Lorelei went to Jack's cabin to work on the portrait.

Jack had been distant with her ever since the evening she'd been up on deck with Henri, and she had begun to wonder if he'd put aside his desire to seduce her. Though that thought should have made her happy, she couldn't help but wonder if there was a way for her to breach the uncomfortable gulf that had sprung up between them.

This morning, Lorelei was early to his cabin. Sarah

hadn't felt particularly well and Alice had wanted to help Mavis with her mending. Left alone, Lorelei had decided to work on the painting while Jack went about his usual routine, receiving his daily report from Tarik and going over their bearings.

As they parted, Sarah warned her that Jack wouldn't be in a particularly good mood this morning since he'd spent half the night in the galley drinking and playing cards with her husband and a couple of other men. She'd told Lorelei that Jack was always an ogre when he didn't get a full night's sleep.

Deciding even that would be a welcome relief from his quiet mood of late, Lorelei opened his door.

She froze.

Still asleep, Jack lay on his bed, his nude body partially entwined with his red satin spread.

Her breath caught in her throat as her gaze drifted across the curve of his muscular back to his bare hip and down his long legs, which were covered with light, golden hairs.

He was beautiful. She watched the gentle rise and fall of his chest. His tawny hair was free and draped becomingly about his face, which was relaxed and almost boyish in repose.

Her first instinct was to slam the door and run, but she couldn't get her feet to obey. Not when what she truly wanted was to step closer to him and take a better look.

What would the harm be? He was sleeping quite soundly; she could hear his faint snore from where she stood. No one would ever know she'd been here. She certainly would *never* tell anyone she'd been here.

Go on, Lorelei. Do it.

Easing the door closed, she bit her lip, debating a few minutes more over the madness of moving closer to a sleeping lion.

As was typical, her foolishness won out. Lorelei tiptoed across the room until she stood over him.

Her heart pounded in fear and wonder, and something else she didn't want to think about. Never had she seen any man so glorious.

The curve of his shoulders highlighted his sleek, strong muscles. His face was covered with the morning's stubble and she yearned to trace it with her finger. Instinctively, her hand moved toward him and it was only the fear of waking him and being caught in this mischief that kept her from yielding to her desire. She clenched her hand into a fist and forced her arm to her side.

Long legs extended over the edge of the bed and his feet dangled precariously into thin air, making her question how he could sleep so peacefully in such a state. Glancing up, she followed the curve of his biceps and the perfect muscles that formed his abdomen.

How she ached for the courage to touch him.

She looked back to his lean hips and the light golden hairs that covered his thighs and legs, then the darker curls that ran from his belly button and disappeared under the spread.

What did the blanket conceal?

Was it the same tiny, silly thing she'd seen on Justin?

Surely not. For there was nothing tiny or silly about Jack Rhys.

Too curious for her own good, she reached for the spread.

Without warning, Jack shifted.

Stifling a squeak, Lorelei darted across the room, horrified that he would awaken and catch her gawking at him like some depraved sneak-thief.

Oh, she would never hear the end of this if he caught her peeking!

But he didn't wake, she realized after several terrifying seconds. Instead, he draped his arm over his eyes and continued to sleep on.

Relieved, she took advantage of her sudden good fortune and quietly made her way from his room.

Lorelei didn't dare breathe again until she was safely tucked away in her own room with the door closed tightly behind her.

She trembled all over. Never in her life had she seen anything as marvelous as Jack Rhys. He was the perfect male.

Well, there would certainly be no portrait painting this morning. At least not until Jack put on some clothes, and even then she wasn't sure if she could ever look at him again without her face bursting into flames. How on earth could she ever banish the image of all that skin . . . of his long eyelashes laying against his cheeks?

Of . . .

Oh, bother!

Gathering up her sketch pad and charcoals, she decided she would take in some fresh air and practice the new cross-hatching technique Henri had shown her yesterday. That would take her mind off the captain.

Maybe she'd sketch Billy, or Mavis and Alice while they worked. Yes, that would definitely distract her from the bronze skin and golden hair and other things a woman of gentle breeding should never think of.

Jack came awake to the rude pounding of a pickax swinging viciously against his brain. Over and over it hit until he could scarcely open his eyes.

Groaning, he shielded his gaze against the morning sun and damned himself for drinking so much. None of it had chased the wench from his thoughts.

All it had done was make him want to strangle her for the new agony in his skull.

You brought this on yourself, old man.

He'd wanted to kill the fire in his groin and he had certainly succeeded. How could he possibly think of sex when his brain was being pulverized and his throat was drier than the Sahara in August?

With a grimace, he pushed himself up.

Ah hell, he thought to himself, why was he mad at her? 'Twas his own stupidity that had him head-first in that barrel of ale last night.

"Seduce her, Jack," he mumbled to himself as he splashed cold water over his face, then sluiced it through his parched mouth.

Aye, he'd get her all right and this time, he wouldn't be dumb enough to let her escape.

Hours later, Lorelei frowned at her hand as if it were the betraying beast that caused all her problems.

Well, it did, in part.

Why couldn't she capture that perfect shape of

Jack's back as he lay on his bed? The sun had just been peeking in and had highlighted his golden skin tone.

She bit her lip and closed her eyes to concentrate. She could see it as plainly as if she were still in his room and yet every time she attempted to sketch it, it eluded her.

You shouldn't be sketching a man like this, her mind chastised her as she opened her eyes and bent her head to try yet again.

But then, her reason argued back, great artists had done such since the beginning of time and if she truly wanted to learn how to sketch people, this was what she needed to do. Michelangelo had sculpted David, Botticelli painted Venus. There was nothing wrong with the human body so long as it was portrayed artistically. She was merely celebrating the form of Jack's physique.

Nothing wrong with that. Nothing at all.

Methinks the lady doth protest too much.

"Get out of my mind, Jack," she whispered to the voice inside her head.

Blowing a stray tendril of hair out of her face, she looked up. Henri and Billy were busy raising sails for speed, or at least that's what they told her. Kesi, Mavis, and Alice were washing clothes while a few of the sailors would occasionally take buckets to the large barrel in the center of the deck to be filled with wash water for the decks.

"What are you doing?"

She turned to her left to see Kit approaching too fast for comfort. Embarrassed, she quickly shuffled the page where Jack was lying partially clothed beneath her sketch of Alice. Heaven forbid Kit should see what she was up to.

"Just working on a few sketches."

"Oh," he said, looking terribly crestfallen.

"What are you about, Mr. Kit?"

He shrugged his thin shoulders and dragged one foot in a pretend line before him. "Well, I wanted to help with the sails," he said, glancing to where Billy was. "But Billy won't let me. Next I tried to help make ropes with the hemp, but Bart said I'd just make a mess of it. I went to the galley to talk to Peter, and he said he didn't have time. I guess you're busy, too."

How she remembered those endless days of childhood. 'Twas the one thing she hated most about being an only child. Grown-ups were forever off doing their business while she would spend hours alone playing dolls and tea.

"I'm not particularly busy." She looked to the knife and piece of half-carved wood in his right hand. "Are you making a soldier?"

"You can tell?" he asked, his face a study of amazement as he immediately perked up.

Before she could say anything, Kit ran to a small box not far away and brought it over to her. Meticulously, he pulled out tiny wooden soldiers and lined them up into two groups.

"I made all of these." He pointed to one group. "They're the Regulars."

His voice spoke his thoughts loudly.

"The bad guys?" she asked, hiding the humor in her voice.

"Always." Then he handed her five soldiers. "These are the pirates. I did this one to look like Henri."

Lorelei studied the one he referred to. It was probably five and one-half inches tall and so intricately carved that it was breathtaking. She could even see the individual hairs of Henri's beard. It was a stunning likeness.

She looked at the others. "This one must be your father," she said, indicating the pirate that looked most like Jack.

"Exactly!" he beamed.

"You know," Lorelei said, as she put four of them down on the deck and kept the Jack pirate in her hand. "We could use some of my paint to paint them."

"Really? Henri never would let me have any. He said I'd just waste it."

"I don't think it would be a waste. Let's have fun, shall we?"

Jack cursed as he came on deck and the sun hit him full in his swollen eyes.

"Are you all right, Captain Jack?" Kesi asked from his left, where she stood washing clothes.

"I'm dead," he said, his voice hoarse. "At least I wish I was."

Alice wiped her hands off on her white cotton apron and approached him. A smile hovered on the edges of her mouth, but she had the sense to stifle it. "I'll go get you something for the pain."

"An executioner and his ax would help."

She ignored his words and headed toward the galley. Pressing his fingers against the throb in his temples, Jack walked along the deck, taking in the day's activities and waiting for Tarik to join him with the report.

He was halfway across the deck before he caught sight of Lorelei, on her knees with her back to him.

She was bent over low, giving him a most pleasant view of her rear. Aye, the soft yellow cambric curved around her and brought a new stinging pain to his loins.

Renewing his curse, he started to turn away, but caught the sound of her laughter.

"If you do that, you might kill one of them," she said.

Jack frowned. What the devil was she talking about?

"We'll just use a little powder in the lock," Kit said. "It should just be enough to blow it open."

"But you would blow off a leg."

"Naw. It'll just leave a bit of a scar. The captain did it when Wayward Hayes captured him in Jamaica and he's still got his arms."

Jack smiled at the pride in Kit's voice. The hint of laughter in the youthful tone.

Lorelei had been right. He did love the boy dearly.

How could he not? Kit was everything he had ever wanted to be as a child—innocent, kind, and most of all loving. Fate had denied him those luxuries and he'd be damned before he let anything tarnish Kit's smile.

"I think your father was merely making up tales to amuse you, Kit," Lorelei said as she finished painting a wooden soldier that looked like Henri.

His gaze darkened in jealous anger.

Kit lifted his chin, his green eyes snapping fire. "It's the truth. Tarik was there, you can ask him."

"Don't be angry with me," she said in the kind of loving, indulgent tone a mother would use—the kind of tone his own mother had never used with him. "I know for a fact that your father is brave and honest."

"And terribly handsome," Jack added.

Lorelei turned around with a gasp. Closing her mouth, her gaze narrowed. "Terribly conceited. That one I'll grant."

"I was telling her about how you escaped Wayward Hayes," Kit piped in as he absently laid aside a brush of blue paint on the deck. "She doesn't believe that you blew up your irons." He rushed to Jack and pushed back the cuff of his shirt. "Show her your scar."

Jack dutifully rolled back his shirt sleeve to reveal the burn mark on his left hand.

Her brows furrowed, Lorelei sat back on her heels, then reached out. Jack steeled his body in preparation for the tingling shock he'd receive the moment she touched him.

As if sensing his thoughts, she froze her hand just above the scar. So close to him, but not quite touching.

Go on, he begged silently, wanting to feel even that tiny part of her flesh against his own.

"It looks like it must have hurt," she said, quickly dropping her hand back to her lap.

He dropped his arm and sighed in irritated disappointment, "I've certainly had more pleasurable experiences," he said, while thinking, *like dancing with you in my arms.*

Kissing her lips.

Her neck.

Her . . .

"Were you scared when he caught you?" she asked, intruding on his pleasant thoughts.

Jack fastened his cuff back around his wrist. "Not really. There's nothing in life I fear."

"Nothing?"

He shook his head.

Kit gave her a superior look. "I told you the captain is perfect. Cunning and—"

"And you wonder why I have a big head," Jack said, giving Kit a light hug. "With this one around to always tout my abilities, 'twould be impossible to be humble."

"Practice," Lorelei said, arching a haughty brow, "I'm told, makes perfect."

Jack laughed. How he loved matching wits with her. He'd never before met a woman so quick.

"Billy!" Kit shouted in Jack's ear.

Wincing, Jack let the boy go.

Kit raced along the deck to Billy, who was just about to take a sail up the fore mast. "You said I could help you the next time you hung a big sail. Can I, huh? Can I help you hang the sail?"

Billy looked up at Jack, who nodded.

"All right, Kit," Billy relented. "But you have to be careful."

"I'll be careful. Just you watch. I'll be as careful as . . . as . . . as something that's really careful, that's what."

Jack laughed, then turned back to Lorelei, who had risen to her feet. She had her arms crossed over her chest as the light breeze tickled her hair. Her face bore just a trace of pink from being out in the sun without a hat or bonnet. The color looked good on her.

"Now what was this about my being honest and brave?" he teased her.

She looked to her right while she squirmed. "You heard that, did you?"

"Hmm."

Her gaze shifted back to his for an instant before she looked somewhere else. "It was for Kit's benefit. I couldn't very well tell him what I really thought of you, now could I?"

How he loved teasing her, especially when it brought out the provocative blush that was creeping over her face as she looked anywhere but at him.

"And what is it that you really think of me?"

Clasping her hands behind her back, she squinted her eyes toward the ocean. "That you're arrogant."

He smiled. "I'll grant you that."

Her gaze drifted to his before she looked away again. Lorelei appeared to be giving the matter much thought. "Irritating," she said plainly.

"I can be."

A twinge of anger darkened her eyes. He could tell she didn't care for his ready acquiescence to her insults. "Infuriating."

His smile widened. "I try to be."

This time, she met his gaze levelly. "Why are you being so accommodating?"

He shrugged. "You're speaking the truth and I never argue with truth."

Jack leaned forward and placed his hands against the railing behind her, trapping her between his arms. The scent of lavender rose up from her skin and idle strands of her hair tickled his face and neck as the wind blew them about. "Do you wish to know what I think of you?"

"Definitely not," she said primly.

Jack leaned forward a tad to take in more of her

intoxicating perfume. When he spoke, his voice was a hoarse whisper. "I find you delectable."

"Excuse me?" She quickly diverted her gaze.

"Beautiful. Exquisite." Jack breathed the words in her ear as he brushed the back of his fingers over the softness of her neck.

She quivered. Beneath his fingertips, he could feel her pulse quicken. How he ached to kiss her, to feel her nails dig into his back.

If only they weren't in full sight of his crew.

And his son, he realized with a start. Licking his lips, which ached to kiss her, he pulled away.

"Billy!"

Jack turned at the sharp scream to see Billy far above deck, hanging by his foot. Kit was tangled in the rigging, clinging to the mast for dear life, and Alice was running about below them like a mad-woman.

"Help!" Alice screamed again. "Someone help him!"

Without thought, Jack ran toward the mast where Billy dangled.

Lorelei looked up the rigging to where Billy was tangled in ropes. It looked as if he'd tripped on his way up and one of the ropes had caught about his ankle.

He swung in a macabre arc upside down about fifty feet above the deck.

Her mouth dropped as her heart pounded in sheer terror.

When one of the men started to climb up, another one grabbed him by the arm. "The rope's giving way. It'll snap before you get halfway up."

Alice was running from man to man begging each one to save her husband.

Jack took a moment to survey the scene, then he grabbed a rope off the deck and coiled it quickly about his body. He climbed up the mizzen stay to the mainmast, then secured himself to the cross-beam as he tried to reach Billy.

Her throat dry, Lorelei didn't know what to do. Kit was still upright and clinging to the rigging above Billy, his young face ashen.

Dear Lord, please, she prayed, *don't let them die.*

What on earth had happened?

Jack's perch on the cross-section looked about as tenuous as Billy's situation. Still, he appeared calm.

"Billy," Jack said, his loud voice somehow soothing as he unwound the rope from around his shoulders and lowered a piece to Billy. "Take a deep breath and reach for the rope."

"I can't!" Billy shouted, his voice filled with terror.

"Yes, you can," Jack assured him, making her wonder how he could remain so serene while death faced him, his son, and one of his crew. "Besides, if you don't take the rope, Alice will run off with Davy."

"I'll kill them both," Billy snarled an instant before he grabbed the rope.

Jack had just pulled him upright when the rigging broke from under Billy. The heavy, tangled ropes and sail fell with a rush to the deck. Billy screamed in agony as the rope against his ankle was pulled taut. For a moment, she feared both he and Jack would be pulled to their deaths.

The sail hit the deck with such force that it jarred the boards under her feet and sent a rush of air over her. Lorelei stared at it, realizing that if it had broken even a second before it would have killed Billy.

Billy was screaming and twisting as he sought to maintain his grip.

"Cut the damned rope from his leg!" Jack snarled.

Tarik rushed forward to oblige. As soon as the rope was cut free, Jack stumbled back into thin air.

"Daddy!" Kit screamed from his place in the rigging at the same time Lorelei gasped Jack's name.

Jack had lost his footing, but somehow he managed to catch himself against the mast and not lose his grip on Billy.

Time seemed suspended as Billy hung far above the deck, whimpering in pain while Jack attempted to right himself and find solid footing again.

Why wasn't someone helping them?

Kit started toward Jack.

"Stay away," Jack warned and she saw the fear and confusion on Kit's face as he stared at his father, who was just a few feet away, powerless to help him.

Lorelei whispered a prayer for them.

And then, somehow, Jack found his footing and slowly he began to lower Billy toward the deck. Alice ran to her husband, sobbing as she threw herself into his arms.

Still dazed by what she'd witnessed, Lorelei watched as Jack dropped the rope, then made his way to Kit, who hadn't moved. Together, they made their way down the rigging to the safety of the deck.

This time when Jack surveyed his crew, she saw the raw, untamed anger that creased his brow.

"What the hell were you doing?" he asked Billy.

"The rigging broke under me, Captain."

A sailor of about thirty came forward with a piece of the rope from the fallen rigging. "It was just weather damage, Captain," he said, holding it up for Jack to see.

Jack grabbed the piece and studied it. When he looked up at his crew, Lorelei realized this was the fearsome face of Black Jack Rhys that made grown men shake in terror. "How many times do I have to tell you to double-check the rigging?"

The pirates all looked sheepish.

Shaking his head, Jack dropped the rigging. "Someone clean up this mess." He looked over to Billy. "And you, take the rest of the day off and calm your wife before she loses that baby she carries."

Jack started toward Lorelei. "Now I'm sober," he muttered irritably as he neared her. "But my head still aches."

"You," she said, enunciating every word slowly and with emphasis, "are insane."

Jack ignored her as he handed Kit over to Kesi. "You," he growled at Kit, "are not allowed to climb the rigging again until you're grown."

"Aw, Captain. I wasn't the one who fell."

"No, but you could have been." Jack looked at Kesi. "Take him below where he can't get into trouble."

"But I wasn't in trouble!"

Jack's face would have melted ice. "You will be if you don't obey me."

Kit pursed his lips in an effort not to say anything more as Kesi led him to the deck ladder.

"I thought you were dead," Lorelei said, taking the three steps that separated them.

Jack turned to look at her. "You mean you hoped I was dead."

"No," she corrected. "In spite of what you think, I don't want you dead, Jack. And I'm glad you weren't hurt."

Jack watched in stunned surprise as Lorelei turned around and left him standing in the middle of the deck. Her words rang in his ears. And in that instant something vile and terrifying whipped through him. It was stupid, really, just a vague thought no doubt dredged up from his past.

Yet it was there, tormenting him.

What would it be like to have a woman like Lorelei actually care for him? To have her scream out for someone to help him the way Alice had done for Billy?

To know that if he'd tumbled to the ground, she would have mourned for him?

In spite of his denials with Lorelei, he knew what love was and he knew it did exist. At least it did for other people, if never for him.

Love was when someone loved you more than they loved themselves. It was when your life was more important to them than their own.

No one had ever given him that. Ever.

And no one ever would.

Lorelei doesn't care if you die this instant, his mind whispered. *Why should she?*

Thadeus would have cared, he argued back. As did Kit.

"*You're worthless, boy,*" his mother's voice whispered in bitter, drunken anger. "*Absolutely worthless. I should have killed myself the minute I found out I carried you. But I was stupid. I thought I might actually be able to love you. God, what a fool I was. If not for you, I'd have had a decent life. You ruined me and you will always ruin everything you touch. It's the curse of your father's blood."*

Jack closed his eyes against the truth. It was his curse and it tainted everything about him.

Someone touched his arm. He turned to see Sarah standing behind him with a mug held in her hands. She urged him to take it.

"Thank you, Sarah."

She motioned to ask him if he were all right.

"I'm always fine, aren't I?"

She shook her head no.

Jack would have laughed, but he didn't quite feel up to it. "Lay aside your fears. There's nothing wrong with me a good dose of your brew won't cure."

She arched a doubtful brow and asked him if he were thinking of Lorelei.

"No," he answered. "I was thinking about the past, which is a great waste of time."

She nodded.

"Sarah?" Mavis called from the deck ladder. "May I borrow you for a minute?"

She excused herself and Jack went to find a quiet corner of the ship where he could let his head pound in peace and think no more thoughts of his past, or of the petite redhead who made him yearn for things he knew he couldn't have.

Lorelei sat at a small table in the galley taking her afternoon tea with Kesi, Alice, Mavis, and Sarah. Jack had retired to his cabin and no one had seen much of him.

"Well," Mavis was saying as she placed her china teacup back in its saucer on the table. "I'm certainly glad Billy is all right."

"But you, Alice," Kesi said in a chiding tone, "should have told us you were pregnant."

Alice blushed. "I was going to tell all of you later today. I only told Billy yesterday. He must have told Jack last night while they were drinking."

"We'll be having a fine celebration," Kesi said with a smile.

Sarah pointed to Lorelei and spoke gently with her hands.

"I'm sorry, Sarah," Lorelei said. "You're moving your hands too fast. I don't understand."

Mavis cleared her throat. "She says she's worried about Jack."

Lorelei frowned. "Jack?"

Sarah gestured.

"She say he's different lately," Kesi translated. "He doesn't keep to himself as much."

Lorelei turned to stare at Kesi.

Kesi shrugged. " 'Tis the truth. He hardly ever spent much time with the rest of us, except for Kit."

"I think he values his privacy," Lorelei said.

Alice sipped at her tea. "I think he's lonely and doesn't know how relate to people."

Lorelei laughed at the thought. "I honestly don't believe that's the problem. He seems to adapt to people with remarkable skill."

"No," Kesi corrected as she chose another tea biscuit. "He adapts to situations with remarkable skill. As for people . . ."

"He hides," Alice finished for her. "Oh, he'll drink with the men and is friendly enough, but when it comes to talking about himself or what he likes to do, he's as silent as a tomb."

Lorelei nodded in agreement. That was certainly true enough.

"But you," Alice said. "You, he treats differently. He actually seeks you out to speak with you."

"Only to torment me, I assure you."

Mavis leaned forward. "And does his presence torment you?"

Lorelei blushed.

Alice laughed. "Just what we thought!"

"I am spoken for," Lorelei said sincerely.

"You may be spoken for," Mavis said, "but it doesn't change the fact that you like Jack."

"He's nice enough," Lorelei agreed. "Sometimes anyway."

But in spite of her denial, Lorelei knew the truth. She was attracted to the scoundrel. Terribly.

She enjoyed his company. He was, dare she admit it, quite fun to be around.

"None of it matters anyway," Lorelei said. "He's only around me so that he can seduce me."

Mavis laughed. "We know. He is a man, after all."

"Aye," Kesi said, joining the laugher. "I've never seen a man yet what didn't chase after a woman."

Alice directed a piercing gaze to Lorelei. "But the question is, do you wish to be caught?"

11

I should say not," Lorelei answered emphatically as she placed her cup on her saucer, then returned them both to the table.

"Phew," Alice said with a smile. "That be a lie and well we know it. There's not a one of us here who hasn't done her fair share of staring at that man."

All of them blushed.

"Well?" Alice insisted. "Haven't we?"

"He is a handsome devil," Mavis said.

"Handsome and charming as sin itself," Alice agreed. She leaned forward over the table and again turned that piercing stare to Lorelei. "Now admit it. You have thought about him at great lengths."

Heat stung Lorelei's cheeks. "This topic is completely inappropriate."

Alice smiled and tilted her head as a mischievous gleam shone in her eyes. "Maybe, but haven't you ever wished you could ask a woman what it was like to be with a man?"

If her cheeks got any warmer, Lorelei was sure they would explode. "I know the details," she said primly. "Thank you very much."

"Really?" Mavis asked.

Lorelei nodded.

"You've been with a man?" Kesi blurted out indelicately.

"No!" Lorelei gasped. "My grandmother told me what . . ." She cleared her throat. "Well, you know."

"Your grandmother," Alice said with a laugh. "I bet she didn't tell you—"

"Alice," Mavis said with a warning note in her voice as she came to Lorelei's rescue. "I think you've embarrassed the girl enough."

"All right," Alice said, taking a sip of tea. She looked back at Lorelei. "But I tell you this. If I'd had a chance to see Jack in his altogether before I met my Billy, I most certainly would have taken it."

That was it, Lorelei was definitely going to burst into flames. Alice's words brought forth an image of Jack lying in his bed that she couldn't banish, and with it came a burning deep inside her for him that was most overwhelming.

"If you'll excuse me, I think I should retire to my room," Lorelei said, quickly pushing herself up.

She needed to get away from them and from horribly inappropriate images that were terrorizing her. Well, the images that should be terrorizing her, but the most horrific part of all was the fact that none of it was terrible. She actually liked thinking of Jack that way.

Liked thinking of Jack taking her into his arms and . . .

She shut the door to her room and collapsed on

the bed. "Stop it, Lorelei!" she breathed sharply to herself.

Think of Justin!

She mentally summoned an image of him in his uniform. Aye, he cut a dashing figure. Tall, proud and . . .

Boring.

Really, Lorelei, she could hear Justin's stiff accent in her head as he chastised her yet again. *Do you not find me pleasing?*

Yes, she thought in answer. *You are quite pleasing.*

But? he asked again.

But he wasn't Jack. His presence didn't make her feel hot and cold at the same time. Around Jack she felt alive and vibrant. Alive and completely feminine.

Against all her arguments and sanity, she wanted her pirate more than she had ever wanted Justin.

"No, no, no!" she insisted. It wasn't true. Justin would come here soon and rescue her, then all would be as it should. Jack would be out of her life and she would be thrilled over it. Yes, yes she would.

Yet her body reacted of its own accord. Her hand reached out to the sketch pad on her mattress and pulled it to her. She flipped to the page where Jack was and she studied her progress.

Aye, his back had just that curve. And sunlight had added a golden sheen to his skin.

His long hair draped down his strong neck. His hips . . .

She just couldn't get his buttocks right.

Closing her eyes, she tried to imagine it.

It was no use.

Even more frustrated now, Lorelei set her drawing

aside. She needed to get another look at his buttocks.

Lorelei! What are you thinking?

"I'm an artist," she whispered to herself. "I just want to paint what I see."

Only she hadn't really seen that part of him. That part had been hidden by the spread.

She heard Jack leaving his cabin.

Before she could think better of it, she tiptoed to her door and eased it open. Jack had just passed her door and she poked her head into the hallway to watch his . . .

He stopped, then to her horror turned around.

She was caught!

Embarrassed and horrified, she opened the door wide as a sudden thought came to her to explain her behavior. "It squeaks," she announced as she swung the door back and forth. But the dreaded thing didn't make a single noise.

She abruptly stopped the idiotic movement before it gave her away completely.

Jack cocked a brow. "The door squeaks?"

"Mmm," she said, glancing at the hinges. "I was wondering if I could fix it."

"With charcoal?" he asked as he dipped his gaze down to her hand.

She clenched the charcoal in her fist as she tried to think of a believable lie.

You're caught!

Refusing to yield victory, she lifted her chin. "Why, yes. It's the latest thing." She opened the door wider, then pretended to oil the hinge with her charcoal.

Jack took two steps closer, a half smile hovering

on the edge of his lips. "Why are you flushed?" he asked and by the gleam in his eyes, she swore he knew what she'd been doing.

She swallowed. "It was . . ."

Think of something!

"Hot in the galley."

"Was it?" he asked.

"Very hot," she finished.

Hotter than he could imagine.

Jack folded his hands behind his back and looked up at the hinge she pretended to grease. "Would you like me to fetch some lubricant for the door?"

"Uh . . . no. I think the charcoal worked. See." She swung the door back and forth again. "No more squeaking."

Just a whole lot of squirming as those steely gray eyes delved into her own.

"Very well then," he said, his eyes laughing at her. "I shall leave you to your . . . matters." He turned and walked away.

Lorelei dropped her gaze to his buttocks.

Ah, there was the curve she'd been trying to capture. The muscles were tight and his derriere was—

Not moving.

Lifting her gaze, she saw him looking at her with an amused smile on his face as he stared back at her over his shoulder.

"Do you like what you see?" he teased.

She stiffened. "There's a stain on your breeches."

He twisted around so that he could look. "Where? I don't see one."

"Oh, it must have been the way the light was striking it."

"That must be it." He mocked her with his tone.

Embarrassed to the very core of her soul and with her face burning as sharply as if she stood before a raging inferno, Lorelei gathered what little dignity she could muster. "Good day, Captain."

"Good day, Miss Dupree."

Lorelei turned and walked with as much grace as possible into her room.

Once the door was safely closed, she threw herself on the bed and curled up into a tiny, mortified ball where she laughed out her humiliation until tears fell.

"He caught me," she breathed into the pillow. Could anything be worse?

He knew she'd been looking at his . . .

Oh, if only someone would kill her now and get it over with.

Jack was smiling as he crossed the deck. So, the little wench was interested in him after all.

Now how was he going to play his next hand?

Lorelei still hadn't finished the portrait of him. That was one way to lure her into his room.

Nay, he wanted something more subtle.

More subtle, hell. All he really wanted to do was call her to his room right this instant and quench the fire ripping through his loins. If he didn't take her soon, he was going to go mad from the need.

All right, Jack, he said to himself. *When it comes to seduction, you're the master. What would you do?*

Dinner. That was the key. He'd pay Klein and the boys to play a little music on deck while he left his windows open. She liked to dance and he was going to show her dance steps she'd never before known existed.

Aye, tonight she was his.

"Kit," he called, seeing his son bothering Pierson while he worked on repairing the sails. "I have a mission for you."

Kit ran to him. "A mission, Captain?"

"Aye, I want you to deliver a message."

Lorelei closed the door behind Kit. So, Jack wanted her to eat with him tonight. It had been awhile since he last made that request. And she remembered all too well the last time they'd shared a meal.

That stupid wager! Make him fall in love with her, indeed. What had she been thinking?

Well, tonight she had another plan. Forget their wagers. What she wanted was to finish her private drawing without him knowing about it. And she knew just the way to render the mighty captain helpless to her whims.

Tonight was the perfect opportunity.

Chewing her lip, she went back to the galley. Luckily all the women were still there and talking.

"Kesi?" she asked from the doorway.

They all turned to look at her.

"I'm sorry for interrupting," Lorelei said as she shifted in the doorway and prepared herself for yet another dreaded lie. Never in her life had she stooped to such measures! "I think I'd like to try that sleeping syrup you were telling me about."

"Want to get some sleep, do you, child?" Kesi asked.

"Yes, I really do."

Kesi excused herself and Lorelei led her back to

her cabin. Lorelei went to where she kept the bottle in her chest and pulled it out. Holding it up to the light, she noted it was a rich reddish brown that should blend nicely with a cup of wine. "How much do I take?"

"Just a spoonful. Anymore and it'll make you sick."

Lorelei turned the bottle in her hand, trying to see the thickness of the liquid. "Does it taste terrible?" she asked, knowing if it did, Jack would know her game immediately.

" 'Tis sweet-tasting actually. Mix it with wine and you'll hardly taste it at all."

Thank goodness.

"Thank you. I shall put it to good use this night." Lorelei felt terrible over the partial lie she offered Kesi, but if she told her the truth, she'd never have given it to her.

Then again, Kesi might have.

She didn't know why, but the four women seemed somehow determined that she and Jack should like each other much more than was proper.

Kesi took her leave to go order a bath drawn for Lorelei. And Lorelei began making preparations for dinner, or more to the point, preparing her concoction for Jack.

Hours later, Jack was ready for his conquest to begin. The table was set with the best china, silver, and crystal. The windows were open and already the men were playing. He looked quite dashing in his best clothes.

All that was missing was Lorelei.

Satisfied with himself, Jack clasped his hands behind his back and glanced to the door that separated this room from his cabin. He smiled.

He'd scented his sheets in expectation of her surrender. There were a few candles strategically placed around the room for lighting, and in a few hours he would be feasting on her like a starving beggar.

A timid knock sounded.

His body reacted instantly to just the thought of her entering his web. "Come in."

And she did. Like the fly to the spider.

Jack crossed the room to greet her. She wore a delicate cream gown that highlighted her skin. Her hair was caught up into a becoming halo of auburn curls that hung down over the column of her throat.

He bowed low before her. She raised her hand, which he brought to his lips for a kiss. "Rose again?" he asked as he inhaled the sweet, seductive scent.

She smiled warmly. "You said you liked it."

Take her! What are you waiting for?

Patience, he reminded himself. Now was not the time to pounce.

Though he wanted to. He really, really wanted to. And it was taking every ounce of his control not to force the issue with her.

"Dinner is already served?" She asked aghast as she looked at the food on the table. "Am I late?"

He shook his head. "You're right on time. I just didn't want us to be disturbed."

"That makes two of us."

Her words took him by surprise and ignited a slow burn in his blood.

"Careful, Lorelei. 'Tis a dangerous game you play.

Don't make an invitation unless you want me to accept it."

By the light in her eyes, he could tell she had another flirtatious remark hovering on the back of her tongue, yet she withheld it. And deep inside he found himself wishing for a moment he was Justin. That he could spend time with an unguarded Lorelei who wasn't afraid to let all her charms be seen. How much more enchanting would she be?

Then again he decided it was best she withheld herself lest he truly lose control.

Jack took her to her chair and held it out for her. The silk of her dress rustled as she moved and the soft feminine sound struck a chord in him. Never before had he been so attuned to a woman.

But this one . . . this one he could feel with all his senses and she set fire to each and every one.

Even though it was the last thing he wanted to do, he left her at her seat and took his chair at the opposite end. "You look beautiful tonight."

"Thank you," she said as she folded her linen napkin into her lap. "I would return the compliment, but I think you're well aware of how well you look."

"You think so?"

"You're too arrogant not to."

He laughed as he folded his own napkin. "I was wondering how long you could carry on your facade of being nice to me."

Lorelei frowned.

"Is something the matter?" he asked.

"No. . . . Yes." She looked up at him, her gaze puzzled. "I don't know why I act the way I do around you, Jack. It's never been in my nature to torment people and yet when I'm around you, I can't seem to help myself."

He could feel a tick begin in his jaw as he thought about her words. "If it makes you feel any better, my mother always told me I brought out the worst in people."

Her look turned to one of bewilderment. "Why would she say such a thing?"

Lifting his wine glass, he sighed. "It's true, is it not?" He took a sip of the robust sweetness before he spoke again. "At any rate, I've no wish to talk about it."

She leaned her arms against the table and leveled a probing stare at him. "You never wish to talk about yourself. Why is that?"

"I'm a boring subject."

"Hardly. You may well be the most fascinating person I've ever met."

"Well, well," he said with a short laugh. "It looks as if you complimented me after all."

"And you are avoiding my question."

He took a deep, long draught of his wine before he set it back on the table. This wasn't going the way he planned and he wasn't about to confide in her or anyone else. "Which was?"

"Why don't you ever talk about yourself?" she insisted with the same tenacity a hunting dog would use to follow its prey. "I've spent hours with you and I know very little about you. I don't even know which of your books you like best to read."

She gave him a calculating stare. "Are you afraid that by telling me things about you that you'll give me some kind of power over you?"

He laughed at the absurdity.

She stiffened. "It is true, is it not, that knowledge gives one power."

"Perhaps, but it has nothing to do with my answer."

"Then tell me."

Jack sat quietly for a minute. What would it hurt to be honest with her?

He weighed the answer for several seconds before he spoke. "Very well. If you must know, I don't talk about myself because no one ever cared enough to listen."

"What do you mean?"

"Think about it, Lorelei," he said, his tone conveying his boredom over the topic. "How many times a day do you ask someone how they're doing? Their world may have just shattered and yet they look up and say, 'Fine, thank you, and you?' No one cares to hear other people's problems. 'Twas a lesson I learned early in life."

"Hide your feelings and move on."

"Exactly."

"And if someone did care?"

"I'm sure that someone would not be you."

"How do you know?" she asked. "If you never reach out, no one will ever take your hand."

He sneered. "If I never reach out, then no one can ever *bite* my hand."

"What a frightening world you live in, Jack," she said, her face mirroring her words. "I can't imagine never telling people how I feel."

"I can certainly attest to that."

Instead of angering her, his words brought a dull glow to her eyes. "One day I'm going to get something personal out of you."

He curved his lips into a half smile. "On the day I go down on bended knee and declare my undying love."

To his surprise, she laughed at his words. "You were right. I can't imagine you ever doing such a thing. You're far too proud and cynical to ever do anything like that."

Jack directed his gaze up to the ceiling as if speaking to heaven itself. "At last the lady sees reason." He looked back at her. "Does this mean I win our wager?"

She paused, as if debating her answer. When she spoke, her voice was low and soft. "No. It just means we both lose."

Her words hit him strangely and he didn't know why. He wasn't even sure what he felt. It was just . . . discomforting.

They ate in silence for awhile. The night wasn't progressing as he'd planned. But then nothing that involved Lorelei ever went as he planned. She had a damnable way of turning things around on him.

Lorelei watched as Jack ate his dinner. He really was elegant and proper in his manners.

Wherever had he learned such decorum? He spoke as if educated in the finest European schools and he dressed as if he'd been raised at court.

She took a bite of her roasted chicken. He was such a strong man. Not just physically, but inside as well. He was like steel, and she couldn't help but wonder what could make someone like him. Surely it would take the very fires of hell to forge someone so strong.

And yet he knew how to give kindness. Somehow in his isolated world, he had learned to be decent and caring.

It was so strange to her that a man who lived his life in violence could ever show compassion.

How she wished she understood him.

Once she finished eating, she leaned back slightly in her chair with her wineglass in her hand. It was only then she noted the tiny gold hoop in Jack's ear. She couldn't help smiling.

Jack paused. "What is it?"

"I was wondering about your earring. You've worn it the entire time we've been at sea. But you didn't wear it at my party."

Humor danced in his steely gray eyes. "That would have been a dead giveaway to my identity, don't you think?"

"True." She took a sip of wine. "Why do you wear it?"

He shrugged. "There's an old sea legend that says the only way a pirate can get into paradise is to bribe his way in. We wear gold to help pay the fee."

"Then why is your piece of gold so small?"

"I've been told there's not enough gold on earth to pay my bribe."

"Is that truly how you feel?"

"I said it was an old legend. I never said I believed in it."

There it was. That odd note in his voice that denoted he was closing himself off from her. Closing himself off from his feelings. "You're hiding from me again." It bothered her very much that he was so adept at it. He must have been practicing the habit all his life to do it so naturally.

The music stopped for a moment, then started back with a slow ballad.

"Would you care to dance?" he asked.

"Yes," she answered honestly. "I think I would."

He moved to her end of the table and held her chair while she stood. He took her by the hand and led her to the small clearing away from the table, which was closer to the windows. When he pulled her into his arms, so wonderful and strong, she feared she might faint.

He was really too handsome and delightful for his own good.

And for her own.

She looked up into those guarded eyes that betrayed nothing of his thoughts or feelings and remembered how charming and boyish he'd looked while he slept. The candlelight played in the golden highlights of his hair and cast a soft glow to his skin. His hands were strong and yet gentle to her hand while he led the dance with expert skill.

"You know what I'd like?" she asked.

"For me to take you home to your father?"

"Besides that."

"I can't imagine."

She bit her lip for a moment, testing her courage. Did she dare say it? Before she could cower out, she spoke. "I would like, for one moment, for you to let me inside you."

His look turned devilish. "Funny, I was thinking the same of you."

Her cheeks burned. "You're wicked, Jack."

"Just beguiled."

As am I.

And she was. Being here in this room alone with

one of the most notorious men alive, dancing in the arms of a bandit who had more charm than the devil himself, it was all she could do not to give him what he wanted.

What would it feel like to run her hands all over the beautiful body she'd seen?

What would it be like to lie with him and have him educate her in the pleasures of sexuality? To experience all the sensations a man could make a woman feel. . . .

Kiss me, Jack, her mind pleaded.

But if he did that right now, she might be his.

As if sensing her thoughts, he looked down at her, his eyes fastening on her lips.

"I love when you stand close to me," he murmured. "I can feel your breath fall against my neck and it sends chills and fire all over my body."

She should be shocked, but instead his words thrilled her.

Take me, Jack.

Luckily, the words lodged in her throat.

He dipped his head to her lips and she opened her mouth for his taste. Their breath mingled.

And a loud knock sounded at the door.

Jack's curse rang in her ears. "The devil take you if this ship's not on fire," he roared.

"Ca-Captain?" Kit's voice stammered through the door. "I'll come back."

Jack looked immediately contrite. "Come in, Kit. I thought you were someone else."

He stepped away from her as Kit entered.

Lorelei swallowed, trying to regain her composure while she shook all over from her need and inappropriate wants.

Thank goodness Kit had come when he had. Another moment and she might have . . .

She didn't want to think about what she might have done.

Jack looked at her from over his shoulder. "I'll be back in a few minutes."

She just nodded as he closed the door behind him. Her hands cold and trembling, she pulled the small vial of Kesi's sleeping syrup from between her breasts. Now was her chance to use it, and use it she must. If for no other reason than to safeguard her virtue.

Pouring the concoction into his wine, she stirred it with her finger, then returned the vial to her cleavage.

While she waited, she went to the windows to stare out at the sea. Moonlight splashed against the waves. There was such tranquility out here with the ocean sounds to lull her.

She heard the door open behind her. Turning, she saw Jack watching her.

"Was he all right?" she asked.

"He thought one of those heads had found its way into his room. It turned out to be the head of a wooden horse he broke a few weeks ago."

She laughed.

Jack came nearer and her laughter died on her tongue. Her heart hammered in fear of what she might do if he took her into his arms again.

"Would you bring me my wine?" she asked.

He paused.

"I would like to propose a toast," she said before he had a chance to deny her request.

His look turned suspicious. "A toast?"

"Yes."

He picked up their glasses and brought them over to her. Lorelei tried to keep her panic down as she stared at the tainted cup. There was only a slight shake to her wrist.

"And what toast is that?" Jack asked.

"I wish to toast the . . . the sea. May it always be so . . . so beautiful."

Jack glanced at her from the corner of his eyes. There was something amiss here and when he took a drink of his wine, he knew immediately what it was.

The wench was trying to drug him! There was no mistaking the taste. It was Kesi's disgusting brew that she used on wounded sailors when their laudanum supply ran low. A concoction he'd built up a tolerance for years ago.

What could Lorelei hope to gain by rendering him unconscious?

She couldn't escape him. There was nowhere on board this ship she could run to.

Henri! he thought, his gaze instantly dulling. She was going to Henri.

He froze at the thought, then dismissed it. Henri had more sense than to impose himself on a woman Jack had already claimed. Nay, there was something else she wanted. Something he hadn't thought of.

But, he would soon find out. Tipping the goblet back, he drained it.

Lorelei swallowed her panic as she watched him finish off the wine.

How long would it take to work?

Jack put his hand to his brow as he frowned. "I feel so strange."

Had she given him too much?

"Are you all right?" she asked, terrified she might have unwittingly hurt him.

"I . . . I think I need to lie down."

Moaning, he stumbled slightly. "Oh, the pain in my head. I need to get to my bed. But I don't think I can do it alone."

Please don't let me have hurt him, she begged silently. "I'll summon Tarik to help you."

"Ooh." He gasped. "I . . . don't know if I can wait that long."

He stumbled again.

Fearing there was no time to get Tarik, she offered him her shoulder. "Lean on me and I'll help you."

Jack draped his arm around her shoulder and leaned against her. "It's through that door," he said, inclining his head to the door to her right.

She headed for it.

In no time at all, she had him in his cabin and on his bed. No sooner did he lie down than he was out cold.

"Jack?" she asked, shaking him. "Jack, are you awake?"

Her answer was a soft snore.

Relieved, she sat down next to him. The scent of sandalwood hovered around her and she realized the smell had increased when he flopped down on the bed.

Leaning closer to the spread, she sniffed.

She saw red, and it was not the color of the spread. "You rake," she accused him as he lay there. "You thought to get me in this bed tonight, didn't you? Well, who's the clever one now?"

Lorelei rose to her feet and stared down at him. He was quite exceptional lying there so quiet and vulnerable. She could do anything she wanted to him and he would be powerless to stop her.

The thought sent an unexpected thrill through her.

Yielding to temptation, she ran her fingertip over the gentle curve of his jaw. His skin was so different from her own. It was firm and . . . masculine.

"I would never do this if you were awake," she whispered. "But I've wanted to do it for a long time."

She touched his hair and marveled at its silken texture. The honey strands were laced with brown and gold. He was definitely the forbidden object of her desire and she would take great pleasure finishing her sketch.

She smiled at the thought. Until it occurred to her that she couldn't finish her drawing with him fully clothed!

"Oh, no. You're still dressed. What am I going to do?" she whispered.

You could undress him.

Oh no, I could not!

Why not? He's not going to wake up and no one would ever know.

Biting her lip, she wondered if she really had the courage to go through with this.

No, she didn't.

"I'll get Tarik to do it." Yes, that would be the proper thing to do.

"Stay put, Jack," she said, then went to find his quartermaster.

A short time later they returned. "He was drunk

you say?" Tarik asked as if doubting her words.

"He drank a lot at dinner."

A deep frown drew his brows together into a deep vee. "Drank what?"

"Wine."

Tarik scoffed at her. "There's not enough wine on board this ship to make Captain Jack pass out."

Trying to look innocent and praying she was carrying it off, Lorelei shrugged. "He must have had something else before I arrived then, because you can see he's quite asleep."

Tarik approached the bed skeptically. Once he assured himself Jack was still breathing, he shook his head. "All right, Miss Lorelei. I'll tend him. You go on back to your room."

Turning around, she quickly retreated.

As soon as the door closed behind her, Tarik moved to undress Jack.

"You so much as touch a button and I'll have you gutted."

Tarik froze as Jack opened his eyes and gave him a heated glare. "I thought you were unconscious," Tarik said, crossing his arms over his chest.

"You know me better than that." Jack sat up and ran his hand over his jaw as if he could still feel Lorelei's touch. "Let's just say I'm having a bit of fun with our guest."

Tarik laughed. "All right then, I'll be off."

As soon as he was alone, Jack quickly disrobed and returned to his bed. His little vixen had wanted him undressed for some reason, and by God, he was going to lie here for her if it killed him.

And it bloody well might.

12

Lorelei waited quietly in her room until she was sure Tarik had had enough time to undress Jack and return to his cabin. Time seemed to move slowly as she clutched her sketchbook and charcoal in nervous hands.

She shouldn't do this. It was wrong and well she knew it. But then she'd always been a bit improper, and a bit too curious for her own good.

As soon as she heard footsteps crossing the front of her door, she carefully eased it open enough to peek outside.

No one. Not in any direction.

Very well then, this is it.

Her heart in her throat, she eased the door open enough to let her through, then headed down the short distance that separated her from Jack.

Tiptoeing into his room, she set her sketchbook and charcoal down on his desk and crept toward his bed. He lay on his side, facing her, with the spread pulled up over him. His loose hair fell over part of his face and he breathed quietly.

"Are you still asleep?" she asked, giving him a slight shake for good measure. "Jack? Jack, are you awake?"

He didn't answer.

Satisfied, she smiled. Oh, this was wonderful. At last he was hers and she didn't have to worry about battling him. She could do most anything she wanted to him and he would never, ever know. In truth, she liked this feeling of power. It was probably the only time anyone had ever had such power over Jack. And she was going to enjoy it.

Pulling the spread down, she exposed his torso.

She yearned to run her hand over his lean ribs, to feel his hard muscles in the palm of her hand. But she didn't dare touch him. She wasn't sure how deeply he slept and the last thing she wanted was for him to awaken to her touch.

No, she would just arrange the covers like they were the morning she'd found him, and then she could finish her picture and be gone.

With that thought in mind, she lifted the bottom of the spread to expose his long legs and feet.

Retrieving her sketchbook, she compared his pose to her drawing.

"Not quite right," she whispered. She set her book down in front of Jack's chest and adjusted the material over his hips. As her hand brushed against his abdomen, she felt his body stiffen beneath her left hand.

She squeaked and jumped back.

Was that his . . . ?

Her face flamed. It must be.

What does it look like?

I'm not going to find out.

Please! He'll never know.

But *she* would, and quite frankly she didn't know if she could look him in the eye after she'd looked him in the ... Well, she wasn't about to, and that was all.

Forcing herself to pick up her sketchbook instead of the cover, she went to pull his chair closer to the bed. She took a seat and began her drawing.

Jack watched her from beneath his lashes. It took every ounce of control he possessed not to move, and he still wasn't sure how he'd kept himself still when her hand had innocently brushed up against him. Even now his gut burned with furious need. A need that had only gotten worse when he had been sure she was going to pull the covers back and reveal him.

Only she hadn't.

The little vixen had only wanted to draw him. He couldn't believe it.

Women. There was no understanding them.

Relaxing his body, he watched the way her brow furrowed as she worked. He'd loved watching her these past weeks. Watching the way her arm curved as she manipulated the charcoal and paints. The grace she used as she blended colors.

How could Justin not want her to pursue something she obviously loved so well and had such talent for?

If she were his woman, he'd ...

There was no use thinking about what he'd do. She wasn't his. Could never be his.

All he could do was savor her body and try to

hold on to her memory. And it would be one he'd treasure until some enemy ended his life.

Finally she looked up and he could tell she was finished. She held the pad up and compared it with him.

"Perfect," she declared. "I finally got it."

How he wished he could say that.

Lorelei stood and moved over to the desk so that she could pack up her charcoal. She was completely satisfied with the results of her drawing. Of course, Jack would kill her if he ever learned what she'd done.

But it had been worth the risk.

She traced the line of his hair on the paper, remembering how it had felt under her hand.

"It's a wonderful likeness."

She gasped at the deep voice resonating by her left ear. "You were awake!"

"The entire time."

Horror engulfed her. She turned around to face him, only to realize he was standing naked before her. Her eyes wide, she quickly turned back to face the door.

"Don't be afraid of me, Lorelei," he said, running his hand through the curls on her neck. "I'm not going to hurt you."

"You're naked."

"So I am."

Heat stole over her cheeks. She'd never in her life had such a conversation, and at the moment, she didn't like it one bit! "Would you please put some clothes on?"

"If it would make you feel better . . ."

"It would."

He trailed his finger down the back of her neck. Chills erupted all over her body. Her breasts tingled at his touch. "Turn around, Lorelei, and face me."

As if she had no will of her own, she obeyed him. Still, she didn't dare look down. Resolutely, she kept her gaze locked on his face.

He took her hand in his and placed it against his bare chest. She could feel his heart pounding against her fingertips and palm as a thousand shards of desire pierced her body.

"I want to make love to you, Lorelei," he murmured, leaning his head down until only a hand's breadth separated their lips. "I want to feel your body against mine and to touch every part of you."

And then he kissed her. Hot and wet, his lips covered hers as he plundered her mouth and stole her breath. His kiss was demanding and fierce, yet somehow tender and welcome.

Lorelei clung to him.

She felt his hands at her back, unlacing her gown. She knew she should stop him, but for some reason she couldn't tell him no. Didn't want to tell him no.

He lifted her skirts.

Lorelei trembled as he deepened his kiss. She heard the whoosh as her hoops fell from beneath her dress and landed in a puddle at her feet. Jack moved his hand to her buttocks and she gasped at the foreign sensation of a man touching her there.

"I won't let you go tonight," he whispered as he pulled away from her lips.

Her gown slipped to the floor.

Afraid, Lorelei stood before him wearing nothing save her petticoat and corset. She wanted to run and yet she didn't. Part of her wanted this, demanded this. Against all reasons and arguments, she wanted this night with Jack.

Jack scooped her up in his arms and carried her to the bed. "Jack, I—"

"Shh," he said as he laid her gently against his sheets. "Forget about everything else. Tonight, there's only us."

He buried his lips against the sensitive flesh below her ear and she moaned in pleasure as a needful ache throbbed through her.

What was this burning, bittersweet pain he caused?

Needing to quench it, she reached for him, running her hands over the flesh of his back, where she felt his strong muscles ripple beneath her palms.

He rolled her over so she sat on his stomach and quickly removed her corset and petticoats. He sucked his breath in sharply as her breasts were bared to his sight. "You are so beautiful," he moaned, lifting himself up to take her right breast into his mouth.

Lorelei gasped in pleasure as his tongue flicked over the taut nipple. She buried her hand in the soft waves of his hair, cupping him to her.

Once more he rolled her in the bed until he pressed her down against the mattress. Jack pulled back from her and stared down at her as he separated her legs with his thigh. She felt him warm and wet as he probed the center of her body with the tip of his shaft.

"I want you as I've wanted no other," he said

between clenched teeth. "And I wish you knew how much it's killing me not to take you."

His words confused her.

He closed his eyes as if he were being tortured.

"Jack?"

"It's all right," he whispered. "I just have to get . . ." He took several deep breaths. "Control."

His hand trembled as he reached up to cup her cheek. "I don't want to hurt you."

She kissed him for the tender concern.

He fell against her, and she savored the feel of his entire body pressing against hers, the strange feel of his hips between her legs.

This was her Jack. Her pirate and her . . .

Lover, she thought, startled by it. This night would change her forever. She would never go back to being the same innocent girl he'd captured that night at the inn. After this, she would be a woman in every sense of the word.

And though it should terrify her, it didn't. She wanted Jack to be here. Wanted him to be the man who taught her the intimate details of this aspect of life.

To her disappointment, he left her lips and trailed kisses down her neck to her breasts. A thousand needles of pleasure pulsed through her with every touch of his tongue and hand against her flesh.

He moved his hand over her hip and down to the throbbing ache at the center of her body. She moaned as he separated the tender folds of her body and stroked her intimately, bringing peace to the burning need.

"Like that, do you?"

"Yes," she groaned.

He smiled. "What if I told you it gets better?"

"I wouldn't believe you."

His stomach quivered against hers as he laughed. He trailed his lips down her ribs, to her stomach. Lorelei arched her back as he ran his tongue over the sensitive flesh of her hip and more pleasure assailed her.

She was going to die from it, she was certain. How could anyone survive this . . . ?

Jack moved his hand from between her legs. Before she could whimper her disapproval, he took her into his mouth.

Her eyes flew open.

"No, Jack!" She gasped. "You can't."

He kissed her inner thigh, looked up at her, and gave her that dazzling smile that never failed to warm her. His finger circled the throbbing core of her body in an intimate caress and he gave an impudent nip to her thigh.

"Trust me, Lorelei. You want me to do this."

And before she could protest further, he returned to her. Lorelei bit her hand at the fierce pleasure that erupted through her. Never in her life had she felt anything so intense, so wonderful.

His tongue teased her while his finger continued its slow assault.

She wanted to scream out for help and still he kept on giving her pleasure. Her body quivered and spasmed as he quickened the strokes of his tongue. She buried her hands in his hair, pushing him closer to her as she pressed her feet against the mattress to bring her body closer to him. And just when she was sure she would perish from it, her body burst into a thousand glowing embers.

Lorelei screamed with release as the entire room spun about her.

Jack lifted his head in triumph. Somehow, he'd survived touching her, and now it was time to claim his prize. With his entire body trembling, he pressed her back against the mattress. He didn't want to hurt her, wished to all that was holy that he could take his pleasure without it, but he couldn't.

Biting his lip in guilt, he separated her legs one more time and plunged himself into paradise.

She tensed as pain intruded on her pleasure.

Jack froze. "I'm sorry," he whispered in her ear, trying to offer her comfort. "Are you all right?"

Lorelei took a deep breath as her body adjusted around him and she marveled at the strange fullness of him inside her.

They were truly joined. She wasn't sure if she should be all right.

"If it hurts too much, tell me and I'll stop."

She stared up at him. Concern for her was etched plainly on his face, in his eyes. He meant his words.

Imagine a pirate saying that to his captive.

Reaching up, she brushed his long hair up over his shoulder, then moved her hand to the tiny gold hoop. "I'm all right," she said, smiling at him.

Relief relaxed his features and he slowly began to move against her hips. The stinging ache of her body was compensated by the knowledge that Jack cared for her. That he had considered her feelings above his own needs.

That knowledge brought so much joy to her that she felt as if she could fly. She meant something to him. She wasn't just another woman in a long list of lovers he'd taken.

She was different.

His strokes quickened as he buried himself deep within her, and she reveled in the feel of his body inside hers. Whether he admitted it or not, he was sharing a part of himself with her, and she wondered if it would change him as much as it was changing her.

Lorelei bit her lip as pleasure once again began to override the pain. Over and over he slid into her, until he finally groaned.

He pulled himself out of her and spilled his seed on the bed next to her hip. Jack collapsed on top of her, his breathing ragged in her ear.

"Thank you," he whispered once he'd regained his composure.

She wiped the sweat from his forehead, then kissed the flesh of his brow. "You were right. I had never imagined anything like it."

Instead of the smugness she expected, he looked ashamed.

"Jack?" she asked as he pulled away from her.

He didn't say anything as he left the bed, went to his trunk, and pulled on his clothes.

Lorelei frowned. Clutching the sheet to cover herself, she sat up. What was the matter with him? She'd assumed this would make him ecstatically happy. Instead, he acted as if he'd just walked into a tavern full of Regulars. "Jack, what is it?"

He didn't say anything, nor did he look at her. He just walked quietly out of the cabin.

* * *

Once on deck, Jack dragged his hands through his hair as he cursed himself for the base-born bastard he was. He'd thought claiming her would make him feel better. Quench the insatiable inferno of his body.

But it hadn't. It hadn't accomplished anything except make him hate himself for what he'd done to her.

And for what? For vengeance?

For . . .

For himself.

He sank down under the shelter of the railings and hung his head in his hands. He was no better than those craven bastards who bid on the young girls who had first come to the bordello.

How many times had he listened to those girls cry over the deed and complain about the pain? 'Twas why he always avoided virgins. He had never wanted to prey on innocence. Never hear a woman cry because of something he did to her.

"Jack?"

He looked up to see Lorelei standing in the moonlight. Her hair was down around her shoulders and her pale gown shimmered. She looked like an angel and it took all his control not to cross himself.

Why had she come to him?

No doubt she hated him, and he deserved her hatred.

But the worst part of all was that he still wanted her. Even after having her, he wasn't satisfied. His body was already stirring again.

"Why did you come out here?" he asked.

"I was worried about you."

He snorted at the very idea.

She knelt down beside him and brushed his hair back from his face. He stared at her, amazed that she showed him such tenderness. He couldn't remember the last time a woman had touched him that way.

He leaned his head into her palm, relishing the soft feel of her skin against the stubble of his cheek.

If he closed his eyes, he could almost pretend he was someone else. That he was . . .

But he wasn't someone else. He was Jack Rhys. Pirate. Murderer. Purveyor of sin and of death.

He could offer her nothing.

Not even himself.

"I wish you'd talk to me," she breathed. "Tell me why you look so troubled."

He laughed bitterly. "You sound like Morgan now."

"The man who's following us?"

He nodded. "You sort of met him the night I kidnapped you. He was the one who tried to talk reason into me." Leaning his head back, he stared up at the stars. "I should have listened to him."

She dropped her hand to his shoulder as she sat down by his side. "Jack," she said, her tone chiding. "I had a choice in the matter."

"No, you didn't. You were innocent and curious and I preyed on you."

Silence hung between them for several seconds, and when she spoke, her voice was quiet and held an amazed tone to it. "So, you do have a conscience after all."

"Amazing, isn't it?" He looked at her and saw the tender look in her eyes. The tender look he didn't deserve.

'Twas her hatred he deserved, not her comfort.

She reached down and took his hand into her own. "A few weeks ago perhaps," she said, lacing her fingers with his. "But it's not so amazing now."

"Oh, God, Lorelei, you don't know," he said, tightening his grip on her hand. "You don't know me. You've no idea what it's like to be me."

"I would like to try."

And for the first time in his life, he wanted to talk to someone. To tell her what was inside him and have her soothe it. Could she?

Trust no one at your back unless you want a knife in it. 'Twas the pirate's first code and a lesson he'd learned firsthand. He'd never even trusted Morgan to that degree. But in spite of his arguments, he wanted to trust her.

Without thinking, he reached out and drew her into his arms. He held her between his knees, her back to his chest. Inhaling the sweet scent of her hair, he leaned his cheek against her head and curled his left arm about her.

Lorelei closed her eyes at the tenderness of his embrace, praying that this one time he would actually open himself to her. Patiently, she waited.

When he spoke, his voice was nothing more than a whisper. "I never wanted to be a captain, Lorelei."

She opened her eyes, but resisted the urge to turn and look at him. "Then why did you?"

"After Robert Dreck retired, his crew voted me into the position."

"But you seem to enjoy the position and you do it very well."

"Perhaps. But I was quite happy being a boatswain."

"Then why didn't you decline?"

"That is easier said than done. I'd led the crew to victory several times when Robert was injured and they probably would have gutted me had I refused."

She cringed at the thought. "How terrible."

"Pirates generally are."

She relaxed against his shoulder and inhaled the sweet scent that was Jack. "Not you," she breathed.

"Now you're deluding yourself," he said with a hard edge to his voice. "I assure you I well earned my reputation."

This time she did yield to the impulse to face him. "No, you didn't. I saw the entries in your log. You paid men to tell those stories."

He shook his head. "I've done that as well. But I've also committed a lot of crimes in my day, including murder."

13

Lorelei pulled back from Jack, aghast at his confession. Could the man holding her so tenderly really be capable of murder? True, he was a pirate who'd been rumored to have killed hundreds in cold blood, but that was a legend. Surely the man she'd come to know would never do something so horrendous. Not without good cause, anyway.

"You killed someone in cold blood?" she asked bluntly.

His face betrayed nothing of his feelings or thoughts. He nodded.

"Why?"

Jack looked away and now she saw the sadness and remorse inside him. "He killed my mother." His voice was empty. He stated it like some simple, innocuous fact.

"What happened?" she asked, wanting to understand.

Jack sighed and leaned his head back. She could

sense he wanted to withdraw from her, to speak no more about a subject that was so close to him.

She waited patiently, hoping he would learn to trust her with the truth.

To her amazement, Jack repaid her patience. "He owned the bordello where my mother worked. When I was eight, she sold me to him for the price of a new pair of shoes, then ran off with some sailor."

Even though he didn't move, raw emotion seemed to bleed from every pore of his skin. Lorelei closed her eyes in sympathetic pain. No doubt he'd carried that secret all these years.

She couldn't imagine the callousness it would take for a mother to not only abandon her child, but to sell him on top of it. What other horrors must there be within him?

"Four years later," he continued, "she returned. Baxter took her back in, but by then the years had taken a terrible toll on her beauty. She was so pock-marked and scrawny that no one wanted her. One night when she failed to . . ." His voice trailed off and he shifted his gaze to the side of the ship.

Jack's stern face showed the strain of a man who had seen hell firsthand and had barely lived to make it back to earth. "She hadn't earned any money that night. In a rage, Baxter killed her for it."

Dear Lord, what horrible things he'd seen. Horrible, dreadful things he must have known. And then to have his own mother murdered by the man who owned him. . . .

She couldn't imagine anything worse.

"You killed him afterward?" she asked, jumping to the most logical conclusion.

Jack shook his head. "I was too afraid of him at

the time. All I did was carry her body outside and bury her in the tiny plot reserved for dead prostitutes."

Her stomach wrenched at the thought as a vivid image played through her mind.

"Oh, Jack," she whispered, reaching up to touch his face. "I'm so sorry."

Tears welled in his eyes, but he quickly blinked them away. "Don't be. I survived it, which is more than I can say for my mother."

Had he? His body had survived, but not his heart. His mother and what she'd done to him had torn that from him long ago, and Lorelei wondered if anything could revive it.

They were quiet for a little while as Lorelei sifted through her tangled emotions and the awfulness of his past. There was still one question she had, and though part of her didn't want it answered, she felt she needed to know. "When did you kill Baxter?"

He rubbed his hand over his chin, then brushed the stray tendrils of her hair down her back.

"Two years later," he said simply. "I was cleaning out the chamber pots when a young girl was delivered to Baxter. She was probably no older than twelve, and he took her into the room where he inspected his new *merchandise*." Jack curled his lip at the word. "I could hear her screaming and begging for his mercy. He just laughed like the evil bastard he was, and then I heard him start slapping her."

Anger and hatred flared in his eyes, and she could feel the agony of his memories.

"Something inside me unfurled," he whispered. "And when next I came to my senses, he was lying dead at my feet and I was covered in his blood with a dagger in my fist. The girl started screaming again, and I ran off and jumped aboard the first ship I reached."

She could see the scene so plainly, imagine the terror Jack must have known as a young boy. Still, it wasn't cold-blooded murder. It was wholly justifiable.

"That's not murder, Jack. You saved that girl."

His eyes turned dull and he yielded a heavy sigh as if somehow resigned to his fate. "I was a slave who killed his master. There's not a court on this earth that would spare me for the crime."

Her throat tightened as the truth dawned on her. He was right. Though it was wrong, in the eyes of the world, he would be considered a murderer.

But he would never be such to her. She knew him better than that.

Lorelei laced her fingers with his.

Jack gave a light squeeze, then brought her hand up to his lips where he placed a gentle kiss on the back of her fingers. "You've no idea how many women I saw ruined by men like Baxter, men like my father."

He frowned as he stared down at her and again she saw the raw pain on his face. "And tonight I realized for the first time that I'm no better than any one of them."

"That's not true," she insisted.

"Isn't it? We both know I ruined you tonight. Justin won't have you when he finds out."

Chewing her bottom lip, she diverted her gaze to the deck of the ship. That was one part of all this she wasn't looking forward to. How on earth could she confide such a thing to Justin? It would devastate him.

"He certainly won't be pleased," she agreed.

"You're so naive."

"Perhaps, but I've known Justin all my life. He's a good man and he will still honor me."

Jack tensed and malice shone in his eyes. "You still plan to marry him?"

She fell silent as she thought the answer over. Marrying Justin would probably be the wisest course of action. No one would ever dare shun her so long as she was his wife. Nor would they openly torment her.

But that wouldn't be fair to Justin. Nor to her. Her loyalties now lay somewhere else.

"No," she said at last. "I can't marry him now. He'll no doubt argue the point, taking the blame for it all upon his own shoulders."

"I seriously doubt that."

"You needn't doubt it," she said, sitting up and taking offense at his slander of Justin. "He will blame it all on his scheme gone awry."

Still, disbelief showed on his face. Lorelei wished she could convince him of the truth, but he wasn't about to listen to her. She'd learned that much about him over the last few weeks. Once he got that look, there was nothing that could sway Jack Rhys's point of view.

"So then," he asked. "What's to become of you?"

"Don't worry about me." She smiled at him, certain of her words. "I have a father who loves me, and whatever scandal comes of this, I shall survive it."

Sighing, he looked up at the stars as if exasperated by her. "If you only knew how many strong women I've seen broken. I was *so* wrong to take you."

And it was then Lorelei made a dreadful, frightening discovery.

She was in love with Black Jack Rhys. Completely, utterly head over hills for the pirate.

The thought terrified her, and yet sitting in the moonlight listening to him spill his soul to her, how could she not love him?

In spite of whatever crimes he'd committed, he had a good heart. A generous heart. He cared for her and he was sorry for his actions.

But with the thought came a new fear. Could he ever love her back?

Could someone who had known such atrocities in his life ever accept what she wanted to give him?

She vowed to find some way to reach him. There had to be a way to make him see reason, to make him realize that he could be loved, that she could and did love him.

She leaned her head against his knee and thought over what he'd told her tonight. His words drifted over her, until one part in particular stood out.

She sat up with a gasp. "You know who your father is?"

He looked startled. "What?"

"You said your mother was ruined by men like your father. How would you know that?"

He shifted his gaze to the deck and tensed all around her. "She told me so."

She tilted her head suspiciously as every instinct in her body told her he was hedging. "And she told you who your father was."

He had that look in his eyes like he wanted to run again. She prepared herself to grab him if he did.

Instead, he answered. "Yes, I know who he is."

Her mouth dropped. Even though she'd guessed the truth, hearing it spoken aloud still left her shocked.

Completely baffled, she stared at him. "Then why didn't you go to him for protection after your mother's death?"

"I didn't have to," he said blandly. "He showed up at the bordello one night not long after she died."

Lorelei frowned. It didn't make any sense. "He came to get you?"

Jack snorted. "He had no idea I was there, but I knew him on sight. How can you forget the face of a man you once worshipped? Someone who was the night and day to you. A man you wanted to be just like when you grew up."

No! Now the full tragedy of his life hit her. He'd once cared for his own father as much as she cared for hers. But something had happened. Something had destroyed their loving bond.

"What did he do?" she asked.

His gaze hardened. "I begged him for a guinea to buy my freedom."

"And?"

"He told me to leave him alone."

"Oh no, Jack," she gasped. "He didn't."

"Aye, and when I went down on my hands and knees to beg him for it, he kicked me like I was a dog trying to piss on his boots."

Tears choked her. There was so much pain in his eyes that it took her breath. Dear heaven, no wonder he was so hard to reach. She couldn't imagine anyone treating a child like that, let alone having to live through something so horrendous.

She blinked away her tears, knowing they wouldn't please Jack. Nay, he was a strong man and wouldn't welcome her show of weakness. And right now, she wanted his trust more than she'd ever wanted it before.

"That's why you bought Kit, isn't it? Because of what your mother and father did to you."

He nodded. "And that's why I will never allow him to know the truth of his mother."

Lorelei cupped his cheek in her hand. She could feel the tautness of his jaw as he held his emotions in check and she admired his strength.

No wonder he denied knowing his father. Such a person should be hung, drawn, and quartered!

He rubbed his stubbly cheek against her palm and she pulled him into a hug. He tensed for a moment, then surrendered himself to her touch.

His arms came around her, drawing her closer to him and he turned his face to hers. Seeing his desire to kiss her, she opened her lips in invitation and he took it.

His kiss was warm and sweet and intoxicating. Against her hip, she could feel his desire for her as his body stirred.

Jack pulled back slightly and nibbled her bottom lip.

"'Shall I compare thee to a summer's day?'" he whispered. "'Thou art more lovely and more temperate; Rough winds do shake the darling buds of May, And summer's lease hath too short a date.'"

She smiled at him, warmed by his quote. "Come back to bed with me, Jack."

And before she could blink, he rose from the

deck, scooped her up in his arms, and took her back to his cabin.

He didn't release her until she was beside the bed. "Shall I fetch us more wine?" she asked.

He arched a suspicious brow.

She laughed. "Untainted wine, then."

"If you wish."

She went to the dining room and when she returned, she caught him flipping through the pages of her sketchbook. "You really are very talented," he said as she handed him his goblet.

"Thank you." She took a sip of her wine.

Jack took a sip of his, then reached his hand out and fingered her cheek. His gaze searched her face and she wondered what it was he sought.

"I could devour you," he said at last.

She should be shocked and offended by his words, but in truth they delighted her.

Smiling, she said, "Then do so."

A slow smile spread across his face.

Jack set his goblet down and pulled her to him. He dipped his head down to the swell of her breasts over the neckline of her gown and trailed his tongue over her flesh. Lorelei gasped in stunned pleasure as her body immediately ignited.

Straightening, he took her glass from her hand, placed it next to his, then led her back to the bed. This time, they took their leisure undressing each other.

"You are wondrous," she whispered as she wrapped her legs around his bare waist.

He leaned down to kiss her. As he started to enter her, Lorelei pulled back. "Wait."

He frowned.

She reached out to run her hand across the muscles of his chest and licked her dry lips. He had shared himself with her tonight and she wanted to do something special for him. Show him how much he'd come to mean to her.

"I want you to tell me what you like, Jack."

His frown deepened.

Lorelei forced him to roll to his back, then straddled him. She could feel the deep ridges of his stomach pressing against the most intimate part of her body. It was wondrously erotic and sent ribbons of desire thrumming through her body. His groan radiated through her.

He reached up to cup her breasts, but she caught his hands and pushed them back to the mattress.

"No, Jack. It's my turn."

Jack stared at her in wonder as she boldly dipped her head to his throat and flicked her tongue across his Adam's apple. He tried to cup her head, but she still held his hands beside his face. His body molten, he sucked his breath in sharply between his teeth.

With a thoroughness that astounded him, she explored his neck and chest with her lips, her tongue. And every time he felt the hesitant stroking, he thought he would die from the pleasure. No woman had ever treated him this way. They merely took what he gave them and were as eager for him to leave as he was to be gone.

But not Lorelei. Her delicate hands caressed his stomach before they moved lower. Writhing in ecstasy, Jack gripped the headboard in his fists as she took him in her hand and explored the length of his manhood.

Until she started laughing.

Lifting his head, he stared at her. "What's so funny?" he demanded.

"You are."

Offended, he pushed himself up on his elbows.

"It does tricks!" She laughed, then trailed her hand lightly over the tip of his shaft. Of its own accord, his body strained for her touch, then retreated as her hand left him.

Joining her laughter, Jack relaxed. "May I offer you some advice?"

She looked up with wide eyes.

"Never, ever laugh at a man's . . . piece during sex. We don't like that."

She bit her lip and looked at him from under her lashes. "I'm sorry. I couldn't help it."

"You're forgiven, but—" The words died on his lips as she bent her head down and took him in her mouth.

Jack threw his head back, striking it against the wood of his bed. But he didn't feel the pain. All he could feel was her mouth working magic on him.

Closing his eyes, he placed his hand on her head and savored the most pleasurable moment of his life. No woman had *ever* done that to him. Never.

The pleasure was so intense, he could swear he saw stars, and considering the fact that he had most likely just given himself a concussion, he probably did.

Lorelei's laugh drifted to his ears once more. "I take it you like that."

He couldn't speak as she trailed her tongue back up his body. Jack watched her every movement, awed by the brazen innocence of her.

And to think he had believed he could teach her lessons!

Cupping her head in his hand, he brought her lips up to his. "I need you," he breathed. "Now."

She straddled his waist and leaned over him. Her rich auburn hair formed a canopy over them as he lifted her hips and then set her down on top of him.

They moaned simultaneously. She tried to move her hips, but it only succeeded in driving him out of her. Jack ground his teeth in frustration before he sat up and leaned her back. This time when he entered her, it was slow and easy.

Lorelei bit her lips against the exquisite feel of him filling her. She lifted her hips to draw him deeper inside.

How she longed to scream out her love to him as he pleasured her. Pressing her lips together, she promised herself she wouldn't do it. Not now. Not during this victory. She didn't want to do anything that would drive him away from her.

He moved faster against her hips, his strokes more furious. Then she felt him leave her as his body shuddered and shook.

Covered in sweat, he rolled to his side and pulled her against him. "I'm sorry I couldn't wait for you."

She smiled up at him. "Don't be. I wanted to pleasure you."

Disbelief glowed in his eyes as he leaned forward and kissed the tip of her nose.

She rested her head on his chest and listened to his heart settle down to a regular beat.

"Why do you pull out of me?" she asked.

His body grew rigid a moment before he relaxed. A little, anyway. "I don't want to make you pregnant."

She turned her head over so that she could look at his face. "Do you always do that?"

"Always."

"Well then—"

"Lorelei," he said quietly. "This really isn't something I wish to discuss with you." He brushed his hand through her hair, spreading it out over his chest. "Is there nothing that embarrasses you?"

She traced idle circles around his chest. "There are many things that embarrass me. I was just curious, and my grandmother always told me I should never fear questions."

"She was right. 'Tis the answers that are most often frightening."

She rolled her eyes at him.

Jack gave a contented sigh and closed his eyes.

"Are you going to sleep?" she asked.

" 'Twas my plan."

"Do you wish me to leave?"

When he opened his eyes, his look burned her. "I wish you to stay right where you are."

Settling down, she closed her own eyes, then moved to trace small circles in the hairs below his belly button. The tiny hairs curled around her fingers, teasing her with the memory of their union.

"Lorelei," Jack whispered hoarsely. "If you continue to do that, neither of us will have any sleep tonight and you shall be terribly sore come morning."

Balling her hand into a fist, she shifted. "Sorry."

"Don't be. It was quite pleasant. I just don't want to hurt you."

She tucked her arm up under her side and watched him as he drifted off into sleep.

Lorelei had learned much this night. Much about Jack and even more about herself.

You're wanton.

It should have shamed her, but it didn't. For some unfathomable reason it seemed right that she should be here with Jack.

I'm going to make you love me, she vowed silently. *Somehow, Jack Rhys, I'm going to make you mine.*

Jack came awake to the smell of sandalwood and roses. For a moment he thought he was dreaming as he felt the soft body molded to his.

Only it wasn't a dream.

The morning was real as had been the night before. He looked down at the auburn curls spread across his chest. Lorelei still slept on top of him, her breasts pressed against his side. She was truly beautiful in his arms. He'd never before awakened with a woman in his bed, let alone one sprawled atop him.

Yet he liked it. He liked the way her breath tickled his chest, the way her hair slid against his flesh.

Raising his left hand, he ran his finger over the soft lashes nestled on her pale cheeks. Even now he could remember the way it felt to kiss her there. The way it felt to penetrate her body.

You're a madman. Women bring nothing but sorrow.

As if that would be a change for him, he thought bitterly.

Through the open windows he could hear his crew going about their daily activities. By the sound of them, it was probably just after noon and he really should be out on deck listening to the morning report, taking calculations. But he had no real desire to leave Lorelei's embrace.

In fact, all he really wanted to do was replay last night's tryst.

A knock sounded on his door.

Unfortunately, it was not meant to be.

Sighing, he carefully slid himself out from Lorelei's arms and made his way to the door. Jack cracked it open to see Tarik on the other side.

"There's a storm brewing, Captain. I thought you might want to come take a look at it."

"Give me a few minutes."

"Aye, Captain."

Jack closed the door.

"Is something wrong?" Lorelei asked as he neared the bed.

Jack paused to stare at her. She lay in the bed with his spread pulled up high over her breasts and her auburn hair tousled about her. He'd never seen anything more appealing. Anyone more inviting.

And she had asked him something. But the devil take it if he could remember what.

"I'm sorry," he said, reaching for his pants. "I didn't hear what you asked."

"I asked if everything was all right."

Jack laced his breeches. "It's fine. There's a storm moving in. Probably just a squall."

He sat on the bed to pull on his boots. Lorelei came up behind him and encircled his waist with her arms. Her bare breasts were pressed tight against his back, burning him through and through as his body instantly ached for hers.

"I'm not sorry about last night, Jack, and I don't want you to be either."

He reached back over his head and cupped her

head with his hand. Closing his eyes, he savored her scent, her feel. "I pray you don't suffer for it."

"If I do, it will have been worth it."

He let go of her and moved away. "This isn't a game, Lorelei. Women have been beaten, jailed, and killed for being unchaste."

"I know," she said with a hint of laughter in her voice. "My grandmother tutored me well on what can happen to women who give their passion free reign. She even warned me about handsome pirates named Jack."

Lorelei sobered as she caught his menacing glare. "Never fear for me. I have people who will watch over me. I *will* be fine."

Jack traced the line of her jaw with the backs of his fingers. How he prayed she was right.

Worst of all, though, he couldn't find it in him to resist her. She was like some enchanted spell that had captured his battered soul.

He was truly selfish. He admitted that.

"Kiss me, Jack."

He obliged. Sweet Jesu, she tasted so wonderful. Her scent filled his head.

"Captain!" someone bellowed from the deck.

Reluctantly, he pulled back from her. "I'll be back."

The afternoon dragged on slowly while Jack stayed busy with preparations. The sky grew increasingly dark until Jack ordered her below. Now in the galley, Lorelei was helping Sarah and the others prepare enough food to last several days should the storm not abate, and she was currently wrapping the potatoes Sarah's husband had prepared.

"A fire's the worst thing that can happen to a ship," Mavis told her.

Alice nodded. "Aye, we'll have no lights tonight, that's for sure."

Kit inched into the galley with a bundle of clothes and set them on the table next to Lorelei. She looked at him with a questioning brow.

"The captain said you'll be needing something other than your skirts while we've got a storm," Kit explained.

Puzzled, she looked to Mavis, who concurred. "Forgot to tell you about that. We all wear trousers in case the ship goes down."

Lorelei dropped the potato in her hand as horror filled her. "What?"

Alice caught the potato as it rolled across the table and handed it back to Lorelei. "You never know in this kind of weather. I personally have never been aboard a sinking ship, knock on wood." She rapped the table three times. "But 'tis better safe than sorry."

Kit narrowed his gaze on Lorelei's hooped skirt. "Those skirts of yours make a nice anchor. Not what I'd want wrapped around my legs if I had to swim for it."

He turned to leave, but Mavis caught him by the arm. "Where are you taking refuge tonight, Mr. Kit?"

Kit puffed out his chest like a proud peacock. "I'm bunking with the sailors. I don't need no woman coddling me. I'm a man, Mavis, or haven't you noticed."

She laughed. "You're a whelp, that's what you are."

He stuck his tongue out, then ran for the door.

Mavis sighed at his departure. "There are times when I swear that boy is as mature as an old man, and other times when he hasn't got the sense of a three-year-old babe."

Alice froze, her face a mask of shock. "Good Lord, Mavis. He is a grown man after all!"

They all burst into laughter.

And so the afternoon went until the storm started and the women went to change into trousers and shirts. Lorelei even left off her corset, since Mavis had advised her not to use one. In the event she had to swim, she would need all the breath she could get.

Lorelei didn't like that thought one tiny bit. However, an afternoon without her tight laces was beginning to appeal to her.

By evening, the ship was being buffeted unmercifully. All Lorelei wanted was to see Jack and have him alleviate the fear gnawing at her, but he and Tarik stayed topside, hoping to guide the ship through the storm while she and Kesi sat in Kesi's cabin trying to keep their minds off of their men.

There was no real light except when lightning would flash and illuminate the room. They both sat on the bunk, holding onto grab rails cut into the side of the wall.

"How long do you think it'll last?" she asked Kesi.

"Not long, I hope. I hate these things."

"So do I." Lorelei searched her mind for a game or song that could possibly take her concentration off of morbid thoughts. She had to do something or she was going to go mad from it!

"How long have you known Jack?" she asked, hoping for a long story from Kesi.

Kesi fell silent as if debating the answer. "For quite a while now. Eight, nine years it seems like."

Just her luck Kesi wasn't in a chatty mood.

Lorelei tried again. "And has he ever told you anything of his parents?"

Kesi shrugged. "Only what his mother did. To my knowledge, he knows nothing of his father."

Could the woman answer anything with more than a sentence or two? Lorelei bit her lip and tried to think of something else that might yield a longer answer.

"And what of Morgan?" she asked as she thought about the ship that was still trailing them. "What is he to the captain?"

More lightning flashed and a loud clap of thunder shook the room.

Kesi waited for it to die down before she spoke. "Ya want the truth, or do ya want to hear what the two of them tell people?"

"Both," Lorelei squeaked, needing Kesi's conversation now more than ever.

Kesi shifted slightly. "Well, child, if ya were to ask one of them, they would tell ya Jack captured Morgan's ship and was about to kill the boy when Morgan refused to flinch as Jack positioned his sword for the kill. Then they'd tell ya Jack so admired Morgan that he spared his life and let him sail with his crew."

"And the truth?" she asked to prevent Kesi from pausing in her telling of the story.

"Morgan had jumped ship to escape the British

Navy. One of the officers recognized Morgan, and he and several others were in pursuit of him. Morgan dodged into an alley at the same time Jack was leaving a tavern. They collided and Jack pulled his sword on him, until he saw the English. Deciding they were a better target for his anger, Jack went for them. They fought the officers off, and afterwards Jack asked Morgan if he'd like to sail with us."

Now that was the last thing she'd expected to hear. "Morgan wanted to be a pirate?"

"Not really," Kesi admitted. "He wasn't happy with Jack once he found out who Jack was, but Jack has a way of getting what he wants out of people."

"I've noticed."

Kesi laughed. "Well, child, ya can't fault a flower for attracting bees. Jack is just charming and charismatic by nature."

He certainly was that.

"Kesi, I want the truth from you. Is Jack as bloodthirsty as his legend says?"

Kesi gave a pregnant pause before she spoke. "Aye, Jack has been bloodthirsty, I won't lie and say otherwise, but then a cornered fox can seldom escape the hounds without bloodshed. When given a choice, he shows mercy. When cornered, he draws blood."

Another flash of lightning streaked through the night, followed by a deafening roll of thunder. The ship shook mightily and it felt as if it might capsize. Lorelei gripped her grab rail as tightly as she could and prayed for deliverance.

For several seconds they sat quietly until frantic voices intruded.

"The ship's afire!"

14

Dripping wet and furious, Jack watched as fire consumed the main sail. Grinding his teeth, he cursed his luck. There was no way to put it out; not as fast as it traveled.

Defeat weighed heavy on his shoulders.

His ship was lost.

"You'd think in this gale it wouldn't burn," Tarik shouted as they pulled the tarps from the rowboats in preparation for the crew to flee.

His men were quick and fairly orderly as they launched the boats over the side, then climbed down to take their places inside them. It was strangely quiet. No one was shouting or screaming. The whole scene played out like some strange dream.

Jack turned to Tarik. "It'll take down the whole ship."

And it would. Jack knew it as well as he knew the sea.

At least Morgan would be able to see the fire and he would know what had happened. The *Roseanna* should be able to pick up their survivors. It would be a tight fit on Morgan's ship, but they weren't that far from the island.

"Captain!"

Jack turned to see Kit running toward him. Without thinking, Kit threw his arms around him and almost knocked Jack off his feet as the boy's full weight hit him square in the chest. Jack hugged him close for only a minute before he pulled Kit away, threw the boy over his shoulder, and carried him over the side to the ship's main boat where Alice and Billy were waiting with various members of the crew.

"You three stay together," Jack ordered.

"What about you?" Kit asked.

"I have to make sure everyone gets off the ship."

Before Kit could argue, Billy and the other men took the oars in their hands and started rowing the boat into the swirling black water.

Clinging to the climbing rope on the side of the ship, Jack watched them until the next boat came crashing down almost on top of his head.

Quickly, he climbed up the side of the ship as more of his crew climbed down to the boat.

Once on deck, he patted Tarik on the shoulder. "You and Kesi take this one and I'll get in the third."

Tarik didn't argue.

Lorelei stood on deck next to Kesi, her face ashen.

"It'll be all right," Jack told her. "We have three boats and only sixty-five crew members. The squeeze will be tight, but there's room for everyone."

She nodded. He tried several times to urge her into the boat with Kesi, but each time she met him with a firm refusal.

"Not until you come with me," she insisted.

Her answer angered him more each time she used it.

Once the deck cleared, Jack and Lorelei made their way to the last boat. As she stepped into the boat, Jack looked back at his beloved ship while flames spread through the rigging and across the deck.

"Whew," Merrimen, one of his boatswains, breathed as he picked up a set of oars. "That was as close to hell as I ever want to come."

Peter, one of his carpenters, looked up as Jack jumped to the boat. "Did anyone make sure Ernie was told?"

Jack froze. "Where was Ernie?"

"Passed out on his bunk," Merrimen said.

"In this storm?" he shouted, angered that one of his men would act so foolishly.

"We didn't think nothing of it, Captain," Merrimen explained.

Suddenly, Jack heard Ernie screaming from the deck. He looked up to see his boatswain engulfed by fire an instant before Ernie jumped into the water.

Without thinking, Jack dove over the side and went to help his crewman.

"Jack!" Lorelei screamed as she realized what he was doing. He paid her no heed.

Rising to her feet, she tried to see him in the water.

"Sit down!" Peter snapped at her. "You'll tip us over."

Her heart pounded against her breastbone as she

desperately searched the waves for some sign of the men. "We have to go back for them."

"Not bloody likely," Peter snapped as he and the others continued to row. "That ship's got stores of gunpowder on her. She'll be exploding before long and the further we're from her the better off we'll all be."

"But what about Jack?" she asked, stunned that his men could leave him behind so easily.

"The captain knows how to swim and he knows how survive," Merrimen snapped. "Now sit down or I'll throw you overboard meself."

He didn't have to. Lorelei jumped into the water to follow after Jack.

Waves crashed all around her in the storm as she swam. Lorelei struggled to keep her head above water, but each wave seemed larger than the last until she was certain she was drowning. She lost all sense of direction and could no longer see anything that gave her a clue as to where she was or where any other boat or person might be.

Dear Lord, what had she done?

No one could survive this.

Not even Jack.

Panic consumed her, and just as she reconciled herself to the inevitable, a hand grabbed her arm.

"What are you doing here?" Jack yelled.

She wanted to laugh in relief. "Looking for you."

Without a word, he wrapped his arm around her chest and pulled her back against him as he swam through the water. Lorelei surrendered herself to his power, too grateful and relieved to protest.

More waves crashed over them, but Jack didn't seem to notice as he pulled her toward the boat she'd left.

A loud explosion rent the air.

"Take a deep breath," Jack shouted.

She barely had time to comply before he dragged the two of them down, far below the waves.

Lorelei panicked.

What was he trying to do, drown them?

She wanted to fight him, but the way he held her she couldn't. She opened her eyes and all she could see was black all around her. Feel the water creeping in through her body. It was stifling. Terrifying. Her lungs burned and she desperately fought her panic, which urged her to open her mouth and scream.

Just when she thought she could stand no more, they started to rise. Pain pounded through her throat and sides as she struggled not to take a breath to ease the burning sensation of her lungs.

Then suddenly they broke the surface.

Lorelei gulped the saturated air into her starving lungs.

Pieces of burning wood and ship remains were scattered all around them.

Just as Peter had predicted, the ship had exploded. Jack grabbed a piece of passing wood and released her to it. "Hold on to this for a second."

He disappeared.

"Jack!" she called, terrified of losing him after all they'd been through.

He didn't answer.

Lorelei felt like a twig being tossed about by an insane wind as she searched the rains and water for a glimpse of one of the boats or of Jack.

Nothing.

Panicked tears choked her. What would she do without him? How could she ever survive this storm?

Just as her terror was about to overtake her, Jack returned. He had a larger piece of wood that appeared to be a portion of one of the decks. "Climb up," he said, then helped her up on top of the wood.

As soon as she was in place, he lifted himself out of the water and joined her on their makeshift raft.

The waves continued to toss them about and threatened several times to overturn them.

"You didn't find Ernie?" she asked as Jack tightened his grip on her.

"No," he said. "I thought you were him when I found you."

"I'm sorry, Jack."

He pulled her into his arms and held on to her. "It's all right, Lorelei."

He gave her a tight squeeze. "Someone is bound to find us in the morning."

For some reason, she believed that when he said it, though her logic argued otherwise.

Sometime in the middle of the night, the storm abated. The sky was still too dark to see anything, but the waves settled down, and for a time Lorelei slept.

By morning, the sun had returned and with it came no sign of the boats or of Morgan's ship.

Lorelei didn't bother to ask Jack what it meant. She already knew. Without food or water, they wouldn't last long.

As if reading her thoughts, Jack offered her an encouraging smile. "They'll be looking for us."

"I know, but the question is, will they find us."

He took a deep breath as he toyed with the edge

of his boot. "Kind of makes you wish for a smaller ocean."

"Or a bigger raft."

He laughed.

Lorelei licked her parched lips as she scanned the horizon for the millionth time seeking some sign of rescue. "Have you ever been caught out like this before?"

"No," Jack said as he, too, scanned the ocean around them. "This is definitely a new experience. You know, being a pirate, I usually have a ship."

In spite of herself, she smiled at his misplaced humor. "I'm sorry it sank."

"You'll be even sorrier in three days if we're not found." Her face must have shown her horror at his words, for he quickly added, "I didn't mean to say that. It was uncalled for."

"But 'tis true," she said, her chest growing tight from the fear that assailed her.

He pulled her against him and they lay down on the raft, watching the blue, perfect sky above them while their raft traveled of its own accord across the waves.

"I'm scared, Jack," she confided, needing him to soothe her nightmare. "I don't want to die, especially not like this."

He leaned up on one elbow and stared down into her face while he stroked her cheek. "There's really nothing to worry about, Lorelei. I swear to you that we are not going to die out here."

"How do you know?"

His hesitation showed in his eyes while he grappled with his explanation. When he spoke, she was completely unprepared for his disclosure. "I know where I'm meant to die and it's not out at sea."

She frowned at him. "How do you know?" she repeated.

He looked away. "Years ago, when I was only a few years older than Kit, I visited a small island. There was this one spot not far from the lagoon and when I walked over it, I knew instinctively that it was the exact spot where Jack Rhys would die."

Her frown deepened. It was so uncharacteristic of him to think of such a thing. Surely Jack Rhys, a man who made his own destiny, was not superstitious?

"And you honestly believe that?" she asked.

He traced the line of her frown until she relaxed her face. "I know it sounds ridiculous. But Thadeus always told me you can't defy fate or destiny and I know deep in my soul that my destiny is to die on that spot."

"And where is this place?"

"*Isla de Los Almas Perdidos.*"

"Is that where we're headed?"

He nodded. "It seemed the perfect place for a confrontation."

She sat up, angered at him and terrified that there might be some truth to his words. "I can't believe you! What you're telling me is that you were going to commit suicide?"

"No," Jack said as he folded an arm under his head and continued to stare up at the sky above him. "I was fulfilling a prophecy. I have no intention of allowing Wallingford to win. I assure you, I *will* fight for my life."

There was something in his eyes that betrayed his words. "But you don't believe you'll win."

He shifted his gaze to hers and she could see the

conviction deep inside him. "I don't care if I win so long as I bury my sword in Wallingford's gut."

She closed her eyes in frustration. What had the admiral done to him that would make Jack so willing to sacrifice his own life for the sake of vengeance?

"I don't understand why you hate him so."

Jack let out a long sigh. "In truth, I don't want you to understand. This is my fight with him, not yours."

"And this fight is worth your life?"

"Obviously."

She growled in her throat, aching from the need to strangle some sense into the man. "I would sell my soul to get off this raft so I could stomp away from you, Jack. You are the most frustrating human being I've ever had the misfortune of . . . of . . ."

"Being marooned with?"

She glared at him.

Light danced in his eyes. He was laughing at her! By the very heavens, the man's audacity had no limits.

"How can you be so lackadaisical when it comes to your life? I for one would hate to see you die. And what would happen to poor Kit?"

He rubbed his hand over his chin. "Morgan would take him. We've already discussed it."

"You would trust your son to him?"

"I would have to."

She released an aggravated breath and folded her arms across her chest. There was no talking to him. Like all the men she'd ever known, Jack had set his course and wouldn't be swayed, no matter the soundness of her logic or arguments.

Did all men have to be so stubborn over stupid matters?

Lying back down, she allowed Jack to encircle

her with his arms. Oddly enough she felt safe, even though they were facing almost certain death.

Oh Jack, she thought, *why can't I make you see all the wonderful things I see when I look at you?*

How she wished they could plan a future together like she'd hoped to do with Justin.

Closing her eyes, she could well imagine a pleasant home with children running around her feet while Jack read to them. She could see herself in his study painting him in a chair with a little boy and girl sitting in his lap.

But that wasn't Jack. He was a pirate and a man as untamable as the sea.

Don't give up hope, Lorelei. He's worth the fight.

After all, how many people had told her Justin would never come up to scratch?

Get your head out of the clouds and see reality, Amanda had said to her. *Why on earth would a Wallingford marry the daughter of a by-blow?*

She'd wanted to punch Amanda in the nose for that. But Amanda had been right. Justin had always been concerned with prestige and titles.

And still she'd won him.

Which meant she could win Jack, too.

Provided they didn't die.

hours passed slowly as they drifted on the raft baking in the sun. Lorelei had returned to sleep a short time ago and now Jack sat watching her as he cradled her head in his lap. Her face was turning a darker shade of pink from the sun and he wished he had something to preserve her skin or ease the ache of the burn she was developing.

She should be home right now, planning her wedding. And though he hated the very thought of her sharing her life with Justin, he would rather she do that than perish on a raft out in the middle of nowhere.

Raking his hand through his hair, he cursed himself. He should have never brought her into his life. She was too fine and precious to ever share a moment with a man like him.

Jack clenched his teeth, angered at himself and at the fickleness of fate.

It was strange, but looking at her just now he could almost believe in love. At least for the first time in his adulthood, he found himself wanting to believe in it. To believe that maybe she could love him.

He reached out and touched her tiny hand. It was so small in comparison to his and yet she possessed a strength of spirit that could crush him as easily as he could crush her fingers with his grip.

Jack looked up at the clear sky above and the scorching sun that was beating down on her delicate skin.

"Lord," he whispered, the words stinging his parched throat. "I'm rather sure you haven't much care for the likes of me. And even though You and I are strangers, I would be deeply obliged if You could spare her."

He glanced down at Lorelei who slept almost peacefully. "I would make a deal with You, Lord, about how I'd never pirate again or that I'd give up the sea or something ridiculous like that, but we both know I'd never keep it. So instead of lying to You, I would just rather be honest and ask that Lorelei survives."

Even if it was without him.

He just didn't know if he could survive without her.

Not that it mattered. He hadn't been lying when he told her of his dream. He was going to die there. He just hoped she didn't die before he did.

Looking out at the sea, he tried to see any sight of one of the boats or of Morgan's ship. But all he saw was endless waves of blue.

Leaning his head into his hand, Jack waited for a miracle that he was fast beginning to doubt.

After Lorelei awoke, they didn't talk much that day. Each one was lost in their own thoughts and regrets while they sought to preserve their dry throats.

When night finally fell and gave them a welcome relief from the fierce heat of the sun, they curled up together to fight the sudden chill.

Sometime after midnight, they both slept.

Lorelei woke first to the bright morning sun. Her mouth was drier than the worst drought and her stomach rumbled for food. Wishing she could sleep through the misery, she lifted her head to search the waves yet again.

Through bleary, scratchy eyes, she saw . . .

Trees?

She jerked upright.

"Jack!" she shouted, shaking him. "Jack, there's land!"

Jack sat upright so quickly, they bumped heads.

"Ow," she snapped, rubbing the tender spot below her temple. Jack didn't pay her any attention as he looked in the direction of the island they were approaching.

"I'll be damned," he said under his breath. "Come on, let's swim for it." He rolled off the raft and splashed into the water.

Too delighted and relieved not to obey, she followed after him. They weren't that far from shore and it only took a couple of minutes to make it to the small beach.

For several minutes, they lay in the surf, allowing the water to splash over them as they enjoyed lying on something that didn't rock beneath them.

It was land! Lorelei thought gleefully. Solid, wonderful, beautiful land. There were trees with shade and if her throat wasn't so dry, she would laugh out her surging giddiness.

Jack was the first to find enough energy to rise. Lorelei rolled over to watch him climb the tree nearest them and drop two coconuts to the ground.

She pushed herself up from the surf and went to pick the coconuts up. She rubbed the coarse husk, wishing for a way to break it open. "How are we going to eat these?"

He pulled a dagger out of his boot.

"With relish," he answered, taking one from her hand and slicing it open.

He handed her one half. Lorelei drank the milk, too hungry and thirsty to care about the fact that she actually hated coconut. At this moment, 'twas the best food she'd ever tasted.

In no time at all, they finished off both coconuts.

Jack wiped his dagger off on his wet sleeve, then returned it to his boot. "Now we just need to find a small stream and some meat."

"Aye," she agreed. "Water would be wonderful."

Jack lightly touched her burning face. "I need to

find some aloe or another plant that'll ease your burn."

Before she could respond, Jack removed his dagger from his boot, then scraped the leftover pulp out of the coconut shells. "Do you know how to dig oysters?"

"I grew up in Charleston," she said. "Of course I know how to dig oysters."

"Good." He handed her his dagger and the two bowls he'd just made. "Go dig us up some while I find water. You can put them in this and I'll be back as soon as I can."

Taking the dagger and shells, she headed toward the beach to complete her task.

By noon, Jack had found water, and they had feasted on oysters, berries, and a small quail Jack had managed to capture. Contented, Lorelei sat next to the small stream that was located about two hundred yards from the beach. Lush trees and flowers kept the area shaded and tranquil.

She bent over the stream and rinsed the salt water from her hair while Jack watched her.

He lay on his side with his long legs stretched out toward her. His shirt was torn where the sleeve joined his left shoulder, and one of his muscular knees protruded from the rip in his breeches. He wore two days' growth of beard on his face and she couldn't resist smiling.

"What?" he asked.

"You look like a pirate. All rough and worn. All you need is a peg-leg and a patch."

He laughed at her. "I've always been fortunate enough not to take many wounds to my face and head. Thadeus used to say it was a miracle, since my head was so swollen by stubbornness and vanity he didn't know how anyone could miss it."

She joined his laughter as she twisted her hair to drain some of the water from it. "Who is Thadeus?"

His laughter died and a deep sadness came over his face. Lorelei paused combing her hair with her fingers to touch his leg with her hand. "Jack?"

He sighed and plucked a blade of grass from the ground. Twirling it through his fingers, he stared at the stream. "Thadeus was my mentor, and the closest thing to a father I ever had."

"Was he one of the men at the bordello?"

"God, no." He looked up at her as if the very thought offended him to the core of his being. "I met him after I killed Baxter. I knew if I were to live I'd have to join the first pirate ship I could find. I figured pirates, unlike a navy or merchant crew, wouldn't mind the fact that I was wanted for murder. Robert Dreck was about to set sail when I stumbled onto the docks."

"Robert Dreck?" She remembered Jack mentioning him to her before, but she didn't recall ever hearing his name from Lord Wallingford or any of the other naval officers she knew. "I've never heard of him."

"That's because he never wanted fame. He went into piracy simply for profit with the intention that after he made his fortune, he would retire and live a life of luxury."

What a romantic idea. "Did he?" she asked.

"Yes, he did."

Lorelei returned to combing her hair with her hands. "So, you met Thadeus on board Robert's ship?"

He nodded. "I was fourteen and bitter with

hatred. Robert wasn't sure if he could trust me, or trust some of his crew with me either for that matter, so he told Thadeus to take me in hand and show me what I needed to know."

"I bet he had his hands full."

"You've no idea," Jack said with a snort. "The man was a paragon of patience. To this day I don't know how he kept from killing me the first year we knew each other."

Satisfied she had most of the serious tangles removed, she braided her damp hair. "Why?"

"To say I was disrespectful would be mild. Thadeus was a small man, no taller than you. Bald-headed, with only a few tufts of gray hair left around his ears. He had these spindly arms and legs, and wore a pair of spectacles. More scholar than sailor, I couldn't imagine why Robert wanted him as part of the crew. I never knew the man to get drunk or curse, and everywhere he went, he toted a book with him."

"You admired him." She could hear it in his voice.

"Not at the time. I thought he was a coward who was afraid to stand up for himself. Of course, there wasn't a man on Robert's ship who teased him for it, except me. I was too blind and stupid to see what the others knew."

She cut a small strip from the hem of her shirt to use as a tie for her hair. "What changed you?"

Jack tossed the piece of grass into the stream and watched it drift away from them. "I had gone off with a group of the crew to a local tavern and Robert had sent Thadeus in to retrieve us. There were pirates there from several other ships and when Thadeus walked in they burst into laughter.

"Three of them started poking at him with their hands and swords, and trying to pull his book from his hand. He ignored them and came to where I sat. I wanted to kill the men tormenting him. When I started to draw my sword, Thadeus grabbed my hand and told me that if I killed everyone who annoyed me, I'd soon find myself alone. I was so angry at him. I called him a craven bastard and I said I hoped they did cut his throat."

His tone was remorseful with a hint of shame in it. She couldn't imagine the man she knew being so rude to anyone.

Jack sighed, then continued his tale. "When it became obvious Thadeus wasn't going to play into their bullying, the three men left him. Thadeus had just told us of Robert's orders to return to the ship when a young woman screamed."

"It was the three sailors?" she asked.

"Aye. They had turned their attention to one of the serving wenches. One of them had pushed her face down on a table and was about to rape her when Thadeus drew his sword." He gave a bitter laugh. "I couldn't believe my eyes. Until then, I thought he wore his sword just for show. It amazed me that he knew how to hold one. But what struck me most at the time was the fact that he showed no anger. No emotions at all. He calmly walked up to the group and told them they had a choice. Let the girl go or die."

Those were almost verbatim the same words Jack had used the night he had saved her from a similar fate, and that told her more than anything else the extent of Thadeus' influence over Jack's life.

"The sailors drew their swords on Thadeus?" she asked.

"Yes. The girl ran and I watched, too stunned to move as Thadeus disarmed two of them and wounded the third. He used moves with his sword that I had never seen. And the speed with which he dispatched them amazed me even more.

"It was then that I realized I wanted to be the man he'd tried for a year to make me."

She smiled. "So, he's the one who taught you to read."

"To read, to think, to behave, to appreciate things in this world other than myself. He made me the man you see before you today."

There was so much love in Jack's tone, on his face. She could tell he worshiped Thadeus like a father.

"Where is he now?" she asked.

"He died a short while ago."

"Oh, Jack, I'm so sorry. What happened to him?"

15

It was on the tip of Jack's tongue to tell Lorelei who had killed Thadeus and how.

The words were almost out of his mouth before he stopped himself. What good would it do Lorelei to know what manner of man Wallingford was? It would be selfish of him to make her hate a man she so admired. And if the truth were known, he didn't want to see the hurt in her eyes.

Let her have her delusions. He refused to hurt her any further.

"Thadeus died in battle," he answered, even though the partial lie caught in his throat and his soul screamed for vengeance.

"Was he on your ship?"

Jack shook his head. "He was a Patriot out to save you colonists from the yoke of England. He always told me that there were causes greater than one man. Causes worth dying for."

By her face he could see she held the same noble

thought. She was such a naive dreamer. So different from the earthy women he'd known.

She still had unshattered dreams and hopes.

Except for one. He'd ended her dream of being Justin's wife. Oh, he could lie here rationalizing his actions, telling himself she was much better off without that spawn of misery, but the truth was she'd wanted Lieutenant Pasty-Face and Jack had taken that from her.

He reached out and gently stroked her reddened cheek.

Lorelei grimaced and flinched from his touch. "No wonder my nurse and father always told me to stay out of the sun. This is terribly painful."

Jack dropped his hand. At least that was one pain he could soothe. "Stay here for a minute. I'll be right back."

He left her and went to find the group of aloe plants he'd seen earlier. He broke a few of the leaves off, then returned to Lorelei.

Kneeling beside her, he squeezed the cool gelatin onto his fingertips. As tenderly as he could, he covered her face with it, then he moved his fingertip over her slightly parted lips.

He could feel her breath tickle against his throat as she gave a contented sigh and closed her eyes, her face a mask of bliss.

Instantly, his body reacted to her seductive look. Fire beat a steady rhythm through his veins. Grinding his teeth against the urge to fall upon her, Jack forced himself to minister to her damaged skin and not to the call of his body.

"That feels wonderful," she breathed, and it almost undid him.

Unable to respond, Jack moved to place the gel on her throat and then down the reddened areas of her chest exposed by her shirt. The reddened area that dipped down to the valley between her breasts.

Lorelei sucked her breath in between her teeth.

Unable to stand anymore, he kissed her. His heart hammering, he laid her carefully down on the grass.

"Dearest Jack," she whispered.

Jack closed his eyes, savoring the sound of his name on her lips. Her voice resonated through him like a caress. No one had ever made him feel the way she did. With her, he almost felt decent. Free. Heroic.

Frightening, tender emotions swelled inside him as he carefully unlaced her shirt and exposed her breasts to his gaze. He wanted to tell her how much she'd come to mean to him and how much the thought of her leaving hurt, but the words lodged themselves in his throat.

Why should he give her false hopes for them when he already knew what lay ahead for them. One way or another, Jack Rhys was dead. Either Wallingford would kill him, or one of his men would do it after Jack succeeded in exacting his revenge.

You could run away with her. . . .

Aye, he could. But to do that would strip her away from her father, whom she treasured. It would deny her everything she'd ever known and all the people she loved.

Not even he was that selfish. He'd taken enough from her, he would take no more.

And if he were half the man Thadeus had been, he'd make her hate him now. Make her glad to see him die. But he couldn't do that either. The thought of her hating him hurt more than any wound he'd ever sustained.

"Jack?" she whispered against his lips. "Is something wrong?"

"No," he said, silencing her with another kiss as he slid her breeches off her.

He jerked his shirt off, his body demanding to feel as much of her skin on his as he could.

Once they were both naked, he drew her into his arms. Lorelei moaned as he dipped his head and took her breast into his mouth. Her hands caressed his scalp, cradling his head against her as he sampled the very fruit of paradise. His blood seemed to boil in his veins, swelling with a need so great he feared it might devour him.

She moved her hands down his body, cupping his hips and pressing him closer to her.

"I want you inside me," she whimpered. "Please."

"Ever as you wish," he murmured before he complied.

She wrapped her legs about his waist, drawing him deeper inside her. Jack closed his eyes as he thrust against her, needing the comfort of her embrace. And when he moved to kiss her, he could swear he felt their two souls mingling.

For the first time in his life, he felt a bond to someone outside himself.

The thought terrified him.

Lorelei threw her head back and screamed out as she found her release. Jack moaned as her body spasmed around his, and her grip drew tighter on his body. He thrust harder now, needing to find the same peace for his body.

She moved her hands over his back, dragging her nails along his spine while she ran her tongue over the ridges of his ear. Jack groaned as his own body erupted into spirals of pleasure and he barely had time to withdraw from her.

He lay next to her, clutching the grass in one hand and her hair in the other. That had been close, and he shook from the fear of what he'd almost done to her. Never before had he come so close to planting his seed inside a woman.

And if the truth were known, he hadn't wanted to withdraw from her. In that one instant before he pulled himself out, his body had almost revolted.

Rolling over onto his back, he promised himself that he would touch her no more. She posed too great a danger to him and he wasn't sure how much longer he could battle the strange feelings she evoked in him.

Lorelei rested her chin on his chest and looked down into his eyes. "You don't think there's anyone on this island, do you?"

Her unexpected question broke his line of thought.

He took her braid in his hand and trailed the tip of it across his jaw. There was something vaguely familiar about the beach where they landed, but he couldn't remember what. Of course, he'd seen many islands similar to this and they all tended to blend together in his memory.

"I have no idea," he finally said. "It would probably be a good idea to scout around and find out."

She jerked back from him and quickly pulled her shirt on.

"I didn't mean now," he said.

"Well, you can lie there naked if you want to, but I have no intention of being caught in my altogether by a stranger."

Jack poked his lip out as she finished dressing. "You know, we could be the last two people on earth."

She paused and looked at him.

"Would you mind if we were stranded here for the rest of our lives?" he asked, not sure where the question came from or why her answer suddenly seemed so important.

"I'm not sure," she answered honestly. "I would miss my father terribly."

"Anything else?"

"Agatha's apple pie and my horse, Samson."

Don't ask it.

And yet he couldn't stop himself from asking what he wanted to know. "What about Justin?"

She looked him square in the eye. "What is it you want me to tell you?"

"I want the truth."

She sighed. "If the truth you're after is whether or not I still love him, then yes. There's a part of me that will always love him."

Disappointed fury squeezed his chest so tightly that he could barely breathe.

Well, what did you expect?

'No, Jack, I hate the imbecile. 'Tis you I love.'

You know better, boy.

His jaw tense, he pushed himself up and dressed. "Aye, I suppose if given a choice you'd much rather be marooned with *him*."

She tugged her shoes on, giving him an irritated glare. "I didn't say that."

Not one to be outdone by her anger, he jerked his pants on and laced the back. "You didn't have to."

Hands on hips, she faced him. "Why are you so angry?"

"I'm not angry," he snapped, snatching his shirt down over his head. He heard another rending of fabric as the tear in his sleeve widened.

"Yes, you are," Lorelei accused. "You said you wanted the truth."

"And you gave it to me." With both cannons of it blasting a hole in his heart.

Why couldn't she love *him*?

Jack froze at the thought.

What the hell? He didn't want her to love him. That would be . . .

Well . . .

Wonderful. Wonderful and terrifying and a whole lot of other things he didn't want to think about.

He started off into the thicket.

"Jack, where are you going?"

"I need to think."

Lorelei folded her arms over her chest as she watched Jack trudge away from her. *Men,* she seethed. *You give them what they want and suddenly they don't want it anymore.*

"Fine," she whispered. "Go off and pout."

Wait a minute, her mind spoke. *Maybe he wanted you to tell him you loved him.*

She scoffed at the very thought of it. Jack Rhys was the type of man who needed no one. He would laugh in her face if she admitted that to him.

Or worse, run for cover.

Nay, to win him, she must make him say it first.

And then another thought struck her. She stood alone in the small clearing on an island she knew nothing about and the only one who had a weapon was quickly leaving her behind!

"Jack!" she called, chasing after him.

She caught up to him a little ways off. The trees and vegetation were much denser now. The sunlight barely penetrated the foliage. The ground under her feet seemed almost alive as she struggled to find the forest floor that wouldn't trip her.

Foreign sounds whipped through the air, some from animals she couldn't even begin to identify, and she suddenly remembered reading stories in books of people who found themselves trapped in quicksand. . . .

As if knowing her thoughts, Jack turned around and faced her. "Leaving you alone wasn't such a good idea, was it?"

She shook her head.

"Come on," he said, draping his arm over her shoulder. "Let's see where this trail leads."

They followed it for close to two hours when suddenly it fanned out into a small town. The buildings were a mixture of huts and wooden and brick structures which reminded her a lot of Charleston. Lorelei gaped as they entered the town.

Men, women, and children bustled all about. She saw a busy smithy at the end of the street. There was a fisherwoman hawking mackerel and shark to passersby, and another man called out for people wanting a fresh drink of water from his cup. At a bordello just to her right, barely dressed women were leaning over the edge of a balcony and calling to the men who passed below them.

The road was filled with carts and horses as people made their way across town.

"I don't believe it," Jack said.

"Jack!" a male voice shouted.

Lorelei turned around as a man rode up to them on the back of a black Arabian stallion. The stranger was tall and lean with dark brown hair and laughing gray eyes. The right half of his face was scarred with what looked like a sword wound.

"Ben," Jack said with a smile as he removed his arm from around her. "I can't believe it."

"*You* can't," Ben inserted. "Morgan told me you went down with your ship."

"I did, and I washed ashore on the other side of the island."

Ben threw his head back and laughed. "Only Black Jack Rhys would have that kind of fortune." He swung his leg over the saddle's horn and slid to the ground. Removing his gloves, he offered Jack his hand.

Shaking Ben's hand, Jack asked, "Where is Morgan anyway?"

"Looking for you."

Lorelei was confused by what was going on. She understood that they had somehow ended up on the correct island, but she didn't know whom the gentleman was, or what he was to Jack.

Jack turned toward her. "Ben Gerrit, this is Lorelei Dupree, my current hostage."

Ben clicked his heels together and bowed low before her like a true courtier.

Instinctively, she raised her hand, which he took, then placed a chaste kiss on her knuckles. "Charmed," he said with debonair flair.

" 'Tis my pleasure," she returned politely.

Jack rudely took her hand out of Ben's grip. "Don't get too charmed."

Ben laughed. "You know me too well."

Jack narrowed his eyes on him and turned his head slightly toward her. "Ben is an old enemy of mine," he explained to Lorelei.

Enemies? They didn't behave as enemies. Completely confounded, she looked back and forth between the two men.

"It's true," Ben admitted. "When I was first appointed governor of *Isla de Los Almas Perdidos*, I swore I'd see this rogue hang. Turns out I was the one who was hanged and Jack here kept the mob from finishing the deed."

"What?" She was stunned by his story.

"Ben has a way of completely alienating everyone around him," Jack said with a hint of humor in his voice. "He'd barely been on the island two weeks before he'd passed so many laws the inhabitants revolted."

Ben cleared his throat. "Yes, well I'm much better at that now."

"Better at alienating people or being revolting?"

"Jack!" She gasped in surprise at his words.

Ben just laughed. "Pay him no mind. He always was surly. I still don't know why he saved me."

Jack folded his arms over his chest. "Because it never hurts to have a public official indebted to you."

"True enough." Ben smoothed the front of his shirt. "You two look like you've been through a shipwreck. I'm sure you'd like to freshen up. Come along and I shall have rooms prepared for you both."

Jack declined his offer.

"Now don't get that look," he told Ben as the man's face fell. "There should be a British Navy ship headed this way and the last thing you need is for them to find out you harbored me. I dare say, I might not be here to pull your neck out of the noose next time."

Ben's face visibly paled. "That is a most excellent point."

"I thought you'd see it my way."

"I shall send word out to Morgan immediately. Several of your crew have taken rooms at Regina's." Ben glanced out toward the docks nervously. "A British ship, you say?"

"Aye, and no doubt armed to the teeth."

Ben pulled his gloves back on. "Morgan should have warned me."

"He most likely didn't think about it."

"Yes, well, I have plans I need to make." Ben gave Lorelei a curt bow. "I bid you good day, *mademoiselle*." He mounted his horse, then headed away from them.

"Did you really save his life?" she asked as Jack led her down the street.

"Aye."

"You are the most remarkable man."

"Hardly." Jack pulled her in the opposite direction.

The streets were fairly crowded with every kind of rough-looking sort. Prostitutes and peddlers constantly approached them, begging their indulgence.

"This isn't a very nice place," Lorelei said as she sidestepped a drunken man who was making his way past them.

Jack pulled her away from the man. "It was named the Island of Lost Souls for a reason. Just stay with me and no harm will come to you."

Well, she certainly had no intention of leaving his side. No, she thought as she watched two men break into a fight, no intention whatsoever.

Jack led her into a large building at the end of the dirt street. It had been blue at one time, but the paint was in bad need of repair.

"Don't worry," Jack assured her. "The inside's much nicer."

And it was, too, she realized as she entered the foyer one step behind him. Expensive gold embossed wallpaper decorated the narrow hallway. Before them was a large, winding staircase.

A huge dining room was to her right and a salon to her left. Jack led her into the salon, which was decorated in the latest style. The chairs and sofas were Chippendale pieces covered in brown and maroon tapestry. Ornately carved tables were set around the room, which was occupied by even more rough-looking men and women, several of whom paused in their drinking and card playing to look up at her.

"Well, well, Jack Rhys lives," came a deep, sultry feminine voice.

A plump woman of about thirty came in behind them. Her dark hair was piled in braids atop her head and her face was beautifully exotic. Her gown was a modest brown color that only emphasized her strange tiger-like eyes. And Lorelei didn't like the way she was looking at Jack one little bit.

"Regina," he said, with that charming smile that made Lorelei ache to kick him in the shin.

The woman called Regina crossed the room and

gave him a large hug that was just a little too long and a little too tight for Lorelei's taste.

"My sweet," she breathed in his ear. "You look dreadful. It's not like you to take after these dogs." She gestured widely to the men in the room.

At last, Jack pulled away from her. "What can I say? I have had a rough couple of days."

Regina cupped Jack's chin in her hand and licked her rouged lips suggestively while she focused her gaze hungrily on his mouth. "You shall have my best room and I will order Davis to draw you a bath and give you anything you need."

Jack removed her hand from his face. "Thank you. I would appreciate that."

It was only then that the woman's eyes slid from Jack to take in Lorelei. Regina arched one finely plucked brow. "Gracious, I thought *she* was one of your men."

Lorelei took a step toward her, intending to let the wench have her full wrath.

Jack took her arm and gave a warning squeeze. "This is Lorelei Dupree. Daughter of *Sir* Charles Dupree, and at present she's my hostage. I shall need clothing and supplies for her as well."

"Ah, Jack," Regina purred. "How I wish you'd take me hostage."

"Another time perhaps."

Lorelei felt her jaw go slack. That was it. She was going to poison the man the first chance she had. Or better yet, strangle him in his sleep.

Regina beamed. She looked back at Lorelei, and the smile instantly vanished and was replaced by a withering glare. "You know where your room is, Jack, and I have a special place for your hostage."

Jack shook his head at Regina, then cast a skeptical look to Lorelei. "I'm afraid she will have to share my room. I don't dare give her any opportunity to escape. She's quite cunning, you know."

And *she* was getting very tired of being spoken of as if she weren't present. Another urge to kick him shot through her.

Regina poked her lips out into a becoming pout. "If you insist."

"I do."

"Very well. Davis will be up shortly."

Jack excused them, then took Lorelei back into the hallway and up the winding staircase.

"'I have a special place for your hostage,'" Lorelei mimicked as he led her down a paneled hallway to the last bedroom on the left. "'I'd like to show her a special place. Who does she think she is?"

Jack opened the door for her and she walked into a clean, well-kept room with a large four-poster bed.

His eyes were alight with mischief and humor. "Why, Lorelei. I've never heard you carry on this way before."

"Oh, just you wait. I'd like to strangle that woman. Not to mention you'd better hire a taster from now on when you dine with me, you randy knave."

Jack closed the door. "May I strongly caution you against any inclination to confront Regina. She isn't above sending *you* a cup of poison if you anger her."

Lorelei paused. "What?"

"She's extremely vicious when crossed."

"Then why did you bring me here? Was it to flaunt your mistress at me?"

He burst into laughter. "My what?"

She saw red. "It's obvious by her greeting that

you two are intimate. I really don't appreciate this, Jack. Not one little bit."

"I can't believe it. You're jealous."

"Yes, I am, you cad."

He cupped her face in his hands and stroked her cheeks with his thumbs. "There's nothing to be jealous of. I came here because it's the only hotel in town where prostitutes aren't soliciting business in the lobby. Regina may be irritating, but she keeps clean beds and the food is almost edible. And as for being intimate with Regina, please give me credit for having some sense."

She looked up at him suspiciously. "What do you mean?"

"I was raised in a brothel, Lorelei, and I learned early on the number of diseases a person can contract from promiscuous women. I've been very careful about my partners, and I can assure you bedding community property such as Regina doesn't appeal to me."

Lorelei curled her lip. "That's so crude."

"Crude or not, it's the truth."

Not sure if that knowledge made her happy or not, she walked stiffly to the other side of the room and took a seat at the table by the window. "Why do you keep telling everyone I'm your hostage?"

"Because the world is an ugly place and if I introduce you as anything other than my hostage, people will judge you harshly."

And that thought bothered him. Greatly. She could see it in his eyes, in the rigidity of his body. And there was only one reason she could think of for him to be like that. "Is that what happened to your mother?"

Though she would have thought it impossible, he

became even more rigid. "Aye, she didn't start out as a whore. She actually had a decent family and a gentle upbringing."

Jack sat on the bed and ran his hands through his unkept hair before he tugged his boots off. "Her father was a major who adored his only daughter. There are times when I'm trying to go to sleep at night that I can recall him. Or at least an image of him."

Lorelei moved to help him pull his boots off. "What happened to him?"

"I don't know."

She gave a deep "umph" as his boot came free and she lost her balance.

"I don't understand," she said as she righted herself and placed the boot by the bed. "If your grandfather loved your mother then why did she—"

"She fell in love with a young naval officer who had the misfortune of already being married. He took advantage of her, and when she became pregnant, he swore to her he'd never let her suffer."

He handed her his other boot.

Lorelei placed it by the first, then took a seat on the bed beside him. "But your father didn't keep his word."

"He did for a time. My grandfather had an estate in Northern England where we stayed. I heard people whisper dreadful things about my mother, but at the time I didn't understand. For all I knew my parents were married and my father was off at sea like any other naval officer. Whenever he could, my father came to visit.

"It was on his last visit that everything changed. He told my mother that he was going to leave his wife. He wanted us to run off with him and leave

England. We were supposed to go to America, where no one would know us and start our life together."

"How old were you?"

"Five. I can still remember him carrying me out of the house in the middle of the night. I felt so safe and I was foolish enough to think he'd never hurt us."

"But he did."

"Aye. 'Twas all lies. He didn't take us to America. He headed out to the West Indies and rented a small room at an inn. He told my mother that he was going to shed his uniform and buy us passage to America and that he would return shortly. He never did."

Lorelei closed her eyes as pain for him washed over her. She couldn't imagine how horrifying it must have been for the two of them. "What did your mother do?"

"She tried to find him, only to learn he'd set sail with his ship. He left us no money and no way home. She was devastated."

Her throat tightened and she started to reach out, but something told her not to. That he wouldn't welcome her comfort right then. "And you?"

"I've hated him every day since," he said, curling his lip. "I watched my kind, sweet mother become an embittered shrew who hated me with every breath she took. And she was right—had I never been born she would have had a perfectly respectable life."

Lorelei frowned, and in spite of her common sense, she touched his hand. "It's not your fault."

Jack shrugged her touch away. "I know," he whispered. "But it doesn't stop it from hurting." His eyes burned into hers. "I don't want to hurt you, Lorelei," he whispered again. "God knows, I don't ever want anything like that to happen to you."

"It won't."

He sighed. "I wish I could believe that."

A knock sounded on the door. Jack sprang to his feet so quickly, she nearly tumbled from the bed.

With a shake of his head, he fell back into his role of pirate and opened the door. Several servants entered carrying a washing tub, soap, water, towels, clothes, and food.

Once everything was in place, they left them alone.

Jack stared at the tub with lust gleaming in his eyes. "You go ahead and take your bath. I need to find my men."

"We can share."

"Don't tempt me." His smile was dazzling. "So long as we're with people who aren't loyal to me, I need to protect your reputation as much as I can."

"Bully that," she said flippantly. "I would rather have you."

"And I would like to have you over and over," he said, his gaze dipping to her breasts. "But unfortunately, it will have to wait."

He pulled the key from the lock of the door. "I'll lock you in. It'll make it look more authentic."

And with that, he was gone.

Bemused and disappointed, Lorelei stripped her clothes off and submerged herself in the hot water as she thought over what Jack had told her. She couldn't envision what his mother must have gone through to have been so betrayed by the man she loved.

How she longed to give Jack the love his mother had denied him. To show him that she would never betray him.

"Oh, Jack," she whispered. "I love you so much."

If only there were some miracle that could erase his past and give her hope.

It didn't take Jack long to round up his crew. Only Tarik and Billy were missing. Both of them had gone with Morgan to look for him.

His men had been bursting with questions about what Jack had planned for their future, and of course he'd told them he'd buy a new ship.

But in truth all he wanted to do was find some quiet, safe haven where he could be with Lorelei.

Stow it, Rhys, you're used to disappointment.

"Captain!"

He turned at Kit's shout. With Alice and Kesi escorting him, Kit ran down the stairs, through the salon, and launched himself into Jack's arms. Jack stumbled back as ninety-five pounds hit him like a cannonball.

"I knew you'd make it," Kit shouted in his ear as Jack hugged him close.

It was only then Kit realized what he'd done. Clearing his throat, he quickly extracted himself from Jack's arms and straightened up like a rough and ready pirate.

He gestured to Kesi and Alice with his thumb. "The women didn't think you'd survive. But I told them otherwise."

"That he did," Kesi said, ruffling Kit's hair.

Kit bristled under her attention and stepped away from her. "Is Lorelei with you?"

Jack stifled his humor at Kit's discomfort. "She's above, changing into new clothes."

"Glad to hear it. I wasn't so sure she'd make it, being a girl and all."

"Like her, do you?" Jack asked.

Kit shrugged. "She's not bad for a woman."

"Well, if you'll excuse us," Kesi and Alice said. "We'll go visit with her."

Once they were alone, Kit looked up at him. "Are you going to marry Lorelei?"

"What?" he asked, momentarily stunned by the unexpected question.

"I overheard Alice telling Kesi you're in love with her. Are you?"

He didn't know how to answer the question. "Love has nothing to do with it, Kit."

"So, you're just bedding her."

Jack scowled at his son. What the devil had gotten into him? "Keep your voice down, pup. And no, I'm not just sleeping with her."

"That's what it looked like on board the ship."

"Well, we're not on board the ship and everything's different now."

"Oh," Kit said. "That's too bad then."

"Why?"

"Because I think she loves you."

16

What on earth had made Kit think she loved him? That thought churned in Jack's mind as he bathed himself.

Kesi and Alice had taken Lorelei below to eat while he made himself a little more presentable.

Over and over he thought about various moments he'd spent with Lorelei. Could Kit have seen something he missed?

Sure, they enjoyed each other's company. Lorelei even seemed to like their verbal sparring.

But love?

What would Lorelei's love look like? Could it be the way she leaned a little closer to him when he spoke to her? Or was it the way a certain fire seemed to light her eyes when they were together?

It's lust, you fool. Don't kid yourself.

What did Kit know. He was only a boy. A pup. And here he was, a grown man obsessing over the words of a child.

Aye, you're a fool to ever believe a woman like that could ever care for a man like you.

Lorelei sat at one of the tables with Kesi, Alice, Mavis, Kit, and Sarah while they sipped tea and sampled some of Regina's biscuits. They'd ordered food for her and a tray to be taken upstairs to Jack.

"We've been terribly worried about the two of you," Mavis said as she stirred cream into her tea.

Alice passed the sugar bowl over to Mavis. "Especially after we found Ernie and there was no sign of either of you."

"You found Ernie?" Lorelei asked, delighted he had somehow survived.

"Aye," Mavis said, swallowing her sip of tea. "He was hurt and cussing like a bandit, but he survived."

Regina brought the food to their table. She sneered at Lorelei before looking over to Alice. "I'm surprised to see you break bread with the likes of her. I thought you hated these rich snobs as much as me."

"Now, Gina," Alice said. "Don't be mean. Lorelei is quite nice once you get to know her."

Regina raked her with a withering stare. "I'll just be glad when she's out of here. She's ruining my atmosphere and stinking up the place."

Remembering Jack's words about Regina and the poison, Lorelei pushed her plate away as the bitter woman stalked away from them.

"Why does she hate me so?" she asked Alice.

"Jealous harpy." Alice set her cup aside. "She's been after Jack for years, but he's never so much as given her the time of day."

Mavis patted Lorelei's arm. "She also likes to pretend she's the by-blow of this rich English earl, so any time she spies a real lady, she gets nasty."

Kesi motioned to Lorelei's discarded plate. "Go on and eat, Lorelei. Gina knows better than to hurt ya, child. Jack would have her head and she well knows it."

Lorelei had barely taken a bite when a rough group of sailors came in.

"Oh, heaven," Alice gasped. "It's Gory Galbraith. There'll be nothing but trouble from this."

Lorelei wiped her mouth with her napkin. "Who is he?"

"The meanest-spirited pirate who ever drew breath," Kit answered. "He makes Blackbeard look like a saint."

"I think we best be going," Alice suggested. "I'll take your bread, Lorelei. You get the bowl and we'll go upstairs to my room."

"Wait," Mavis whispered to them. "He's seen us. Don't move and maybe he'll leave is alone."

Only it wasn't to be.

The four men came straight to their table. "Well, well, what have we here?" the one who appeared to be the leader said.

"Looks like a bunch of doves, Captain."

"That it does," Galbraith concurred.

One of the pirates leaned over Alice and took a rude sniff. "They don't look like no soiled doves, neither. And they don't smell of sex or sweat. I think we have some real ladies here, Captain."

"You must be wrong, Leo," Galbraith said. "Gina wouldn't let no ladies into her place."

"They're ladies, all right," Kit said. "And if you mess with them, you'll have me to deal with."

The captain straightened and narrowed his beady stare on Kit. "What did you say, insect?"

Kit rose slowly from his chair. "I said for you to leave them alone."

"Kit, sit down," Mavis snapped. "You're going to get hurt."

"That's right, pup," the Captain said. "You better listen to the old crone. I make my meals off of little rats like you."

Unwilling to stand by and see her friends abused, Lorelei spoke up. "Insect, pup, or rat. It certainly seems to me that you don't know what he is, so maybe you should leave him alone."

The captain turned his attention to her.

Gracious, Lorelei, you should have kept your mouth shut! Why not just call him a smelly rhinoceros wart while you're at it?

"Did you say something to me?" Galbraith asked.

"No," Lorelei said with a gulp.

He wiggled his finger in his ear as if cleaning it. "Funny, I could have sworn I heard you speak."

Maybe it's the dirt clogging those nasty things you call ears.

Lorelei bit her lips closed to keep from saying it aloud.

The captain turned Kit's chair over, dumping the boy onto the floor. "Oops," he said. "Looks like you need to find yourself a new chair."

His three men laughed.

That was it. Caution aside, she wasn't about to let these men pick on a boy and do nothing about it. "And maybe you need to find yourself some new manners."

The captain snaked out his arm to her and

grabbed her wrist. "Maybe I ought to teach *you* some manners."

"Let me go." Lorelei tried to pull out of his grip, but it was no use.

The other women sat at the table, unsure what to do while Kit fled the room.

"Ach now," the captain said. "Why don't you come over here and make it up to me with a kiss?"

"Forgive me," Lorelei snapped as she tried again to wrest her arm from his grip. Her entire arm burned. "I really don't need a purgative at present."

His grip tightened even more. Against her protests, he pulled her into his lap. Struggling against him, she shrieked her outrage.

Just as his fetid breath fell against her lips, she was freed.

Lorelei jumped back and saw Jack holding the captain's head back in his fist while he balanced the blade of his dagger against Galbraith's bearded neck.

The man's eyes hardened. "Well now, Jack Rhys. How is it you got past my men?"

Jack didn't seem to hear him. Instead of answering, he pulled the dagger from the captain's throat, lifted it up and started to plunge it straight into his chest.

A scream caught in Lorelei's throat.

An instant before Jack made contact with the captain's chest, Jack turned the blade aside and sliced air with it. "If you ever lay hands on what's mine again, as God is my witness I'll lay you down dead."

Jack jerked the chair out from under the captain, spilling the man to the floor. "Go on, get out of here and don't turn around until you're on your own ship headed out to sea."

Cursing, the captain shot to his feet. "I'll kill you for this."

Jack stiffened. "Then go ahead and try."

It was then the captain looked around and saw his men lying unconscious on the floor. The color faded from his face.

Kesi, Alice, and Mavis dumped their cups' contents into the faces of the slumbering pirates. They sputtered awake.

By Galbraith's face, Lorelei could see his desire to say something more, but he thought better of it. Gathering his men, he left.

Her entire body trembling, she breathed deep in relief.

Jack caught her up against him. "He didn't hurt you, did he?"

Before she could answer, Mavis, Kesi, and Alice spoke at once.

"You were wonderful, Lorelei."

"Did you hear what she said?"

"I thought Jack was going to kill him!"

Jack ignored their words and continued to look at her. "Are you all right?"

"I'm fine. Really." She hugged him close. "Thank you for coming."

His laugh reverberated through her. "Oh, my little Lorelei, polite unto the end."

Kit jumped into the middle of the women, and began relaying the story of how Jack had rendered the pirates unconscious.

Jack kissed her lightly on the forehead, then addressed the group. "I think Lorelei's had enough excitement for the day."

"I know I have," Mavis said. "You two go on up. I

know you're tired." She put her hands on Kit's shoulders. "I'll see to this one."

Jack took Lorelei by the hand and led her upstairs. Without a second thought, she followed, and it wasn't until they were alone in the room that she finally spoke. "Would you have really killed him?"

His eyes had the cold, deadly gleam to them that marked his sincerity. "For touching you, absolutely."

"Why?" she asked, wanting to hear his reasons for spilling a man's blood for her. Could she possibly mean something to him after all?

"Because I . . ." His voice trailed off and he looked about the room like a cornered fox surrounded by snapping hounds.

"You?"

"I . . ."

She giggled. "For an eloquent man, Captain Rhys, you seem to be stymied for an answer."

And then he was there, standing in front of her, pulling her against him. His lips covered hers and the kiss he gave was one of desperation and power. It took her breath away.

He moved from her lips and trailed kisses over her cheeks and throat.

"Lorelei," he murmured in her ear as he unbuttoned the back of her gown. Her dress fell to the floor. He ran his hand over her chest, raising chills along her body. "I don't want any other man to ever touch you."

"Neither do I," she said as she unlaced his shirt, then pulled it off over his head.

She arched her back as he deftly opened her corset, then slid it to the floor. Her chemise and stockings soon followed. She expected him to carry her to the bed. Instead, he picked her up and placed her on the long narrow table. "What are you doing?" She gasped.

A wicked smile curved his lips as he peeled his breeches off. "I'm going to feast on you."

He climbed up on the table beside her. Just above her head, his food tray was set out, still untouched. Jack reached his hand out to scoop the cream off of a slice of pie.

"Jack?"

He smeared the cream over her breasts and down her belly. Before she could say another word, he dipped his head and began licking the cream from her body. Writhing in pleasure, she ran her hands through his hair. Over and over his tongue stroked her, fanning the flames of her desire until she thought she'd scream from it.

Biting her lip, Lorelei reached for the chocolate part of the pie and spread it over his neck and shoulders, then set about feasting from him. Jack's moan reverberated through her.

And when he pulled her against him and seized her lips, she could stand no more of the sweet torture.

"Now, Jack," she begged as she reached down and took him in her hand. She guided his swollen shaft toward her.

He laughed low in his throat. "That's what I love most about you. You always know what you want."

And then he slid into her. Lorelei moaned in blissful satisfaction as he buried himself deep.

Lifting her hips, she urged him on, whispering to him as he stroked the bittersweet need of her body.

"Faster," she urged, her body spinning out of control.

He obliged, and she felt as if she were on the precipice of some great mountain, about to fall off. Her ecstasy built, stoked by his body.

Lorelei dug her nails into his back as her body erupted and she groaned with wondrous release. Jack moved faster for a few seconds longer, increasing her pleasure all the more.

And then she felt him shudder. For the first time, he didn't pull himself out of her as his own release came.

Instead, he buried himself deep inside her and called out her name.

Lorelei lay perfectly still as the full implication hit her. He hadn't pulled out.

Her breathing heavy, she brushed the hair away from the nape of his neck. "Jack, why did you—"

"God and his saints help me for it," he panted. "But for once I wanted to know what it felt like to give a part of myself to someone."

Tears stung her eyes.

Immediately, Jack slid out of her. "What did I do? Did I hurt you?"

"No," she said as the tears flowed down her temples. "You didn't hurt me, you silly pirate. You just made me happy."

He brushed the tears away with his fingertips. "You are a strange woman."

"I'd have to be to put up with you."

Jack picked her up and moved her from the table to the bed. They spent the rest of the day and night there, exploring each other. It wasn't until the wee hours of the morning that they were disturbed by a sudden knock on the door.

Jack cracked the door open to see Morgan on the other side.

Morgan didn't bother greeting him. His words were clipped and emotionless. "Wallingford's coming. I barely beat him here."

17

Jack felt as if he'd been punched in the gut. Wallingford. It figured. Of all the cursed timing.

"Does Ben know?" he asked Morgan.

"I sent Tarik up to tell him."

Jack nodded. "How much time before Wallingford arrives?"

"An hour, maybe. He has three warships with him."

Jack ground his teeth together. "And I have none."

"You have mine."

"No, Morgan. I appreciate it, but I wanted to make my stand against him and so I shall. I've involved you in this too deeply already and I know how hard you're trying to leave piracy behind. The best thing you can do is to hide yourself until all this is over."

Jack paused and looked back over to the bed where Lorelei still slept. "Just promise me one thing."

"Anything."

"If I die, see to it my wealth is distributed evenly between Kit and Lorelei."

"But Jack—"

"Just promise me, Morgan."

"All right. I promise."

Not feeling a damn bit better, Jack said, "Now you better go hide your ship. If Wallingford recognizes it, he'll skin your hide as well."

"I already thought of that. I had my crew take it to the other side of the island out of sight."

Jack gave a half-hearted laugh. "I taught you well."

"Yes, you did." Morgan took a step back. "I plan to be there when you face him."

"I would rather you not."

"I know. But you need a reliable second there and I'm not some craven beast who would send you out alone."

Morgan's loyalty had never failed to amaze him. He'd never understood it, but for once, he was grateful for Morgan's sense of honor. "Just stay out of my way."

"All right. I will." Morgan headed off down the hallway.

Jack closed the door and leaned his forehead against it. There was no use in wishing for what could have been. He knew that. This was the course he had chosen and now it was his time to rendezvous with destiny.

Walking over to the bed, he watched the early dawn light play against the creamy softness of Lorelei's bare body. Even now he could taste the salt of her skin on his tongue, feel her hands playing against his back.

Their time together had been so brief. And it was

the best part of his life. If he had to die, then he wanted it to be now, with the memory of her still fresh in his mind. The last thing Jack wanted was to go grow old alone while trying to hang onto her memory and the few wondrous days they'd spent together.

This tiny woman lying in his bed had changed him forever.

Pulling the covers over her, he went to dress and wait for the inevitable.

Lorelei came awake to the sunlight streaming in through the window, and to the smell of freshly cooked ham. Savoring the warm aroma, she opened her eyes to see Jack standing in front of the windows, staring out at the sea.

As if he sensed her sudden alertness, he turned his head and looked directly at her. "Good morning," he said with a hint of ill-humor in his voice.

What on earth had caused him to be so grumpy first thing on such a beautiful day?

To her, this day was glorious and she couldn't wait to spend it with Jack. In fact, she'd thought of another picture she wanted to paint of him and she couldn't wait to get started. Especially since her earlier one had gone down on board his ship.

"Good morning," she repeated. "What were you thinking of? Returning to sea?"

Jack leaned with one arm against the side of the window as he continued scanning the scenery. He drew a deep breath before he answered. "No. I was wondering how long it's going to take Wallingford before he comes ashore."

"What?" she gasped, bolting out of bed.

Had she heard him correctly?

Draping a sheet around her, she rushed to the window. Out in the harbor were three English ships. She knew the admiral's as soon as her gaze touched on the crisply polished sloop which had all canons prepped and aiming straight at the island. None of the islanders were about and all the shutters in town had been pulled tightly closed. Everything looked deserted, no doubt in expectation of the ensuing battle.

Lorelei wanted to run. She didn't want to go home. Not now and certainly not like this.

"What are we going to do, Jack?"

The reconciled look on his face terrified her even more than the three ships prepared to blow them all to kingdom come. Dear heaven, he was going to go through with his mad plan after all.

He spoke and confirmed her thoughts. "You are to dress and eat your breakfast while I wait on Ben. Then I shall go down there and meet them."

Horror filled her. "You can't."

"I have to."

Closing her eyes, she prayed for an answer to keep him from this madness. Did she mean so little to him that he was now prepared to end his life over some insane need for vengeance? "Please don't do this," she begged, trying to reach that part of him she knew did care for her.

"Would you have me run, then?"

"Yes," she said, hoping to sway him to common sense. "You and I could run away and find someplace where—"

He stopped her words by pressing his finger to her lips. "Remember what happened to your grandfather? Remember what your grandmother's last words to him were? 'If you had fought like a man, you wouldn't die like a dog.'"

Anger coiled through her. "That's a myth penned by a man who wanted to portray my grandmother as a monster. My grandmother's last words to Calico Jack were that she loved him more than anything else on this earth. That she would always love him and that she had no regrets for the time they'd spent together."

Jack's gaze softened. "If she were anything like you, then I don't doubt that. However, it doesn't change anything. I may have been many things in my life, but I've never been a coward."

Oh, how she wanted to beat him senseless for his stupidity! Lorelei's gaze darkened.

"Fine then," she snapped. "Go kill yourself. But don't expect me to watch."

"I don't." He turned around and headed out the door.

Lorelei slung the sheet to the floor in a mighty rage. How dare he behave this way! Just who did he think he was, seducing her, making her love him, and then throwing his life away?

"Well, I won't let you, Jack Rhys. Do you hear me?" she said to the room as she retrieved her garments from the floor. "I'm not going to stand by and watch you die like my grandmother had to do with her Jack. I won't let it happen this time. At least not without a fight."

Ignoring her breakfast, she started dressing.

Morgan met Jack just outside the inn with Ben by his side. The street was completely deserted as the ocean breeze whipped through town, stirring up tangles of dust.

"Wallingford has agreed to your terms," Morgan said as Jack paused by his side. "He's picking five men to come ashore and take Lorelei while he faces you on the beach. He's chosen swords for the confrontation."

Jack didn't look at Morgan; instead, his attention was fastened in the direction of the harbor as if he could see Wallingford already on shore. "I knew he would." He indicated Morgan's sword, which was hung against his hip. "May I?"

"Sure," Morgan said as he unfastened the buckle, then handed it over to Jack. "Just make sure you kill the bastard with it."

Jack strapped the sword to his hips. "That's what I intend to do."

Ben cleared his throat before he spoke. "I certainly hope you know what you're doing, Jack. You know if you fail, I won't be able to offer you a pardon."

"I'm well aware of that fact."

Ben's jaw tightened and he looked at Jack as if seeing him for the last time.

Ignoring the dire look, Jack led them toward the small harbor, his mind set and his heart heavy. In spite of his best intentions, his thoughts drifted back to Lorelei and the way she'd looked lying in bed this morning, with her hair tossed about the covers and her bare skin against the sheets.

Out of his entire life, he had but one regret.

And Lorelei was it.

Jack ground his teeth together. He mustn't think of her. Mustn't let his feelings intrude on this match, or else he was definitely as dead as Ben predicted. His only hope for victory was his ability to control his emotions.

Deadening himself, he walked across the beach. The water lapped up against the short wooden pier that jetted out into the lagoon. The beach was a natural harbor and ships would anchor a little ways off while their crews rowed ashore.

This morning, there were four boats on the horizon. One a merchant ship that had come in yesterday, and the three British warships that stood like skeletal guardians of doom in the morning light. Even from this distance, Jack could see the activity of the crew as they launched the ship's boats which would bring his most hated enemy into his grasp.

One of Ben's assistants was waiting for them. The thirty-year-old was dressed in a crisp brown suit that almost matched Ben's. "They should be here shortly," he told them.

Jack nodded and watched as the Englishmen climbed aboard the small boat and rowed toward the beach. It took very little effort to make out Wallingford and Justin. Especially Justin, who kept standing up in the boat and leaning forward as if wanting to jump out and swim ashore. Any other time, it might have been comical the way the man popped to his feet, only to have his father snap an order for him to sit down.

Jack tightened his grip on the hilt of Morgan's sword in expectation. With any luck all this would be ended before Lorelei finished dressing, and before Kit woke up to find himself an orphan.

As soon as the boat was close enough for the men to wade ashore, Justin leapt from it.

"You bastard!" Justin roared as he stomped through the waves and unsheathed his sword. He held his polished sword above his head, cursing with every step.

As soon as he reached the beach, he charged Jack.

Unsheathing his own sword, Jack deflected Justin's blow, his body cold and numb, and once again under his firm control. "My fight's not with you."

"Oh yes, it is."

Jack parried two more thrusts. "Don't make me kill you, boy."

Justin's face turned bright red. "You're not man enough to kill me, you craven thief."

"Ouch," Jack mocked. "What a vicious insult."

He shoved Justin away from him and looked to Wallingford, who watched them with pinched, worried features. It had been a long time since Jack had seen the man. He wore his uniform with the same pompous, self-righteous, stiff spine that had marked Wallingford and all his deeds.

"Is this how you fight, old man?" Jack asked him. "You send a boy out to die in your place?"

Wallingford said nothing as Justin lunged for him again. Anger taking a firm root in him, Jack sidestepped the thrust and brought his sword down hard across Justin's blade.

The boy staggered back from the ferocity of the blow and Jack seized the moment to shove him backward with his hand. Justin stumbled, turned slightly, then fell to the ground, landing on his stomach. His sword landed almost three feet away from his outstretched hand.

Kill him!

Jack hesitated, and in that moment of his laxity, Justin scrambled across the sand and retrieved his sword.

Once more, he faced Jack.

Now Justin's face bore a mask of terror and fear that consumed him as he realized fully that Jack was the master and he just a mere pupil.

Everyone on the beach now knew the outcome. It was only a matter of time before Jack ended this and took the boy's life.

They fought for several minutes more, but there was no longer any contest. Justin lacked stamina and skill. Sweat poured down the younger man's face, making lines in the white powder covering his cheeks.

"Nay!"

The horrified plea tore through Jack like a blast of shrapnel. He looked over to see Lorelei being held back from their fight. Tears were streaming down her cheeks as she struggled against Morgan and demanded he let her go.

"Please stop this, please!" Her anguished cries shredded what little soul Jack still possessed.

A part of me will love him forever, her voice whispered in his mind.

And in that instant Jack knew he couldn't kill what Lorelei loved. No matter the consequences.

Letting go the sword in his fist, Jack watched as it arched up and landed blade down in the sand.

The look on Justin's astonished face would have been laughable had Jack not just consigned himself to the gallows.

Breathing heavy and sweating profusely, Justin angled his sword at Jack's throat. "On your knees, pig."

Jack gave a subtle shake of his head as he crossed his arms over his chest. "I bow before no man. If you're going to kill me, then you'll do it while I stand."

"Please, Justin, don't hurt him."

They both turned stunned faces to Lorelei.

Morgan let her go and she rushed toward them.

"What did you say?" Justin asked as she came to a halt between them.

Lorelei wiped the tears from her face. "It's not him," she said, grabbing Justin's hand and lowering the blade from Jack's neck. "That's not Black Jack Rhys."

Wallingford joined them. In all his stiff formality, he surveyed Lorelei. "What are you saying, child?"

Lorelei looked at Jack and swallowed. She took several deep breaths and composed herself before she spoke again. "Black Jack Rhys is dead and this . . . this man saved me from him."

"Lorelei," Justin said in warning.

She turned to face Justin. A silent plea was etched on her face as she addressed her fiancé. "Remember that night in the tavern? You asked me to identify Black Jack. I named him then, don't you think I would do so now if this man were really him?"

A muscle began to tick in Justin's jaw and Jack waited for him to denounce her as a liar.

Wallingford lifted his monocle up to study Jack in detail. After a pregnant pause, the admiral turned back to Lorelei. "Then who is he?" he demanded.

"Ja-jac . . . Jacob," she stuttered as she tried to come up with something. "Jacob Dudley."

Jack lifted a brow at the horrendous name she'd

chosen. Granted, it was on the cusp, but couldn't she have come up with something better than that?

Why not call him Percy Poindexter, or Oscar Gridley?

"Is what she says the truth?" Wallingford asked him.

Jack debated on his answer. She had brazened much to face a British officer and give false testimony regarding a known outlaw. Part of him wanted his confrontation with Wallingford still, but the other part sought to protect Lorelei.

It was that part he listened to. "I would never deign to call a lady a liar."

"Nor would I," Justin added, sheathing his sword. "Now that I look at you I can see that I was clearly mistaken by my bloodlust. You're not the man in the tavern."

"Are you sure about that?" Wallingford asked his youngest son.

"Positive."

Ben came forward with a nervous laugh. "Of course he's not Black Jack Rhys. Haven't you heard that I swore I'd hang that pirate beast if he ever showed himself on my island?"

Jack guarded his look as he turned his head to Ben. Now that was laying it on a bit thick, and not at all to his liking. Aye, he'd make the man pay for that.

Later.

"Well then," Wallingford said with a sniff. "Justin, collect your bride and you . . ." He raked his gaze over Jack. "Come with me. I should like a word with you."

Jack went cold. "I don't think so."

"It wasn't a request, boy. And I suggest you obey."

It was on the tip of Jack's tongue to tell him to go to hell and roast, but one look at Lorelei quelled the impulse. Concern was plainly etched on her face, and if he didn't know better, he'd almost swear he saw love in her eyes.

Of course, if that were truly there, then it was no doubt meant for Justin.

Justin pulled her away from Jack, toward the boat, and it took every shred of Jack's control not to run to her as she looked back at him over her shoulder.

It was only then Jack realized where he stood. It was the same spot that had haunted his dreams for years. The same spot where he had once told Thadeus that Jack Rhys would die.

With an eerie chill skipping up his spine, he followed Wallingford to the boat.

"Don't worry," the old man assured him in that stiff, pompous accent he deplored. "I shall have my men row you back to shore once our meeting is finished."

"As if I would *ever* believe anything that comes out of your mouth, old man."

Even so, Jack followed.

His heart heavy, he watched Justin help Lorelei into the boat before he took a protective seat next to her. Jack wanted to shout in rage and toss the brat out on his arse. That should be *his* place beside her, not Justin's.

But it wasn't.

Why she had saved him, he didn't know. In truth, he wished she hadn't bothered. One sword stroke and all this pain would have ended.

Unable to see the two of them together, Jack took a seat with his back to her.

No one spoke as they made their way to the ship.

Once on board, Lorelei was led away while Jack followed Wallingford to the deck below and into his officers' room. It was a typical study with a large table and chairs set up for meetings. The oak panelling glistened from new polish and sunlight flooded in from the open windows.

Wallingford closed the door securely before he faced Jack. "Why didn't you kill Justin on the beach?"

"Because no matter how much I hate *you*, I couldn't bring myself to kill my brother."

Wallingford folded his hands behind his back as he approached Jack. He narrowed his gaze. "Is that the only reason?"

"It's the only one I plan to give you."

He walked past Jack as if pondering his words, then he turned to face him again. "Tell me why Lorelei lied to protect you."

Jack folded his arms across his chest. "How should I know. I've never understood women and their loyalties."

Wallingford's jaw flexed a moment before he gave a long, tired sigh. "I know you don't believe me, Jack. But I'm very sorry for what I did to you and your mother."

Jack sneered at him. "You're right, old man. I don't believe you."

Tears glistened in his eyes before Wallingford turned his back and cleared his throat. "I want you to know that I really did love her and . . . and you."

Did he honestly expect Jack to believe that? How

could he even say it with a straight face? Especially to *him*!

"I see," Jack said slowly as he sought to stave off the roiling rage that simmered deep in his gut. "So that's why you abandoned us."

"No," Wallingford said, his voice hoarse. "It's why I *had* to abandon you."

What the devil did that mean?

Not that he cared.

"And you think this makes it all better?" Jack asked as his lip curled in repugnance. "Or that it relieves you of your guilt?"

Wallingford faced him with a tormented face and for the first time in his life, Jack saw something other than smug assuredness on those pinched features. "I know it doesn't, and I don't ask for your forgiveness. I deserve your hatred. God knows I hate myself for it."

The admiral's raw emotions gave Jack pause. "Then why did you leave?"

"Because Charlotte found out about the two of you and she threatened to take Adrian and Justin and leave me."

Jack's jaw dropped. That was the last thing he had expected him to say. The bastard had taken them away from any shred of protection and left them in hell because his little wife might take his legitimate heirs and leave!

"What?" he asked in disbelief.

"I was scared, Jack. She could have ruined me."

The urge to strike the man was so fierce that Jack didn't know what prevented him from it. If the truth were known, he'd like to gut the beast. "So instead you ruined us."

"I had to," the admiral insisted as if he could somehow sway Jack over to his twisted reasoning. "I knew if I kept Margaret in England that sooner or later I'd find myself at her door. The only chance I had was to leave her somewhere I couldn't return to."

"I see now," Jack said, seizing him by the throat. "You left us in hell because you were a craven bastard." He tightened his grip, enjoying the feel of the flabby flesh against his palm. "Well, I can most certainly send you there now."

Wallingford's eyes bulged as he tried to pull Jack's hands away. "You don't have to send me there." He gasped with each breath he could draw through his constricted throat. "I've lived there every day of my life. There hasn't been an hour that has gone by that I haven't seen her face or yours."

Jack slung him against the wall, then returned to seize his throat. He held his father against the paneling, waiting for him to draw his last breath and end this once and for all. "Is that why you kicked me in my face when I begged you for a guinea to buy my freedom?"

Wallingford closed his eyes and swallowed. "Dear God, Jack, I didn't mean to do that. You surprised me. I had no idea that you and your mother had gone somewhere else, and then there you were looking me in the face. I reacted without thought."

"And I hate you for it."

"I know you do, and it should give you great comfort to know that I'm dying."

Jack loosened his grip. "What?"

"It's true," Wallingford said, taking Jack's hand in both of his. "It's lung sickness. I've been coughing up blood for some time now, and the doctors have assured me that my time is short. That's why I wanted to speak with you today. I've made provisions for you."

Growling low in his throat, Jack released him. He was no longer sure what to feel. The urge to kill his father was as strong as ever, but there were other emotions that were confusing him.

But one thing was certain, he wasn't about to take anything from this man. Not now. Not so that he could go to his grave peacefully.

"I don't want your damned provisions, old man. Nor do I need them."

"Yes," Wallingford said, straightening his jacket with an imperial tug. "I'm sure you've grown quite wealthy stealing from others."

"It's what I learned while starving in the gutter."

Wallingford flinched, then took a deep breath as if steadying himself. "Fine, give it away then. I know it doesn't relieve my conscience, nor does it make ammends to you. It was just something I had to do."

Jack curled his lip. "And what will good sweet Charlotte say?"

Wallingford's face hardened. "I don't care what she says. She has made my life a living hell for years. Why do you think I've been at sea though I know I'm dying? Because I'd rather be here than listening to her croaky, nagging voice."

In spite of himself, Jack snorted a bitter laugh. Perhaps there was some justice in this world after all.

"You are the image of your mother when you smile."

Jack sobered.

"Would you please answer me one thing?" Wallingford asked.

Jack stared at him in disbelief that he would dare ask anything of him.

"Why did you draw me here?" Wallingford continued. " 'Tis obvious you deplore me."

"I wanted to kill you."

"I see. After all these years you wanted peace."

Jack couldn't let it go at that. Nay, he wanted the beast to know the truth.

"You don't know anything," he growled. "You've taken everything from me. First it was my security, then it was my mother and my dignity. Then six months ago you razed a ship called the *White Dove*, do you remember it?"

"Aye, I recall it. It was a Patriot blockade runner and I did what was necessary to secure the interests of the Crown. Why do you care about it?"

"Because on that ship was the only father I ever knew and you killed him."

A single tear ran down Wallingford's cheek. "I'm truly sorry, Jack. I did not know."

Jack stood back in confusion at the sincerity.

Wallingford walked over to his desk and slid open a drawer. He pulled out an ivory-handled dagger and laid in on the desk. "Go ahead. Kill me. You might as well, and I certainly deserve it."

Stepping forward, Jack reached for it.

Just as he was about to take it into his hand, he pulled back.

Lorelei had bought his life with her integrity and he wasn't about to let his father take that as well.

"You're not worth it."

Wallingford drew a ragged sigh of relief. "I've said

my piece, Jack, and I hope that someday you might find it in your heart to let go of the hatred you feel for me."

"They tell me anything's possible given time." And with that, Jack turned and walked out the door.

Why did you lie, Lori?" Justin asked as soon as they were alone in a small cabin.

Lorelei reached up and touched his cheek. Poor, precious Justin. He'd lost weight, and deep circles marred his eyes. "You've been worried about me, haven't you?"

"Of course I have," he said, placing his hands on her shoulders. "I haven't been able to eat or sleep for fear of what that monster was doing to you."

Guilt gnawed at her. He'd been terrified while she, for the most part, had been enjoying herself. "Jack's not so bad, really."

Justin was aghast. "How can you say that?"

She looked away from him, her heart heavy. She didn't want to hurt Justin. Ever.

But to tell him the truth would crush him.

"After all this, do you still wish to marry me?" she asked him.

"Of course I do. Why . . ." His voice trailed off as color suffused his cheeks. "If he's laid a hand on you I swear I'll—"

"Bleed all over him?"

His look turned murderous.

She stifled the smile that was on the edge of her lips. "I'm sorry, Justin. It's just that I saw your fight and though I love you still, I . . ."

Reality dawned on him. His eyes widened, and horror mixed with disbelief shone in his eyes. "Nay, Lori. Tell me 'tis not true."

"I wish I could, but I love him, too."

His face turned a shade darker. "So much so that you would cast me aside for him?"

Lorelei pulled away from him. Clenching her hands together, she diverted her gaze to the floor. "I'm not casting you aside, Justin. It's just—"

He placed a finger over her lips to silence her. "Say nothing more. I don't want to hear it. I knew how you felt the moment I saw your face when you begged me not to hurt him. Does he know how you feel?"

Refusing to meet his gaze, she murmured, "I don't know."

"Well, at least tell me he loves you."

"I wish I could."

"Oh, Lori," he said, pulling her into his arms. "You know how much I love you, but I would be lying if I didn't say I was relieved by your news."

Stunned, she looked up at him. "Relieved?"

"Aye, relieved that he didn't hurt you and relieved that you no longer wish to marry me."

"Why?"

He pulled away from her and offered her a tender smile. "I'm not what you need. I've known that all along, but you seemed to want me so badly that I couldn't disappoint you. The truth is, you're so lively and daring. I'm just simple Justin who likes to sit quietly while you have always wanted to be the center of attention. Not that that's bad. It's part of why I love you so. But you could never be truly happy with me. And after a time, I am quite certain my boring ways would begin to wear on even your gracious patience."

Her throat tight, she offered him a gentle smile. "You're such a wonderful man."

"But not wonderful enough," he said with a sigh. "Go on, get out of here before I change my mind. Go get your pirate." He urged her to the door.

Lorelei turned around to face him. "Thank you."

His eyes were sad, but he kissed the tip of his finger, then touched the tip of her nose. "Tell him to be good to you, or I shall be forced to bleed on his boots."

She laughed, then he opened the door and pushed her out.

Lorelei reached the deck just a few steps behind Jack. He was heading for the ship's boat. Forgetting her role of lady, she ran across the deck and grabbed his arm. "Hello."

Surprise flickered across his face. "What are you doing here?"

She hesitated. Something wasn't right. Jack looked troubled and . . . well, he looked lost. "I'm going with you."

He looked around them, then shook his head. "You don't belong with me."

"Yes, I do."

"Woman, would you for once see reason. Go home."

She reached to touch him. "But Jack—"

He moved away from her hand. "But nothing. I don't want you near me, and I don't want you touching me. I don't want anything from you except for you to leave me alone!"

She flinched as tears stung her eyes, yet she refused to cry. Refused to let him see how much his words hurt her.

Then her anger set in. She had stared two men she loved in the face and told them a complete lie. She had given Jack his life and this was her reward?

To the devil with him, if that was his attitude.

"Fine then. Leave. You're quite right, I'm home now. 'Tis where I belong. Where I am safe from the likes of you."

Something flickered in his eyes a moment before his gaze hardened. He stepped past her and left the ship behind.

At first Lorelei couldn't believe he'd really left her. Not until she forced herself to walk numbly to the railing and look out at him being rowed back to shore.

It was only then the full impact hit her. Jack was gone.

He didn't care for her. And worst of all, while he was everything in the world to her, she was absolutely nothing to him.

18

Jack didn't dare look back. He could feel Lorelei's eyes on him as if it were a physical touch and he knew if he turned around, he wouldn't be able to leave her. Especially not when the only thing he really wanted was to have her soothe the pain that was pounding through every fiber of his being.

You have to leave her.

And he did. She deserved so much more than he could ever offer her.

This was for her own good. She belonged with her own kind. People who knew how to love someone. People who knew . . .

He didn't finish the thought. Too much had happened this day and he hadn't considered what being face-to-face with his father would cost him emotionally. Right now he was in turmoil and didn't know how to escape it. He just wanted to run away.

Nay, he needed time to think, to sort through this maelstrom of emotions.

$\mathcal{T}$wo days later, Lorelei sat alone in her cabin. Inside herself she wept constantly, and it was getting harder and harder not to let her sadness out, especially when Justin would visit with her. He was so kind and understanding. So forgiving and dear.

Why couldn't he make her heart pound the way Jack did?

Why, oh why wasn't it Justin's scent that haunted her?

And over the last two days she'd discovered just how right Jack had been. She would never have had a happy life with Justin. They would have gotten along for a time, but after awhile their difference in personality would have destroyed that bond.

As her grandmother so often said, 'twas one thing to love a man, 'twas entirely another to live with one.

"Oh, Jack," she whispered, "Why couldn't you love me?" She drew a ragged sigh as she sat alone at the small desk sketching a picture of the man who had haunted her day and night. Then, out of spite, she placed two horns on his head and a dark circle about his left eye.

"Lorelei?" Justin called from outside her door.

She shoved the paper into a small pigeonhole. "Yes?"

He opened the door and leaned in. "There's something on deck you need to see."

She frowned at him. "What?"

Justin looked like a small child who had glimpsed

an early Christmas present and was trying to keep it a secret. "You'll have to see it to believe it."

Perplexed, she rose and followed him topside.

The crew stood ready at their cannons while Admiral Wallingford stared out with his telescope. Looking in the direction he faced, she saw a sloop gaining speed on them.

Only it wasn't just any sloop. It was Morgan's.

"They've raised the white flag, Admiral," a youth called from the crow's nest.

The admiral lowered the telescope and looked to where Lorelei and Justin were standing. "Should I order them blasted from the sea?" he asked.

Lorelei gasped. "Nay."

"I somehow thought you might protest such a move." The admiral turned to his men. "Stand ready to defend, but do not fire upon your lives unless I state so."

"Aye, sir!" they shouted in military unison.

Uncertain, Lorelei watched as the ship drew closer.

How had the admiral known it was Morgan's ship approaching? It hadn't been near the harbor the day he arrived.

As if knowing her thoughts, the admiral stepped forward and whispered into her ear. "I saw Ja—" He paused and cleared his throat. "Jacob," he pronounced slowly, as if catching himself in a slip, "on the deck."

Lorelei stared up at him in disbelief.

He knew!

A moment of horror filled her as she wondered if Justin had betrayed her. And if Justin had betrayed her, why hadn't the admiral ordered Jack taken?

"Is this a trap for him?" she asked, unable to see another reason.

The admiral shook his head.

Unable to comprehend another reason for his mercy, she watched as he walked back to his place and waited for the *Roseanna* to approach.

Once Morgan's ship was broadside, Jack shouted, "Permission to come aboard, sir."

The admiral waited several heartbeats before he answered. "Come aboard if you're able."

Jack let fly a huge, iron grappling hook. It caught and wrapped around the mizzen mast. Lorelei gaped as Jack jumped from the upper deck of Morgan's ship and swung to the main deck a few feet in front of her.

He looked marvelous to her. His long blond hair was free and blowing about his roguish face. He wore a black pair of breeches and high black boots. His white linen shirt was open at the neck and his long, green waistcoat was left unbuttoned and hanging open.

An urge to rush into his arms seized her. All she wanted was to feel his arms about her and have him pull her into a fierce kiss.

But beneath that urge was an even greater one to kick him. After all, he'd left her harshly and she did have her pride.

Jack paused just before her. So close that she could smell the crisp, clean scent of him. "You're angry with me, aren't you?" he asked.

"Why would you think that?" she responded tartly. "I actually enjoy being snapped at and then left behind." Lorelei eyed him with suspicion. "Why are you here?"

He smiled that smile that had never failed to warm her and make her breathless and weak.

Jack gestured like some great stage actor. "Down in the valley, leaves fall from trees, the branches are bare." He sighed and brought his hands together over his chest as he gave her a forlorn stare. "All the flowers have faded, their blossoms once so beautiful. The frost attacks many herbs and kills them. I grieve. But if the winter is so cold, there must be new joys. Help me sing a joy a hundred thousand times greater than the buds of May. I will sing of roses on the red cheeks of my lady. . . ." He took her hand. "Could I win her favor, this lovely lady would give me such joy that I would need no other."

"What are you saying?"

He lifted her chin with his knuckle. "Noble lady, I ask nothing of you save that you should accept me as your servant. I will serve you as a good lord should serve, whatever the reward may be. Here I am, then, at your orders, sincere and humble, gay and courteous. You are not, after all, a bear or lion, and would not kill me, surely, if I put myself between your hands."

He bent down on one knee before her. "I love you, my lady, Lorelei. Marry me and I swear I shall never again do or say anything to harm you and I will slay anyone who does."

She bit her quivering lip. A thousand thoughts and emotions tumbled through her simultaneously. Joy, happiness, and most of all love. Never in her wildest imaginings had she envisioned this man on his knee before her spouting such wonderful words of poetry.

Jack looked about uneasily. "Are you not going to say anything after all that?"

She could feel her face betray her giddiness, while her need for vengeance still stood strong. "And what would you have me say?"

He arched a brow. "That you love me, too, would be nice. Especially given the fact that I look like a complete ass kneeling here in front of you while two hundred men watch."

She laughed as joy exploded through her and yet her vengeance was not so appeased that she could let him off the hook quite so easily.

She pursed her lips as if in serious debate.

He squirmed a little more and looked a bit sheepish.

"Very well, knave," she said at last. "For some reason heaven only knows, I do find you . . . irritating."

Panic flickered in his eyes.

"Forgive me," she said, savoring her power over him. "That's not quite the word I seek."

She could read on his face the fear he had of her next word.

"Irresistible. Aye, that be the word. I find you irresistible."

A slow smile spread across his face. "And?"

She cocked a haughty brow. "Who said there was an *and*?"

"Your eyes say it."

"Oh, very well then. And I love you."

The smile broke full force across his face as he stood and scooped her up in his arms. When his lips touched hers, he claimed her with a passion that stole all the strength from her limbs.

"I'm so sorry I left you," he murmured in her ear. "I swear I'll never do it again."

She held him close and leaned her head against his shoulder, content to stay in his arms for the rest of her life.

The admiral stepped forward and cleared his throat. He looked to Jack. "I take it you'll be joining us for the trip to Charleston?"

Jack shook his head and set her back down on the deck. "She'll be joining us."

The admiral nodded. "I understand. Follow us into port and I shall see to it you make safe harbor, but you'll be on your own when you decide to leave."

Jack said nothing. Instead, he moved to grab the rope he'd used to swing over to the admiral's ship. He returned to her side and took her hand, then led her to the upper deck.

"What are you doing?" she asked.

"Taking you home," he said as he dipped down and placed an arm about her waist. His arm tightened. "Lift your feet."

"Don't you dare!"

But he did. The two of them sailed off into the air, over the ocean, and to the deck of Morgan's ship. Everything seemed to swim around her and she didn't feel safe until her feet finally touched the wooden boards of the deck.

Lorelei's entire body shook with fright. "I swear, Jack—"

"Jake," he whispered as he let go of the rope. His loving gaze captured hers and left her bereft of words. "A fair maiden cast her spell upon Jack Rhys and transformed him into a new man she named Jacob Dudley."

"You truly hate that name, don't you?"

His look was playful and warm. "Something a little more masculine would have been preferable. However, I can console myself with the knowledge that you'll be Mrs. Jacob Dudley."

"And that I surely will."

19

Six months later

Jack stood in the door of his father's bedroom as the butler quietly walked past. He still wasn't sure why he was here, only that Lorelei had asked him to make peace and he would do practically anything she wanted.

Wallingford's eldest son, Adrian, stood at the window staring at him. And Justin, who sat by the bed, looked as if he were seeing a ghost.

"What are you doing here?" Justin asked, his voice almost accusing in its grief.

"Leave us," Wallingford ordered, though his voice had lost its power and authority. "I wish to speak with him alone."

"But Father—" Justin began.

"Do it!"

Reluctantly, they did as he wished. Adrian closed the door and Jack moved closer to the bed.

"Come to see me die to make sure the devil takes me?"

"No," Jack said. "I've come to make peace with you."

"Have you now?" Wallingford asked in disbelief.

Jack clutched his hands together before him as he grappled with his numerous emotions. "I guess it doesn't make sense to hate you anymore. As Lorelei is so quick to say, the past is the past and it can do us no harm unless we let it."

His father wheezed and coughed for several minutes into a blood-soaked handkerchief. When he finally regained himself, he motioned for Jack to come closer.

Reluctantly, he did. He was trying to give the man a little peace, and trying to find some for himself. But it was hard to be here and witness the destruction of a strong man. Even one he'd spent most of his life hating.

"You'll never know how much regret I've had," his father wheezed. "How many times I wish I'd had the strength your mother possessed. In spite of the sneers and ridicule, she stood strong, fortified by her love of me. I was so undeserving of her love." He looked away, his eyes misting. "I should have been willing to do the same for her, but I couldn't stand the thought of losing my commission, my family. . . ."

Jack clenched his teeth as old wounds were gouged open.

His father coughed again, then rasped, "I'm glad you didn't make my mistake. You'll never know how proud I was of you when you knelt before Lorelei and told her what you felt. You're the man I never was."

The unexpected compliment hit him hard and he wasn't sure how to take it. What did one say to such a thing?

"I'm sure she's the reason you're here, isn't she?" his father asked. "You told her about us."

"Aye. I keep no secrets from her."

He nodded. "Women can't help but try to set matters to what they consider right. But I'm glad she insisted."

For some reason Jack was beginning to, too. "I do forgive you, Father." The words were harsh against his throat and yet, once spoken, they seemed to remove some strange burden from his shoulders.

But I will never really understand why you did it. How you could have done it.

Jack buried those thoughts and the words. They were the past, and he was now willing to let it rest.

"Call your brothers in."

Jack obeyed.

Once they were all in the room, Wallingford positioned them around his bed and smiled. " 'Tis a sight I've waited my entire life to see."

He looked to Justin. "Open the bottom drawer of my table and you'll find a sealed parchment."

Justin went and found it, then returned to the bed. Wallingford took it from him and handed it to Jack. "For my grandchildren. I would that they have at least part of what I should have left their father."

Dumbfounded, Jack reached out and took the paper.

His father touched his hand for just a moment, and then he drew his last breath.

Adrian and Justin erupted into tears as they wailed for the father they loved.

Feeling awkward and unsure, Jack made a quiet exit.

Lorelei sat at the window of her drawing room, painting in the fading daylight. It was yet another portrait of Jack, her favorite piece of fruit.

Jack, she thought, warming at the mere thought of him. Her father had been most reluctant to accept his new son-in-law, but after a few days of pouting and prodding, Lorelei had finally swayed his affections for Jack.

Then there was the way Jack had followed him around, making a nuisance of himself and warning her father that he would not stop bothering him until her father gave him a fair shake.

She smiled at the memory.

Lorelei looked up at the large room and stared at the molding on the ceiling. 'Twas a beautiful home Jack had bought for them and she hoped to one day fill the large plantation house with precious children. Especially since Kit had decided to sail with Morgan.

Jack had taken his son's decision hard. But in the end, he'd let the boy go.

Morgan had promised to take good care of Kit and to bring him home at least twice a year. She hoped for Jack's sake that Morgan kept his promise.

She heard the front door open.

Before she could rise, Jack came into the room, his face dour.

Without a single word passing between them, she knew what had happened. "He's dead?"

Jack nodded.

Lorelei rose and went to him. After removing her stained apron, she pulled him into a tight hug. "I'm sorry."

His response came as an even tighter squeeze.

They stood embracing each other for several mintues before Jack finally pulled away from her. "Thank you for making me go," he said hoarsely.

She clutched his hand in hers, delighted that the final confrontation had done him some good. "You feel better, then?"

He brought her hand up to his lips and kissed her knuckles. "In some strange way I do. I feel so relieved. Like the past can harm me no more."

"I'm glad for it."

Jack released her hand and reached inside his coat. He pulled out a sealed piece of parchment and handed it to her.

Lorelei turned it over and studied the Wallingford crest. "What is this?"

He shrugged in that irritating way that often drove her to distraction. "He wanted me to have it."

"And you didn't open it?"

"I thought you might wish the honor."

Resisting the urge to roll her eyes, she broke the seal and opened it. As she scanned the page, anger, relief, sadness, and joy mingled inside her.

"Well?" Jack asked after she finished.

Lorelei debated whether or not she should let him know. But then they had sworn to have no secrets from each other—to be honest no matter the pain.

"Your mother's father wrote to the admiral numerous times over the years begging him to bring you home," she said, her voice cracking at the sadness that settled over Jack's features. "It seems he had no other heir, and when he died eight years ago, he left everything to you."

"What?" Jack breathed.

"Aye. The admiral wrote that he never had the heart to tell your grandfather what he'd done to you, and since he didn't know how to tell you about your inheritance, he managed your estates and money in your absence."

Anger darkened Jack's cheeks.

Lorelei touched his arm lightly, offering him what comfort she could. "He took great care of it all for you. The admiral has also left you a large holding of his in Wales."

"Did he honestly think—"

"Jack," she said, cutting him off. "He's gone now. Does it matter what he thought?"

Jack sighed. "I suppose not."

Lorelei handed him the letter. "You're a wealthy man, Jacob Dudley."

He snorted. "I was already a wealthy man." Jack pulled her into his arms. "But tell me, Mistress Dudley, were I merely a poor sailor bereft of jewels and wealth, would you still have a kind thought of me?"

She smiled. "Most certainly not, sir. For then I would see your thinning hair and poochy belly."

"My what?"

"You heard me."

"Methinks milady hasn't seen my belly in so long that she has it confused with some other man's."

"I but saw it last night, and it was quite the flabby mound I claim."

"Flabby?"

She bit her lip. "Then again, perhaps my memory is not what it once was."

"I should say not."

"Then come, my pirate, take me upstairs and refresh my memory."

His smile was wicked. "Ever as you wish, sweetest. Ever as you wish."

New York Times bestselling author

Christina Dodd

Some Enchanted Evening

0-06-056098-3/$6.99 US/$9.99 Can

Though Robert is wary of the exquisite stranger who rides into the town he is sworn to defend, Clarice stirs emotions within him that he buried deeply years before.

One Kiss From You

0-06-009266-1/$6.99 US/$9.99 Can

Eleanor de Lacy must have been mad to agree to exchange identities with her stronger-willed cousin. Worse still, she finds the man she's to deceive dazzlingly attractive.

Scandalous Again

0-06-009265-3/$6.99 US/$9.99 Can

Madeline de Lacy prides herself on being one of the most sensible young women in England, which is why she can't believe that her noble father has lost his entire estate—*and her!*—in a card game.

My Favorite Bride

0-06-009264-5/$6.99 US/$9.99 Can

When Samantha Prendregast arrives to take charge of six rebellious girls, the vibrant, outspoken governess is not quite prepared to deal with the dashing master of the grand estate.